CRITICAL ACCLAIM FOR
LOUD WATER

"Robby Henson's prose crackles with the raw-boned, rough-edged hardness of the Eastern Kentucky landscape, intensely capturing the desperate victims seeking to escape its unforgiving hold...whether through an act of redemption or an act of revenge. A visceral Southern Gothic Noir."
—Charles Edward Pogue, screenwriter of *The Fly*, *Dragonheart*, and *Psycho III*

"Sins of the past litter the backroads of rural Kentucky in this powerful Southern Gothic Noir. Redemption is a hard thing to come by. Henson writes like William Faulkner's Kentucky cousin and reminds us what great writing really looks like."
—John Morrissey, producer of *American History X*, *Havoc*, and *There Are No Saints*

"A brilliant noir debut with a bittersweet ending."
—Jim Winter, author of the Holland Bay series

LOUD WATER

ROBBY HENSON

LOUD WATER

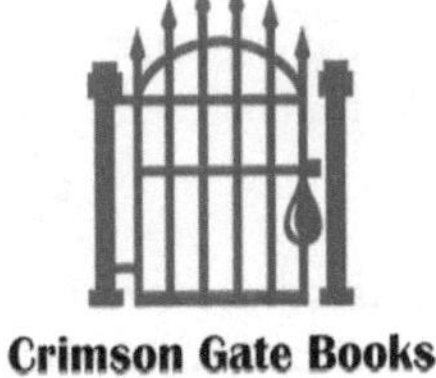

Crimson Gate Books

*"Ain't no use in turning on your light babe,
I'm on the dark side of the road."*
—Robert Zimmerman

Chapter 1

THIRTEEN ROUNDS

When he woke in a narrow room on a metal cot he reached out to touch the child beside him. He grabbed instead the thick arm of a heavy woman with dyed red hair and dark roots pumping air into a small rubber medical bulb. His hand got pushed away. A sensation of pressure constricted his bicep.

"Who done it?"

Slate gray eyes blinked and panned and he found the round-faced C.O. who the inmates at Little Sandy called Smurf.

"You musta' seen who hit you?"

Every strobic heartbeat sent nail spikes into his brain and his throat was August dry but he wasn't about to beg for meds or water and he certainly wasn't about to spill any part of what had gone before. Had he exited the tunnel and why had he even paused to watch a few aimless handball points played between two inked and shirtless Louisville Westsiders? Had he half-turned into a pipe or more likely a sock stuffed with rocks or coins? Was it an old or new grievance? A fish prowling for cred? He didn't care much to know. And here now the right side of his head was gauze-taped and a crackling trilled his ear channel like loud water in a creek after a three-day rain.

Smurf set his clipboard on top of a metal file cabinet to hitch up his pepper spray and walki-heavy belt. Freckles and pimples fought for space on his cheeks and chin. When he spoke his lips hardly moved.

"Can he hear me?"

The nurse gave an unhelpful shrug. Then counted the pulse count and whistled air out of her rubber bulb. Smurf spoke again but all the glassy-eyed inmate got was a low, heavy, continuous, reverberating muffled roar.

***

"It might get better and go away eventually." The nurse said six months later. Her hair cut shorter and dyed a different color. When she said it, he had a finger up his ear, pressing the hole wider, listening to the tone change.

It never did get better. Crit Poppwell had sustained subjective tinnitus in an unprovoked prison yard assault nine years into a fifteen-year bid. Damaged microscopic nerve endings never got right and thereafter with every heavy and deliberate step forward God's mocking wrath hissed into his left ear canal loud as wind rips through the open window of a speeding car.

Life in prison moves on routine. Meal call. Stand and wait. Take a nap. Meal call. Walk to nowhere. Meal Call. Lights out. Only now his non-existence had a grating soundtrack. At first, the buzz had kept him awake nights. He'd been okay with that. Sleep brought dreams of faces he had no business remembering. In the blue hours he'd sit awake, cup a hand over his left then right ear, creating a pulse rhythm like waves crashing. If only Liddy had met someone else. Had a child with someone else.

Had he truly chosen this or fallen to it like bald tires skidding across a bad road? No way to not go through the guardrail. He and his brother had kicked and screamed into being like wildings at the top of Frozen Creek Road. They had gouged and scarred each other's flesh and blackened eyes. They had hand-fished for bullhead under outcrop rocks on the North Fork of the Kentucky. They had briefly found Jesus and got river-dunked, but that didn't stop their wrong turning.

You boys ain't gonna be the death of me, their momma shrieked while shucking leaves off a willow switch. But her vow proved hollow and mostly untrue. Her slackness in paying rent triggered frequent moves from one drafty up-creek tenant shack to the next. They lived six months in a converted tobacco stripping shed without indoor plumbing. Mattress on a dirt floor. Two clip lights and a space heater connected by an orange extension cord to somebody else's outlet. Crit and his brother grew tall in the shadow of tall mountains and twined together like wild vines that got out of hand and broke apart brickwork and killed trees.

Crit stole a car at fourteen and wrecked it. Spent thirteen months at KSR youth detention. He married young. He habitually cheated. He worked low-pay jobs and sold homegrown. He and his brother moved up. Cash and carry. Dilaudid, Percodan, Xylazine, Demerol, Quaaludes, Oxy, Tramadol, Morphine, Methadone, and his specialty—crystalized and sparkling mountain skante. He liked the way meth made him fearless. The way he could take a punch and not feel it. At twenty-one he pulled three years for nearly beating a man twice his age to death with a crowbar. When he got out he blew up his father-in-law's singlewide while boiling down starter fluid. He fathered a child but the miracle of it barely blunted his alcohol and crank-fueled wildness.

And then at age thirty-nine, Crit committed a crime for which there was no forgiveness and got away with it. Sick from the weight of it he celebrated his fortieth birthday with thirteen rounds of Russian roulette. For the last two he'd loaded an extra shell. He would have gone on until the bloody end of it all, but for passing out on Oxy and Ol Grandad. Amped up and never sober in the weeks that followed, he went careless and caught a third strike—possession with intent to sell and possession of a stolen firearm. The Springfield Armory Hellcat in his trunk turned out to be stolen from a Richmond sporting goods store. He'd traded four grams of chunky white for it to a man he hardly knew, but he declined to name names and took the full hit. He met his public defender only twice before sentencing. He spent two years at Roederer up near Louisville, then transferred to Green River. He slumped into his fiftieth year in solitary at Little Sandy for not hearing a C.O.'s order to submit to a random body search.

Age hung on Crit like a shroud but he didn't feel wiser. He was a dead man barely standing. Ear buzzing. Hardly breathing. Abandoned and empty. Locked up and burdened with a single memory that plagued him with unbearable despair. The world was a rancid place full of no-good people, and he included himself and his brother the worst best examples.

There had been times early in his bid when his will to wake to the next morning light had ebbed so low that he picked fights with gang enforcers and Aryan muscle-heads. But word got out that he had a death wish and it got so nobody wanted to do him any favors. Years came and went. He talked to no one. Refused visitors. He rejected alliances and friendships. His current cellmate of seven years didn't even know where he was from. He walked in darkness. His existence moldered into a grim acceptance that he didn't have to kill himself; he was already dead and buried in three and a half acres of steel fencing and guard towers.

* * *

So it came to be that half past morning on a chilly October day two turkey vultures floated on the wind above the razor wire. Crit stood near the walled perimeter in his usual somnambulant state and whistled air through tightly clenched teeth. A soft shushing sound that diminished the imperishable grind. He watched the carrion birds ride a thermal up from the wooded ravine East of tower four, then over and above khaki-clad men lined up early outside the mess hall. He gave up watching when their black silhouettes crossed the sun. He stood without moving, inert and gray as a metal fence pole. A minute later the vultures dropped lower again into his view and curled a lazy ellipse out across a fresh-cut fescue field where cowlicks of cut grass hid mangled rabbits and field mice. They reached the far end and perched atop a high-voltage utility tower. Crit stared through symmetrical chain links and wondered why so few birds in his witnessing ever came to harm from such dangerous perching.

He stood at the fence for well over an hour and then he joined the end of the lunch line.

When he was finishing his meal a fight broke out in the tunnel between the hub and dorm five. The entire prison population went into lockdown. There were only a handful of inmates left in the mess hall, and now they would be there for some time. Crit sat at a metal table anchored into the cement floor. A top-heavy female C.O. the inmates called The Chest jostled past to shoo away the Khakis gathered at the exit door. She was bottom-heavy, too, for that matter. She had a whispered reputation for not writing up inmates she caught jerking off.

Her walki crackled, *medical alert.*

That drew whistles and catcalls from the brotherhood of the hopeless who always seemed to enjoy hearing bad news concerning one of their own.

Crit lowered his forehead onto his hands to nap or not and noticed a black felt tip pen on the floor where the C.O. had passed. Crit extended his state-issued tennis shoe and nudged the pen up under his chair. Such a thing could be traded for noodles or stamps from the four or five inkers who charged. But it had no cap. And he had no need for stamps.

A minute passed before Crit palmed the pen up to his plate. He brought the point tip down onto his napkin. A small black stain slowly inked wider. He moved and furrowed a line without thought on the puckered paper. He scratched and thickened. Curved the line and curled it back on itself into a tight, angry mass of squiggles. It surprised him what his random scratching resembled, and he slashed and jabbed new lines to improve the likeness.

"I work for your brother."

A scrawny fish with a wispy thin beard and hangdog eyes slid into the chair across. Crit blinked and didn't know him, but he should have heard him approach, even with his ringing tinnitus.

"He said I should look you up."

The young man had bad teeth and itched at a bare part of his beard and waited a response.

"Get the fuck away from me," Crit said and stared hard.

The young man got up and moved away.

Crit dropped his pitch-black gaze down to the dark shape on his napkin. A ghoulish thing with wings and claws and dead eyes perched on a high-voltage tower.

Chapter 2

WEDNESDAYS

Sister Nikhael DeKoven wasn't sure she believed in God anymore. But she didn't see his absence as a loss of faith. She had gained faith in the belief that life was precious and humankind was essentially good. She believed in the historical Jesus as a kind of non-Caucasian revolutionary Gandhi who divided loaves and fishes for the poor. As a novitiate she had created a large tempera-and-photo-collage mixed-media artwork inspired by Thomas Aquinas's definition of Christ's ethic as the will to do good to another.

Her progressive inclinations and Rita Marley dreads occasionally ruffled the habits of the more conservative voices in her Dominican order. That and she swore like a truck driver. But even those who challenged her beliefs did not question her enthusiasm to do good works as evidenced by the fact that even after teaching a full load at St. Catharine's Women's College in Springfield, she still found time to teach English as a second language to illegal landscapers at a Louisville community center. And on Wednesdays she drove three hours up the Bert T. Combs Mountain Parkway, nodding out to Bootsy Collins's bass lines to teach art to thieves, murderers, and child molesters.

"How do you feel about what you draw?" Sister Nikhael

asked in a hushed whisper. A fruit bowl reposed on a stool beside her. "Do these apples make you hungry? Do they make you remember another time when you enjoyed eating an apple?"

Suspicious eyes followed her as she moved through and behind the seated inmates who were spread out and scratching wobbly spheres and banana shapes onto sketch paper with charcoal sticks that she had sent copious emails to the warden to gain approval to give to them. They were a mix of young and old. Majority black. A couple of Hispanics. An older Caucasian male had moved as far away from the others as he could to the very back of the industrial gray academic room. His mind and hands were busy and he hadn't noticed her approach. His was a hard-chiseled face you could drive nails with. And a full beard like an Old Testament prophet—the kind of face Rembrandt or Caravaggio put to canvas, she told herself. He had voiced his name at roll call, but this was his first time in her class, and she didn't remember it.

And there on this whiskered inmate's sketchpad was a black crow, struggling to fly. The image caught her by surprise. Each dark scratch and blurry smudge writhed with fury and anguished impossibility, as if the crow had thrown its very being against a strong headwind that rendered its life purpose impossible.

The brutal beauty of this sketch made her step back. She saw that on the other side of the inmate was a barred window and on the other side of that window was a single black crow perched atop a coiled strand of razor wire.

"Shit a brick. That's not the assignment but it's good. Really good."

He looked up with distrust and menace. Several other inmates had turned to watch.

"Can I show the group?"

"I didn't do it to show nobody."

"We're all part of a circle."

The inmate slapped over his sketch like he was washing his hands of it. "If you want me to leave I'll leave."

Sister Nikhael billowed her checks. She met his icy stare with kind eyes. "As good as you are, Honey, you can stay as long as you like."

Chapter 3

BIRDS OF PREY

Time in prison moves on routine. After his third class, Crit changed his routine. He stayed in his cell on Mondays and Tuesdays during leisure time. He didn't walk the perimeter. Or take in the scuffling and arguing at the basketball court. He sat on the cold hard floor next to his cot, back to a cinderblock wall, sketchpad in his lap, and he drew. He drew things without a thought in his head. That started out as nothing and appeared out of nowhere. A hand slapping at a handball. A dirty tennis shoe with a loose string. A lunch bucket pulled up to a guard tower by a hemp rope. Icicles on razor wire. Snow drifts drifting. Dead birds. Snow melting into puddles around a metal fence. April tree branches budding. A half-eaten grilled cheese sandwich. A dirty Styrofoam plate. A mosquito sucking blood. A raised middle finger.

Come Wednesdays, he put his efforts before Sister Nikhael and was always rewarded with a radiant and approving smile.

"Nice. I like it a lot."

Crit stroked his beard and barely made eye contact.

"You do hands really well. Most artists find them impossible. Lots of different parts and angles that catch the light differently. You don't even know how good this is, do you?"

Crit shrugged.

"It's damn good. Wow."

She was able to get him extra paper, charcoal, and pens. She even attempted to get him a watercolor set but there the program director drew the line. Crit could only use color during class time.

She never corrected or told him how to do better. She marveled at what he did and what it was and explained what he was doing in ways that were often hard for him to follow. Negative space and spatial relationships were explained but didn't really stick. Her lectures on figurative versus abstraction sailed past. He did get most of the gist of her explanations about perspective and how the artist must emulate on paper how the human eye sees the world by establishing a vanishing point. Crit took it to mean there was always a black hole behind everything he drew that disappeared into an infinite nothing.

"When you draw something, when you create, it's like a window into, not only who you are, but where you've been and where you're going," Sister Nikhael said to the class. "Creative works are like a map of your life, maps of your soul. Does anybody get what I'm trying to say?"

"Sure," said a felon who was tall and wide like a linebacker. His head was clean-shaven and he had a tattoo of a fist on the back of his stacked neck. Word was he had caught a murder charge for killing his wife. "My map is a bad road both ways."

Several inmates chuckled and most smiled. Crit didn't. He was drawing a cigarette butt smushed into a sidewalk.

"So you already know where your journey leads?"

"Sure, I caught the full bid. When I get out it's feet first."

"That's the story the courts have told about you, and the prosecutors have told about you," Sister Nikhael used her hands when she spoke. "In your creative life, you get to tell your own story. And you get to tell the ending that you want."

Several inmates spoke up to agree and affirm that they felt some modicum of freedom when they drew things or made up poems. Crit paused to listen but found the conversation self-serving and congratulatory.

But he kept showing up. Every Wednesday. Like a wasp that should have perished in November but crawled out feebly in fluke-warm December.

The wall space above his cot became crowded with monochrome and color-washed images. Hands in handcuffs. Rotating ventilation fans. A silhouette in a hallway mopping a floor. Tattooed arms and legs. Bloodshot eyes. Hair-clogged shower drains. Soap suds on a dish. A hand crushing a soda can. Silent screams.

"Hey, Teacher's Pet."

Crit was passing through the tunnel on his way to lunch call. It was February and there was a cold bite in the air. Silvery frost clung to the metal fencing that crowded in on both sides. The felon with the fist on his neck was approaching in a padded khaki jacket that made him look even larger.

"It's like you got her wrapped around yer dick."

They stopped in front of each other. Two feet apart. Air fogged as they breathed. He had Crit by six inches and fifty or sixty pounds. And he had nothing to lose. But Crit didn't worry about any of that. A vein wormed at his temple. His ear sang.

"Look at you, lookin' me hard, like you want to go."

"Keep it moving," said a C.O. who was coming up behind.

The heavy inmate winked and made a kissing sound and moved around and away. "Seeya' later, Teacher's Pet."

Crit had no doubt where this was headed. If not today, soon enough. But he didn't worry or lose sleep over it. Then less than a week later he heard the heavy inmate had nearly stomped a fish from Bowling Green to death in the shower and was isolated for thirty days, and then transferred to Eddyville. Corrections tended to shuffle problem inmates through different prisons to keep them off balance.

Winter thawed into spring. Then came the oppressive heat of summer. Then the leaves fell and winter blew in again. His beard gained inches. Days passed and Crit got older, and each Wednesday, except holidays, he sat in the same seat in the back of Sister

Nikhael's class. Close to the window. Close to the water fountain that hummed louder than his tinnitus. Head bent and his close-set eyes narrowed and intense and inches above his labor of the moment that emerged painstakingly slow like a snake shedding its skin.

He hadn't heard her step up behind him but she was there. And was always there. Each Wednesday except holidays. She watched over as he rubbed and scratched and scraped and blurred charcoal dust into the pores of his sketch paper with a dirty thumb.

"Penumbra," she said.

His eyebrows arched into question marks.

"Halfway between dark and light. It's a word the old Italian masters used to describe the merging of the two.

"Can you spell it?"

She picked up a torn sheet of paper he had discarded and wrote.

Penumbra.

He told her it was a good word to describe a prison umbrella, a thing so rare no one had ever seen one. She laughed out loud and told him that was the first joke she'd ever heard him tell.

That night he taped the scrap of paper with the strange cursive word alongside his wall sketches, while his cellmates snored and coughed and farted.

Chapter 4

SILENT MAGIC

Eighteen months later Crit shaved his beard and trimmed his hair and sat in a molded plastic chair facing a TV monitor and video camera. He hadn't thought much about parole until Sister Nikhael had dug down into the details of his sentence. She informed him he would soon meet his eighty-five and ten requirement, and he should prep for it. When he asked her what business it was of hers, she answered that Van Gogh had had a brother and he needed a sister. She told him that his was a rare talent. She used the word *savant*. Whatever that meant. Apparently he had innate and exceptional skill and brilliance. He worked a piece of charcoal like the best poets sling words. Most of what she said flapped past him without landing.

"So you believe it was your fault?"

The TV screen before him was divided into three vertical boxes and each box held an unsmiling parole board officer who looked like a retired bull cop. The video-link setup allowed officers of the court to drink coffee and eat donuts in the comfort of their own homes or plywood-paneled offices and not drive out to the far-flung corners of the state to give a thumbs up or down to sacred hopes and dreams.

"It was my fault I chose to take drugs and sell drugs and

drink alcohol."

He had been coached to look directly at the blinking red light on the video camera by the bald trustee who ran the camera, a tip he found hard to follow. His eyes kept drifting down to his hands and the floor.

"You completed a S-A-P program?"

He nodded and remembered to say *yes, I did. It got me to look at myself and my bad habits in a better way.*

There was a pause. The skin on his face itched. The officer on the left sipped from a coffee mug. The officer on the right was texting on his phone. The officer in the center picked up a piece of paper. "We have a letter, a recommendation letter here from a Sister Nikhael DeKoven. Can you tell us why she would recommend paroling you?"

"She taught some art classes that got me to focus on a new hobby that became more than a hobby."

"What do you mean?"

Crit rubbed at a charcoal smudge on the webbing between his thumb and forefinger. "Instead of getting into trouble I pretty much stay to myself and draw. And paint."

He was asked to speak louder.

"Instead of getting into trouble I just draw."

"What do you draw?"

It took a moment for Crit to gather an answer. "I draw the darkness of things in charcoal. And then the white of the paper, the part that I don't touch, that becomes the light."

It happened whippet fast. Thirty-six hours later Crit stood in the hub with three plastic garbage bags clutched to his chest. He had been told to stand and wait and watch for a signal from the control center officer a hundred yards distant. Then to start walking. But April winds gusted a dust cloud up from the softball field and Crit's left eye stung and watered from it. The officer appeared to beckon. Crit blinked cloudiness away to be sure.

"Free man walking," an inmate behind Crit chirped.

He had lived amongst a thousand strangers but in an unpeopled place. The wind blew and rattled the chain on the flagless flagpole. The ringing in his ears escalated like a sand blaster in his head and pushed up his unease. He walked a steady cadence. Right foot. Left foot. What troubled Crit Poppwell to his marrow core was not that there, beyond the nearing gate, lay sky and clouds and mud so very different from the dark mud he had wallowed in for nearly fourteen years. Nor was he trembling before an unknown future. He had no future. This he knew without a doubt. What he felt now was each propulsive and trembling stride foreword carried him backward into his own defeated, dreaded, and worthless past.

The road and barns and hills of East Kentucky ribboned ahead of him. Crit rode in the passenger seat beside Sister Nikhael amazed and afraid. His forehead tilted into cool-tempered glass. He had come this way before. Handcuffed in the back of a department of corrections van. It had been the dead of winter then, and these same dark hills had been ragged with snow. Now the tallest trees were still bare but the shrub thickets and clinging-vine underbrush had leafed spring-green, and the days would get longer.

"How does it feel?"

Crit didn't answer and marveled at the mechanical silence of Sister Nikhael's Prius. He had owned only loud cars.

"You paid what they asked you to pay."

Crit shook his head. "I went in on a repeat offender controlled substance and weapons charge. I ain't paid for everything."

"If I didn't believe in second chances, I wouldn't like refried beans so much." She looked over and got next to nothing. But she was used to that. "I want you to keep it up."

"Keep what up?"

"Creating. Drawing. Painting. You've got a gift, Sir. Your work shows the soul of things."

"I just draw what I see."

Not for the first time Crit wondered if this strange woman beside him with the matted hair and glinting eyes was just one more to enter his orbit in hopes of breaking even. All so far had cashed out disappointed.

"You listen to yourself. You can't teach that. Your talent makes me love what I do."

"This car don't make much noise, does it?"

They came in on 15 and turned onto East 30. Jackson was the county seat of Breathitt County. Bloody Breathitt, so named after a coal strike his momma had claimed killed two great uncles. Crit wasn't sure whether that was true, as his momma had been prone to lying for no reason. They passed an old man and wife puffed out in thick winter coats, despite the warming spring weather. The couple had split up to hunt aluminum cans in the ditches on either side of the road. He remembered the man had once fixed a lawnmower for him, maybe twenty years ago or more.

He saw a new Wendy's and a new Hardee's, both with towering signs. The carpet remnant store was gone and where it had been someone was selling pre-fab metal sheds. A Chinese takeout business had usurped the Bun Boy Diner. Downtown was perched on a ridge above the river, where the familiar Breathitt County Courthouse spire rose church-like over everything.

"So you're back on home ground."

She didn't need to tell him that. His pulse had started to quicken ten miles back.

"Turn here."

They pulled off 30 and went up a rutted and potted asphalt drive where an oval sign on a metal pole announced *Sunset Motel*. There was an office with an A-frame roof and four or five rooms with stucco walls of faded tan and brown flanked out on both sides. An old Econoline van and a couple of hard-luck cars that might or might not ever run again sat on weedy gravel. Crit climbed out and stretched and met Sister Nikhael at the back of her car.

"Not exactly the Hilton," she said.

A loud metallic squall announced that someone in the office was torturing an electric guitar.

"Bill's home, I can take it from here," Crit said.

He lifted out his garbage bags. He had not been able to cart out all of his drawings. A few he had given away. The rest that wouldn't fit, years of work, he had tossed into a trash receptacle outside the TV commons.

Sister Nikhael positioned herself in front of him so he couldn't walk around. "Here's what's up. I know some curators who might be interested in your stuff."

"Why?"

"Because you suck. Actually it's because someone besides me needs to know how good you are."

A crazy human wolf howl now accompanied the guitar squalling.

"Do you want me to stick around and make sure this works out?"

"No, thanks. I'm good."

"I'm about to hug you. Get ready for it. Get ready for it."

Before he could dodge or run she stepped forward, wrapped both arms around him and squeezed tight. "I'll be checking in on you."

"I appreciate everything, what you done," he said, because something needed to be said. He wanted to say more, that in his hopelessness she had opened a door, but he couldn't find the words.

She waved. He nodded a stiff, awkward smile and a wave as her car moved away as if by silent magic.

A curtain at the office window fluttered. Crit set his bags outside on a webbed lawn chair. It felt strange, standing and being in an unconfined place that he hadn't traversed countless times like a stuck record and no one watching from a tower. He turned to see Sister Nikhael's Prius drift out of sight. He inhaled and stepped inside.

There behind a cluttered wooden desk was a tallish thin man with curly—almost kinky—gray hair to his shoulders, soul patch, deep sunken eyes, and a Stratocaster knockoff slung high on his chest. He was wearing a leather vest, banana print pajama bottoms, and plastic Crocs. He looked up from texting and his amplifier buzzed.

"Long-ass time muthfuka!'" Wild Bill shouted and pocketed his phone. "You still got yer rock star hair. Fuck the bald-heads, right?" He yawped a power chord.

Corrections had demanded that Crit secure an approved residence to parole out to. With no family to answer the call, he had reluctantly given Sister Nikhael Wild Bill's name and she had done the legwork. Everyone knew that Bill was a bit of an oddball. Many assumed he had scrambled his brains on Ketamine and glue. But Crit had known his whole family to be crazy.

Feedback reverberated and Bill grabbed what was left of a PBR six-pack, yanked one for himself, and tossed the last at Crit.

"What'd you pull, I forget?"

"Fourteen. Almost."

"Thaz a load. You hungry? They never feed ya enough, right? Not when they can make money off starvin' yer ass. I know something 'bout that. Tennessee Department of Corrections took the best seven years of my life." Wild Bill tossed his beer tab in the vague direction of a trash can. "I spent six of it up at Brushy Mountain. I ever tell you that? A hell of a place to send a green-ass kid."

Crit was an hour and a half removed from the razor wire and he was about to hear a prison tale he had heard many times before, many years before. But never while sober.

"It was him or me."

Wild Bill set up the scene, where barely out of his teens, he had shot the son of a Tennessee state trooper, partly over a girl and mostly over drugs. The shot was through and through, and the trooper's son lived, but the law smacked Bill hard and sent him to Tennessee's infamous Brushy Mountain Super Max. And it was there where Bill claimed he had worked on the electric crew for six months with James Earl Ray.

"Nicest guy ever, polite to the guards. Even the nigger guards got to like him. And a hell of an electrician." Wild Bill pulled the plug on his amp to kill rising feedback and then flung his skinny arm at an open Chinese takeout carton. "How about I order another Kung Pao chicken?"

"No thanks, I'm good."

"We got a new chink joint run by real Chinese. Or Japanese. Or some slant-eye muthafuckas. Foreigners takin' over, right? But I'm not complaining. They deliver and I'm gettin' good with chopsticks." He picked up the carton and offered it. "You can have what's left. I can nuke it."

Crit shook no.

"Ya sure?"

"I'm sure."

"So yer room's got a leak and some drywall came down but..."

"I can fix that."

"That's what I was thinking. You can fix a few ends and odds and we forget about the rent."

"I'll pay what I can."

"No worries. *Freedom.* I love that sword-fight movie with that big-ass movie star, what's his name?"

Crit didn't know.

Wild Bill screamed *freedom* again and raised his beer in an enthusiastic toast.

Crit raised his can but his tab had yet to be pulled.

Wild Bill helped carry Crit's possessions down the row of brown doors to the room next to the end and then worked at sliding a key into the lock. Seven was the number on the door.

"We don't get many tourists. Mostly by-the-week regulars. I had my momma livin' out here, actually livin' right here in yer room, but she had her stroke and now she's at assisted living. Eight hundred a month I got to pay on top of her Medicare and Medicaid. Hard nut. I'm like a squirrel in a cage," he said and mimicked a running squirrel.

Crit felt then heard it.

The boom and thrash of thrash metal from subwoofers with

the gain turned all the way up. A new Ford F Series with spoked rims and all black metal flake body and coal dark windows eased up the driveway. It was the kind of ride that announced itself, that said the owner had no fear of the law. Crit had guessed who Wild Bill had texted, even before the dark window slow-rolled half-down and there grinned Chrome Poppwell with sunglasses and peroxided hair that looked like he had paid somebody good money to cut it. Born eighteen months apart, and to different fathers, Chrome looked a smug fifteen years younger than Crit, easy.

"Been a while."

The singing in Crit's ear changed to a louder key.

"My peeps on the inside all told me you told me to fuck off," Chrome said with a smile and cut his loud music in half. "You doin' okay?"

His brother smiled a lot. Even when he was about to do someone damage. He always put everything he had into his smiles. Their eyes stayed on each other while Chrome nodded several times, as if Crit had answered him.

"Leave any boyfriends behind?"

Crit wanted to step forward and smash his brother's fulgent face down to the bones and marrow. But thinking about a thing too long always stops you from doing it.

"Got ya a homecoming present." Chrome handed Crit a boxed fifth of *Crown Royal*. "That shit was mountain water the day you went in."

Crit took the bottle reluctantly. "I meet my P.O. later so I'm not getting too..."

"You need a job? Your P.-O. needs you to work, right?"

Crit looked down at the bottle. "What kind of job?"

Just then the door to number five opened and out stepped a barefoot young woman in baggy UK shorts and cut-off tee. She had an exposed tummy with a belly-button ring, and some kind of reptile tat crawled up her leg. Half of her hair was red and short and the other half blue and long. And all of it was wild and uncombed. She could have been thirty or twenty, with wide eyes on a feral face.

"Hey Baby, party time?" She asked and yawned and looked sideways at Chrome. She had a dried crust of saliva at the corner of her mouth.

"I'll ring you later," Chrome said.

"For reals?"

"Reals."

"This is me smiling," she said, not smiling, and turned back to her room.

"Rennie, you got a new neighbor," Wild Bill said.

"This is me giving a shit," Rennie said and disappeared without looking at Crit.

"Anyhoo," Chrome said, glancing at a dinging message on his phone. "I'm legit, Bra. Got a used car lot. You can fix cars. Change oil. Sweep floors. Basic Mexican labor."

"I don't think so."

Chrome put his phone down and rubbed at his smile. Two of his fingernails were painted black. "My brother just told me to fuck off to my face. But I love him anyway. That's just the way it is with blood, ain't it, Bill?"

Bill gave a feckless nod and said yes and Chrome drove away, slow and loud.

Crit watched him go with something like hatred seeping out of every pore. "Did he have anything to do with you takin' me in?"

Chrome gunned it loud once he was on the highway so they wouldn't forget about him and his tires left a burnt mark.

"Yes and no. He's kind of a silent partner. But I woulda done it anyway."

Bill pushed open the door. When the parole thing seemed less of a joke, Crit had told himself to either steer clear of his brother or kill him. Bill stepped inside. Crit stood where he was, his molars grinding.

Bill put down the plastic bags and looked back at Crit. "Something wrong?"

"If I cross over I'm crossing out the steer clear."
"Steer clear of what?"
Crit stepped on inside.

Chapter 5

BLACK MOLD

When Bill finally left, Crit closed the door, and turned on the overhead bare bulb. A brown and tan acrylic coverlet covered the full bed that took up most of the room. The air smelled of disuse. There was a folded handicap walker leaning against a yellowed wall. There was a chipped veneer dresser with two of the drawers half-open. A mouse had made a nest in the top drawer. A TV that wasn't plugged in sat on it. The window was heavy draped. Chunks of drywall littered the shag carpet beside a bucket of rancid rainwater. He glanced up and noticed black mold creeping out from a soggy hole in the cottage-cheese ceiling.

The bathroom was worse, as someone had used and not flushed the toilet. Crit jiggled the handle. The tank was empty. Crit knelt and turned the supply line valve and heard water spray into the tank. After Crit flushed the toilet twice he emptied the rainwater bucket into it.

He placed the Crown Royal bottle on the dresser and caught sight of his gaunt image in the dusty mirror. He looked like a hobo, or a carnival worker, or one of the rangy homeless men who crawled out of the mountains to panhandle on the streets of Knoxville. His eyes climbed up to the black spores. Suicide by mold did not sound so unappealing, he thought.

Crit sat on his bed and pulled out three sketchpads from a garbage bag. He flipped through his pages of starlings on wires, hopeless hands on barred windows, weeds cracking concrete, a bald inmate grimacing under shower spray. Crit studied each image and his mind questioned what Sister Nikhael had ever seen in them. Crit had used charcoal and black sharpie mostly. Several had been washed with translucent swaths of watercolor that he had been allowed to use only in her classes.

Crit wasn't capable of drawing a straight line, even if someone held a gun to his head. The charcoal stick in his hand had never behaved, so his blank pages exploded with a slurry of slashes and squiggly scratches. The thing he drew evolved from the center, like a black heart bleeding outward. Angry and dense snarls expanded from an exploding core toward a raw depiction of the thing that declared unapologetically what the Sister had called the essence of the thing. She had never asked him why he was driven to scrawl and scratch on paper and so he had not once told her his truth—that when he turned a blank page into a non-blank page, his tinnitus stopped screaming. Hunched over with a charcoal stick in his hand he found silence. He felt dead. He ceased to exist. And that was pretty much the all of it, as far as he could tell.

Hip-hop beats bled through the wall from his candy-haired neighbor. He paced his small room, no bigger than a cell. Left foot. Right foot. Footsteps on carpet sounded different than on concrete. Breathing alone sounded way different than side by side with cellmates. He sat down on the bed and looked at his fingers. He wanted a cigarette. And more than that. He scratched his bare chin. He rose and turned off the light and sat back down in the half-dark. He listened to the thumping beats in the wall. He listened to a car passing. Taylor had been dead fourteen years now. He stood and moved to the dresser and separated the Crown Royal bottle from its cardboard packaging. He refused to look at himself in the mirror and sat back down and tested the heft of the bottle. The way his fingers circled the tapered neck. The amber swish. A gift from his brother.

Oh Taylor, he said.

Crit stepped out of his room, fast and striding. If he didn't do it now it might turn the other way. Straight to a ten-yard dumpster. He flipped the lid up and tossed the bottle in on top of construction debris.

"Mister, something wrong with that bottle?"

Crit turned. His neighbor that Bill had called Rennie stood in her doorway, checking her phone. A band called Bone Thugs N Harmony bragged about pussy and money. Crit shook his head no.

"Well in that case."

She walked past him and tiptoed up to reach the bottle. Her shorts tightened on her behind. She reached more and grabbed it, and returned to her room with a saucy defiant twitch. She looked back over her shoulder at him. Her door closed. Now and then a dog barked. After a moment Crit flipped the dumpster lid closed.

* * *

The sun was trying but was not yet up. Morning mist hung thick in low places. A coal truck rolled to a blinking stoplight. A lazy freight train clanked and picked up speed on its way to Tennessee.

Inside his room Crit sat on the stained carpet using his bed as a table. He had not been able to sleep in this place of strange sounds. The thing he had worked at for five hours straight was of a callused and dirty hand gripping the neck of a Crown Royal bottle. He tilted his head and judged the shape of it, the density of his cross-hatching. Then he went and picked up the leak bucket from the bathroom. Using a wad of toilet paper, he scrapped wet rust out of the bottom and smeared a red-brown earthy paste across the sketch surface. He paused. He wondered if the rust color was a mistake.

Then someone knocked twice at his door.

"You up?

"I'm up."

"You feel like doing something?" Wild Bill asked.

"What time is it?"

"Ten-thirty, about."

It was later than he had thought.

"Doing what?"

Two hours passed and he was up on the motel's flat roof pushing Black Jack cement into tar cracks with the end of a stiff broom. Wild Bill had given him gloves, a bandana and work boots. Then Bill had left him to go do a slow motion, cocked-elbow dance in the wet grass patch between the motel and the highway. Crit worked the oozing tar and watched Bill's strange movements.

Bill had taken off his crocs and was barefoot. His arms went up slowly. His palms thrust out, then down, then upward. He pivoted slowly, then moved a leg out and squatted.

"T'ai chi. That's what the Chinese call it." Bill yelled up to Crit. "I think it means keep stuff movin' so it don't rot."

Crit nodded like he understood, but he really didn't. He rested for a moment on his broom and looked beyond Bill, out across the highway to where the jagged blue Cumberland ridgeline ran South to Hazard. He would have to get used to open vistas without chain-link foregrounds. An Asian delivery man on a bicycle pumped past and glided down the hill. Bill called out a greeting that sounded like *what's up B*. Crit would later learn it was the name of a peppery Asian hot sauce. The delivery man rose up from his seat to slow-climb the next hill standing. Any such delivery man in Breathitt County had to have strong legs, Crit thought.

The next job was fixing the interior ceiling. Wild Bill finished his t'ai chi and helped Crit spread plastic sheeting over most everything in Crit's room, even though there wasn't much to protect or save. Crit climbed up on a ladder and reached through the soggy hole at the center of the spotted mold pattern and felt and marked where the rafters were. Then he used a dull matt knife and a level to cut straight lines around the worst part and pulled down a two-by-three-foot section.

There was an empty room at the very end of the line of rooms that Bill used to store tools. The overhead light bulb was burned out but with the door open Crit could mostly see. They stepped inside, looking for drywall pieces and joint compound.

"I had a pipe bust right after Christmas," Bill said. "Fun times. Had this dude in number four homecooking on a hot plate. He turned the gas heat off. It dropped to minus two and his pipes froze and I only found out when all this water flooded out the bottom of his door. Found him passed out on his bed with two inches of water all around him. I kicked his ass out and had to replace the wall, the pipes and the carpet. My cousin helped with that."

Wedged in behind a push mower were two large pieces of gypsum board and a five-gallon bucket of ready-mix joint compound with a green top. "Had that left over and that mud should still be good." Bill turned on the flashlight on his cell phone to look for a trowel.

Crit pried off the top off the bucket with a screwdriver to make sure the joint compound hadn't dried out.

Bill found a six-inch trowel and Crit hefted the larger drywall panel onto his shoulder. He staggered down to his room and set it down slowly so as not to chip or crack the edges. He then transferred his measurements while Bill sat on a bucket and watched and talked about how he had recently traded a half-ounce of weed for a used Ovation guitar.

"You can borrow it. I'm into electric only these days."

"I don't play no more."

"You can set it in a corner and one day it'll talk you into picking it up."

"I don't think so."

"Guitars are like that, like women in a bar. Speaking of, if you need to get laid, I can help with that."

"How can you help with that?"

"Some of these gals I know just wanna party."

Crit grunted.

"Was that a yes or a no?"

"What do you do for my brother besides run his motel?"

"Not much, a few favors now and then."

Crit made a shallow score line and broke off a drywall rectangle and carried it inside. Wild Bill followed him in and stood on a chair and held it up in place while Crit sank the screws.

"I was supposed to climb the wall with James Earl Ray on his big escape," Bill said. "But I got food poisoning from the shit food, and when the dogs were out chasin' Jimmy's fugitive ass all over East Tennessee, I was stuck on the shitter."

Crit had never heard this part of Bill's Brushy Mountain saga before and wondered if it was true. He anchored the drywall on the perimeter. It might bow some in the middle over time. But Bill seemed okay with that. Crit stuck the trowel in the joint compound bucket and worked the mud as best he could to match the cottage cheese pattern.

When they were finished, Bill packed his tools. "I can take that walker out of here if you don't need it."

"I don't need it."

"Momma don't need it either. She can't walk. Can't eat without tubes. She don't even know who I am," Bill said with a touch of melancholy and wiped his trowel clean with a rag. "There's a store downtown she keeps a lot of her junk in. I'll have to clean that out, too."

Crit climbed down from the ladder and noticed he'd left black tar tracks on the plastic that was covering the floor. He folded the ladder and took it outside and leaned it up beside leftover drywall cuts. Bill and Crit then made several trips back and forth, carrying out tools and the plastic drop cloth. Bill emptied the trowel bucket into the grass.

"You throwin' them away?" Crit nodded at the unused drywall squares.

"I guess so."

"I'll take em if you are."

"Sure. What for?"

Wild Bill didn't wait for an answer. A red pick-up with a tan roof pulled up at the motel office and honked, and Bill jogged toward it and was gone. Crit carried two of the larger drywall pieces inside. He pulled back his curtain and caught sight of Bill handing the unseen driver something. Maybe it was chunky white. A favor for his brother. Maybe it wasn't his business and he closed the curtain.

Crit cleared his charcoal sticks, sharpies and sketchpads off his coverlet and laid one of the drywall panels, white-face-up on his bed. He knelt and picked up a stick of charcoal. His ear sang like a hundred mosquitos trapped inside.

Time passed and the sun shadows moved. Four hours after he'd started it was dark outside and Crit rose, stiff from kneeling. He had worked in the dark and now he turned on the light. The charcoal, ink, and rainwater-sludged human form on the panel was a depiction of a long-haired man practicing t'ai chi. Crit had spent more time than usual on the background. He had even scraped tar off his work boots and smeared it onto the image surface. The figure's contorted body pushed out to the viewer as if free from a curtain of gloom.

When a thing he worked on got close to an ending, Crit would tend to look at it more and work on it less. Then when it was finished, he would hardly look at it at all. He set Wild Bill's image against the wall and went to sleep.

He had bad dreams but he didn't remember them.

Chapter 6

WE'RE NOT FRIENDS

The next morning Crit walked three miles North on 30 toward town. Low clouds hid the massive uplift of the mountains. The old man and his wife had already filled two bags with cans. They were now arguing across the road at each other. A lot of yelling and arm waving. It seemed to be a disagreement over which highway to comb next. He moved past them and crossed a concrete bridge over the North Fork and counted three mobile phone towers.

He walked another half-mile and paused to watch a bulldozer push down a building that had been a machine shop way back and then a farm implement dealership. A cloud of diesel smoke mushroomed about the driver's head, and his heavy blade pushed floor joists and support timbers and broken concrete blocks into irregular piles. With each stamp on the left or right brake and each flick of the hydraulics, the driver changed what was before and what was to come after. *O lucky man.* He reversed and then went forward, toppling the old and useless and pushing things into piles to haul away and discard.

Crit walked farther and the sun climbed higher. Some of the ridge-peaks were now visible through disappearing tendrils of mist.

Passing a muffler shop, Crit was surprised to catch sight of his brother's spoked-wheel truck parked in a used-car lot. Several low-slung Harleys were kick-standed by the open garage door. Just then Chrome stepped out, trailed by two bearded bikers in torn-sleeve jackets. Crit watched from a hundred yards away as his brother kicked over one of the Harleys and flat out screamed into the ugliest biker's face. The man getting yelled at was bigger than his brother but he took it. The other biker pulled what appeared to be cash out of a chained wallet. Chrome took the money but continued to berate them both.

Crit had given his brother his shiny nickname. One day during middle school recess there had been a no-holds-barred game of twenty-one at the hoop court behind Highland Turner Elementary. Chrome had busted the tread off his hand-me-down sneakers and then bloodied a toe, playing barefoot. He lost and whimpered that Crit had had an unfair advantage. Crit spied a plumbing truck parked at the service entrance of the school and then stole a roll of metal conduit tape. He wrapped Chrome's flapping shoe tread in the shiny metal tape like a torpedo.

Crit moved off and away.

There was a new gas island at the Marathon Gas and Go and the place looked as clean-scrubbed and made-over as any high-volume station on I-75. Crit remembered it as a one-pump deal with hubcaps nailed to the sidewalls. During his childhood it had been run by a friend of his momma's who chewed tobacco and lost her leg to the sugar. Her concessions had been bare essentials, including a big jar of pickled bologna that Chrome had always said looked like a jar of dicks. Now Crit was staring at five bright aisles stocked with groceries, auto accessories, wine and beer. A clear Plexi shield encased a Pakistani or maybe Indian clerk who was playing what seemed to be on-line poker on a monitor next to the cash register. The clerk had thick black hair, glasses, and dark stubble like he hadn't shaved in two days.

Crit picked up several cans of Vienna sausages and a box of Ritz crackers. He moved and noticed a watercolor paint set in the school/stationery section. *Living Color* was printed across the cover. Crit opened it. The color pots were dry-cracked and a small brush fell to the floor. The clerk stopped looking at his video screen and watched Crit as he bent and picked up the brush.

"That it?"

"If it ain't, it will have to do for now."

The clerk looked for a price tag on the watercolor set and didn't find one. "Was there another like this with a price tag?"

"Last one."

"I will say five dollars. If you can find another cheaper at Walmart you come back and I'll give you the difference, do you understand?" The foreign clerk smiled to be agreeable.

"I ain't going to Walmart."

"Okay then four dollars. Is this a gift for your child?"

Something dark registered behind Crit's eyes. Loud water flooded the moment. He breathed in half-breaths. The clerk had to tell him the price again before he moved to pay.

* * *

Crit didn't have a watch and worried that he was late. He carried his sack up the hill to town and was now walking past storefronts, churches, and pedestrians who moved like they had places to be. He noticed the newer styles of cars wedged in at the parking meters in front of the courthouse. SUVs seemed to have gotten larger and more bloated since he'd gone in. He checked the address on his state letter and located the one-story red-brick annex directly behind the courthouse.

He knocked. He entered. And now he was watching a medium-heavy, middle-aged parole officer named Brenda Cowan turn away from him to bang on the air conditioner unit that was jammed in her window.

"First time I had it on all year and I think the compressor's shot to snot." Her round face glistened with beads of perspiration. "What's in the bag?"

"Snacks."

"Lemme' see. You wouldn't think parolees would be dumb enough to carry contraband in here, but you'd be surprised."

Crit handed over his sack from the Marathon.

"What's this?" She put aside the crackers and popped open the watercolor set and also dropped the paintbrush.

"I snort it."

"Don't crack jokes with me. We're not friends."

It took her a struggling moment for her meaty fingers to get the brush off the floor and back into its plastic case, the effort leaving her short of breath and sweating more. She handed Crit his sack and rooted up a fax from her cluttered desk.

"There's a part-time job at county sanitation. Afternoons only. Minimum wage. No benefits."

"A garbage man?"

"A part-time garbage man." She handed him a beaker. "I'm gonna have to piss you."

Chapter 7

EYE OF THE NEEDLE

Johnny Cash sang about a grave that couldn't keep his body down on a tape player in a flatbed half-ton that Crit was driving up the pigtail curves of 1098 near Saldee. The man beside him was Eldon Cantwell, a wiry squirrel of a man with a bass-deep voice. Eldon had moved to Breathitt County ten years ago from up near Ashland to pastor a Pentecostal church, but backbiting had done him in, and he'd had to take a job with the county. The songs on Eldon's homemade cassettes were all old-timey gospel and he sang along with every one of them.

"Do you know what constitutes a mortal sin?" Eldon asked.

Crit shook no.

"Gluttony. God hates fat people."

"That so."

"Mark 10:25, the parable about the camel and needle, the camel's a symbol for fat people not fitting in as God's chosen. That message has more to do with the man being fat than rich."

When Crit walked over to county to ask about applying for the part-time sanitation job, Eldon had immediately tossed Crit the truck keys and told him to drive. Crit did as he was told. Doing as you're told was the how to survive long bids in prison. Going against the grain tended to wear you down and out.

"Gluttony is a starter sin to all other sins, if you can't control what goes in your mouth, you're a sponge for the devil."

Crit nodded. He wasn't sure whether he was employed or not or maybe this was a test run. Eldon had not even asked if he had a valid license. His license had expired five years into his bid, but he figured he could get a new one soon enough, and he'd never seen the Breathitt law pull over a county vehicle ever. And then what did it matter if they did? Did it really matter if his parole was revoked?

They had already picked up a discarded sofa and mattress at a trailer park in Quicksand. And then a flattened raccoon off the breakdown lane South of Wolverine. Crit gathered the afternoon shift was mainly to service random calls that came in about illegal dumping and dead-animal removal.

Crit drove around a bend and Eldon pointed up ahead at what appeared to be a large dog that traffic had thumped over repeatedly and pushed to the side of the road. "There she blows."

Crit pulled over. There was a 45-degree drop just off the edge of the road into a sunken fence line. He had to park half-on and half-off the road. He stepped on the emergency brake, and Eldon told him to put on the hazard lights and then had to tell him where they were. Crit climbed out. The air reeked of carrion. As with the previous stops, Eldon's preference was to supervise from the cab. Crit reached the back of the truck bed and saw the dead animal was a Holstein calf about six months old. Tires had crushed and exposed the skull to the bone and teeth, and rusty brown goo puddled the asphalt. A wind-burned farmer in Carhart and milking boots walked over from a rickety barn. Crit knew the land and knew the farmer but gave no greeting.

"Took y'all long enough to get here. His momma's been bawlin' for two days and nights."

As if on cue a mournful bovine lament trumpeted from the barn. Crit kept his head down as he grabbed the scoop shovel off the truck and slid it up under the calf. He pulled and walked backward, dragging the carcass nosily to the truck. The hard part was lifting it without fouling his shirt and pants.

"Hey, I know you. I'm Liddy's half-brother."

Crit tapped the shovel on the road to knock off maggots, ear full of rush and hiss. "I know you are."

"I heard they let you out." The farmer's eyes got small. "You're going to hell for what you did."

Sour decay filled Crit's nostrils. He turned and walked back to the cab and climbed in and started the engine and asked El-don where to next and drove, but all the while he was thinking Liddy must know, too. *Liddy must know, too.* That I'm out.

* * *

Crit walked the three miles from the sanitation garage to the motel in a kind of unconscious daze. Left foot. Right foot. The air had cooled and the sky was burnt embers over dark mountains. Two planets pretending to be stars blinked. He turned up the motel driveway and Wild Bill was lumbering through his gangly Chinese movements in the cool half-dark. A speeding car honked and someone screamed out Bill's name in a smart-ass way and the hollering drew Rennie out of her room. She had a cell phone pressed to her ear and hadn't changed her clothes from yesterday.

"Who the hell was that?" she yelled at Bill.

Bill told her he didn't know or care.

"Pick up dumbass dickfucker!"

Crit glanced over. She was yelling into her phone and her face had a shiny sheen to it. He patted his pockets for his key.

"Pick up, pick up, pick up. Where the fuck you at? And fuck this lame-ass box full ain't takin' no more message bullshit." She slung her arm up as if to toss her phone and caught Crit looking at her. "Mind yer own business, Dickwad."

Crit moved into his room and closed the door. He heard Rennie try to start up a fight with Bill, who gave up on his exercise and went off to his office. Her curses receded and Crit figured she was walking to town. He pulled back his curtain and saw instead that she was stepping into Bill's office.

He closed his curtain and washed his hands because they smelled dead. The only thing he found on the old black and white TV was a Lexington station playing CSI Las Vegas and he watched for a bit, but the fuzzy reception hurt his eyes. He turned it off and finished off a can of Vienna sausages and started a new painting.

As before he sat on the floor and used his bed as a table. It took him an hour to slash out the shape and form and another hour to darken the lines around his subject with a sharpie and crosshatch the shadows. He then trickled water into the watercolor dry pots. He wet the small brush. The first washes dried too red, too blue. Crit experimented with adding some of the rusty sludge from the leak bucket to mute things. It seemed to work, mostly. He brushed and scratched with focused intensity well past midnight, then paused short of breath, hand trembling and cramping.

He stood up and stepped back to see what he had worked on from a distance and wondered if it was done. There on a drywall panel was a desperate young woman with two-tone hair pacing, phone jammed into her ear, waiting for a phone call that never comes.

Something banged his door and Crit leaped up with prison-honed quickness.

"Who's there?"

No answer.

He lifted the drapes. He saw nothing but heard a car. He opened his door and stepped outside into mist and darkness. The only thing moving was a brown Pontiac, already halfway down the hill and picking up speed as it ran the blinking red light.

Then it was gone.

A couple of crickets chirped.

Crit looked about. Bill's office was dark. The road was dark. The mountains were dark. Rennie's red-curtained window glowed bright and her hip-hop beats pulsed from inside like something that wouldn't die. He moved back to his door and noticed a round thing in the shadow of a concrete planter. He bent and picked it up.

A worn and well-used softball.

Some of the stitching had come lose. He moved it into a shaft of light. The name *Taylor* was crudely cut into the leather with a birthday Case pocketknife.

Crit closed his eyes to a flood of rushing noise and wished he could sink into the earth. And be done and gone. Consumed by lava and magma or worms. A dizziness came, and he reached out, but found nothing to tether to.

But he didn't fall.

* * *

Crit barely slept. He lay on his back atop his bed, fitful, fully dressed, holding the softball in his hand, staring up at nothing as the long hours of the night passed. He dozed off a bit just before dawn and dreamed he was still in prison, locked in a solitary cell where he could hear a riot on the other side of his caged door. Shots rang out and guards and inmates screamed echoey screams like they were being butchered. Then somehow he was freed, and he walked alone out into the prison yard. And there was no one—no inmates or guards. Not a moving, living thing. Just him. All others had disappeared like the rapture. The dorms and chapel and gym stood empty with doors banging from gusts of wind. The flagless flagpole rattled. He looked up. The sky was thick with circling black vultures that obscured the sun.

* * *

Crit woke with a gasping cough and sat up. He was sweating. He looked for the softball and it was gone. Was that a dream, too? He searched the wadded coverlet and then found it under a chair where it must have rolled when he dozed off. He picked it up and felt the scuffed leather again. He looked up at the ceiling, at the fine cracks that had dried in the drywall patch. But he didn't see the ceiling or the cracks. He saw the recreation-league softball game. The out-of-focus kaleidoscope of hitters hitting, catchers catching, scoreboard changing, a young boy making a dash for home and losing his cap. Crit's head throbbed and ghosts of his past were jumbling into his dreams and waking actuality. His breathing and heart-rate increased and the veins at his temples pulsed. He stood up dizzy, went to the bathroom, and drank water from the sink, then repeatedly splashed his face with cold water. He was sloppy in shoveling the water and the walls dripped.

Oh, Taylor.

Chapter 8

PENUMBRA

Morning came. Wild Bill knocked and asked through the door for a favor. Crit came out and fifteen minutes later he was riding in Bill's rusty Econoline van down Quicksand Road toward downtown. Wild Bill slipped a Slayer CD into an external CD player bracketed to the dashboard and lit up a joint and inhaled deeply as the music jackhammered. He held the smoke in with his face pinched and offered the joint to Crit.

"No, thanks."

Bill glanced over at Crit, exhaled a gray stream, and then shouted over the screeching vocalist. "You used to talk more."

"Talk more?"

"Before you went in. You were a cock-of-the-walk son of a bitch with too many opinions about everything."

"That so."

"And you never turned down good weed or just about nothin'."

"I got used to not using."

"And so now you like, don't play guitar, don't smoke or drink or..."

"I don't know what I do or don't do, I just don't want that shit now." There was a seam of anger in Crit's voice.

"Right on."

Bill turned at a stoplight. He honked and waved to someone on the street he knew. They passed boarded-up storefronts on Court Street and pulled over in front of a second-hand clothing and appliance store. Bill tossed cardboard boxes out of the back of the van and they carried them inside a dusty shop filled with castoff clothes, dollhouses, toasters, kids toys, coffee makers, and other items in boxes that were double- and triple-stacked against the walls.

"The deal is since Momma had her stroke she can't sell no more," Bill said.

Crit noticed a large velveteen painting of Jesus hands praying. "She sold this stuff?"

"Yep. Folks got their basements chock-full of useless shit but they always find room for more." Bill slipped on finger-less leather gloves. "I paid up three months advance for her, but I figure we clean this crap out, landlord might kick back that last month." Bill scraped a stack of baby clothes into a box.

"Where's it all going?"

"The dump. You see anything you like you can keep it."

Crit walked through a divider door into the cluttered back workroom. There were piles of secondhand items against the left and right walls, and an old Singer sewing machine sat atop a sawhorse table nearly buried under swaths of fabric. There was a huge factory-type window that ran the width of the back wall and filled the entire room with late morning light. Crit moved to the window. He raised his hand and saw the way the light fell on his fingers and palm. A stray cat snarled and flashed out a broken windowpane. Crit put his palm print on the dirty glass. Below him two boys fished at a curl in the river. They had left their cane poles stuck in the mud and were throwing rocks at each other. An idea came. He rubbed his nose and considered the foolishness of it.

"I guess I oughta' hold onto her sewing machine," said Bill. His voice had emotion in it. "She used to make her own clothes.

She once sewed me some britches made out of burlap. I loved my momma awful, but I sure as hell wasn't going to school in burlap pants." Bill reached out and gently touched a spool of thread on the top of the sewing machine.

"How about I hang out here mornings and sell her stuff?" Crit heard himself say.

"Naw, man, we haul it out, I can get that last month."

"You ain't gettin' your last month unless landlords changed their stripes since I been in. And if I sell anything at all, we got less to haul to the dump."

Bill bent his arms into a t'ai chi move. "You just strung together the most words I yet heard you say since you been out."

Crit shrugged and turned back to the window.

"I ain't no dream crusher," Bill said, and then vocalized sound effects to his slow-motion movements that sounded like a clock ticking.

Down below, Crit saw that the boys had given up on rocks and were throwing hedge apples at each other. The large brain-like seedpods were easier to dodge, he remembered from years ago.

* * *

Crit worked mostly mornings and some evenings on it. He sorted through and threw out most of the frayed and unsellable junk. He gathered boxes of scuffed children's toys and left them against the locked door of Jackson First Baptist Church. He organized the remaining items by type and function. He broomed cobwebs off the ceiling and walls. And every moment he worked on the place, trying to get it ready, he was less sure of why he was trying to get it ready in the first place. What he told himself mostly was that if he could set himself up to make some money without the hassle of working for someone else, that was the way to go.

When he finished straightening the front room he started on

the back. The Pakistani clerk at the gas station let Crit have eight or nine empty produce boxes and he collapsed them and carried them to his store. He set the boxes at the base of a large pile of secondhand debris and dug through and culled out pots and pans, a napkin holder, coffee mugs, candlesticks, a ukulele, Tupperware, garden hoses, ancient tennis rackets and cookbooks. He gave a spin to a dusty globe. He doubted that all these things had been owned by Bill's family. The sheer volume of it spoke to the fact that it was the castoff refuse of many other lives.

He opened a leather-bound photo album and neither Bill nor his momma were in any of the pictures. Some of the photos were very old. On the second page there was a black and white image of a dark-haired soldier in uniform with a young girlfriend or wife who had her hair up in a long-ago style. Behind them was a horse tied to a tree. The black and white images gave way to color as Crit turned the pages, and he recognized the couple as they produced children, threw birthday parties and decorated Christmas trees. Crit turned more pages and the children grew older and had children of their own and the couple became older and their postures went and they started wearing glasses and gained weight. The man lost most his hair. The last photo showed the couple perhaps in their sixties or seventies, sitting close together on a porch swing. They weren't smiling but seemed content. The woman was looking off to the side but had her hand on her husband's knee. Crit closed the album and tossed it into the box to take to the trash.

Eldon had reduced his hours to just two afternoons a week and that freed up more time to be uncertain about opening the shop. He swept and washed the floor. He cleaned soot off the back windowpanes and replaced the broken ones with plywood rectangles. The cat would be disappointed. He shook dust out of the curtains. He placed the globe on his sales counter and sometimes, when he was between tasks, for no reason at all, he would give it a spin and stick out his finger and stop it on a country whose name he was totally unfamiliar with and about which he knew nothing.

Later that same week, when Crit and Eldon drove the flatbed to the county dump to dispose of a deer carcass, he spotted a ten-foot section of modular metal fencing leaning against a pile of scrap metal. Sister Nikhael had once shown Crit a photograph of a Louisville group show she had a painting in. The gallery was in an old factory in the part of Louisville Sister Nikhael had called Germantown. And the white walls had been lined with black metal fencing. Crit had been more impressed with the repurposed black wire squares against the white gallery walls than the confusing abstract paintings displayed on them.

The sanitation yard attendant had given Crit the okay to grab the fence, and so after work, Crit went back with Wild Bill and fetched it.

Crit and Bill lifted it off the top of the van and hauled it into the shop and Crit spray painted black over the rust. Then Bill held it up while Crit screwed it to the wall behind the sales counter. He took a step back and imagined it covered with his own artwork. Wouldn't that be something? Or would it? He stood frozen in place for ten minutes and decided that what he was attempting was a terrible idea. He should have left the fence with the rest of the junk and the dead deer at the dump.

He went outside and walked down by the river and stood there. He watched the dull brown current and the occasional drifting log and then looked up at the dark blue misty mountains pocked with telephone towers and the clouds above them and wondered where he should begin to achieve a change in his existence.

In a closet he found a cardboard box full of framed prints of farm scenes, flowers in vases, Jesus with thorns, Jesus with glowing halos, and dogs playing poker. The only print he kept intact was one of the dog poker series. The rest of the mass-produced cardboard prints he pulled from their glass frames and replaced them with his own artwork. It was a strange sensation to press under hard glass that which he had scratched into being. And when he finished framing as many of his works as he could, he boxed them all up and shoved them back deep into the closet. And shut the door. And left them in the dark.

Then the next morning he came in and pulled them out again and looked at each and every one, one by one, and boldly hung them onto the metal fencing behind the sales counter.

He walked the perimeter of his store. Left foot. Right foot. Scratched his nose. Dug a fingernail of earwax. What was he doing? He was a rodeo clown. He was Wild Bill jerking through his t'ai chi moves next to the highway. He was putting it out there like a prancing homosexual in the prison yard. Why had he even suggested taking over the store?

Who are you trying to fool, Inmate?

He never answered himself. But at the end of that first week he found a three-foot by one-foot board and painted it black. He let it dry. He was about to paint a door sign that said…

2nd Chance Collectibles.

He had even penciled out the spacing and checked the spelling with an old worn-edged Webster Dictionary he had found in the back room. He wet his brush and dipped it into white latex. He carefully painted the *two*. And he paused and put down his brush. Put his brush back in water. He took a wet rag and rubbed out what he had painted. He applied another coat of black and had to wait until the next morning to finish the sign.

After it dried he drove lag bolts into it and screwed it over his front door. White letters over black backing.

Penumbra Gallery.

That sign would certainly have local folks talking and guessing.

Chapter 9

TYBO

"I could use a hand," Crit said and tapped on the passenger window.

Eldon stopped singing and sounded annoyed. "What?"

"I got the trash and garbage bags, but I need a hand with the refrigerator."

"Damn, I hate refrigerators," Eldon said, and turned off his tape player and climbed out in no hurry. "I hate 'em worse than stoves. I put in a request to get a truck with a lift gate. One of these days, one of these years."

Eldon took his time sliding on leather gloves with fabric cuffs. He met Crit at the back of the flatbed at the edge of the pull-off that overlooked a wooded ravine. They were way out in the county. Stony pinnacles dotted with shrubby evergreens rose on both sides of the road. The illegal dumper had not even bothered to push the old curved-top refrigerator over the edge and down to where fast water coursed over rocks and the rusting hulks of junked cars. A state sign with bullet holes on a metal post said *No Dumping*.

"You should back it up more."

Crit went around to the driver's side and started to climb in but then he saw the front left tire was half-flat. Maybe more than that.

"Tire's low."

Eldon came over and both men looked at the tire.

"Picked up a nail I imagine," Eldon said.

Crit looked and then Eldon looked but neither saw a nail head in the part of the tire they could see.

"There's a spare under there but I don't know if it's up."

Crit went to the back and knelt and reached under and pushed his thumb against the wall of the mud-crusted spare that was bolted to the bottom of the truck bed.

"Seems low."

Eldon shook his head. "We better try to make a run back to town. Too much slope if we try to change it out here. You think it'll stay on the rim?"

Crit shrugged.

"I'll say a prayer."

They left the refrigerator where it was and Crit maneuvered a three-point and headed back down the mountain. He took the curves more slowly than usual, as all the weight was now on the front tires.

Eldon closed his eyes and mumbled a short prayer about how God had problems many and great, but if he could manage to consider a small humble request from a humble servant to keep their left front tire on the rim, he would greatly appreciate it. Then he opened his eyes and told Crit to head to the Marathon.

Crit nodded. It was closer than the county garage. Crit drove the last four miles on edge and when they finally pulled up to the coin-operated air compressor at the Marathon Gas and Go, Eldon profusely thanked his Lord and Savior. Eldon then fished out two quarters and handed them to Crit.

"Get a receipt."

"For fifty cents?"

"Did I stutter? Get the receipt first," Eldon said sharply and turned up a Doc Watson song on his tape deck. Crit figured he was in a snit over leaving the refrigerator behind.

Crit went in and asked for the receipt from the Pakistani clerk and got a headshake and an explanation that the air compressor was owned by a third party vendor and he made no money off the deal. The clerk even showed Crit the card of the air compressor company. Crit borrowed a pen and wrote out a fifty-cent receipt on a napkin by the coffee pots and creamers. He had the clerk tell him the date and put that on it too. And then he walked out and gave it to Eldon who took it with disdain.

"What's this?"

"A receipt."

"It don't look like a receipt."

"Well, it's the only receipt they're giving out today."

Eldon shook his head but put the napkin in the glove box.

Crit fed the coins, squatted and fizzed air into the tire that was now almost completely flat. Crit was amazed it had stayed on.

And just then a twenty-year-old Celica notchback coupe whined past and braked hard. Crit paid more attention to it when he recognized Rennie in the back seat behind two men who looked like the ugly dogs at a kennel that nobody ever took home. She seemed upset and yelled and pawed and pushed past them to get out. Crit thought she was in trouble. And he stood up.

"Tybo!"

She ran barefoot toward the gas island. Crit saw that a sturdy mountain woman was pumping gas into her large Buick with a young boy, maybe four or five, strapped in a child's seat in the back.

"Hey, Tybo, you havin' a nice day at school?" Rennie asked hyper fast.

"He ain't started school yet," the woman spoke. "And I can't afford daycare."

"Aw'right then, you been watchin' some awesome cartoons?" Rennie asked and pressed her face to the back window.

The boy stared at Rennie and said nothing. The woman put her hand on Rennie's shoulder to turn her. Rennie shook it off.

"No worries. I'll pump gas for you."

Rennie clipped the back bumper and fell and struggled to rise.

The woman replaced her gas cap. "You need to get to church."

"Your last husband went to church," Rennie said in a way that sounded friendly but wasn't.

The woman was now in a hurry to leave. What Rennie yelled next was no longer friendly. "The only reason I'm letting Tyler stay with you is that bastard's cold-ass dead."

The Buick started up, kicked out an oily exhaust cloud and beat a retreat toward 30. Rennie's face tightened, and then relaxed into a grin. She wiped the blue part of her hair from her eyes and waved at the gone car with both hands and kept waving, even after Tybo was long gone.

Crit hunted for the valve cap on the ground and found it and screwed it on.

The men in the coupe honked and yelled at Rennie. She turned from facing the highway and walked back to them. But then she stopped halfway and crumbled at the waist as if God had cut her puppet strings.

"Let's go before it goes flat," Eldon yelled.

Crit climbed back in. And he drove. And when he checked his rearview, Rennie was still at the pumps. Bent over.

Crit turned onto 30, crossed the bridge, and drove toward the county yard. The Doc Watson song ended and the Louvin Brothers started up.

"You sellin' anything out yer store?"

"Not yet," Crit said.

"Who's your landlord?"

"I don't know. I'm kind of a sub-tenant."

"I'm looking for someplace to start my church. If you ever give up on yer place, I might be interested."

Crit nodded and had to slow behind a blue Ford tractor with a bush hog raised up on the three-point back hitch.

"You ever have dark stools?"

Crit checked the highway ahead and pulled out into the opposite lane and passed the tractor. The driver waved.

"Not that I remember."

"My stools been comin' out dark as sin lately. I probably need to see a doctor," Eldon said, and then pointed. "There she blows."

It took several seconds for Crit to see it. A flat-dead something across from Hardee's. Maybe a cat.

"You want me to stop?"

"We missed out on the refrigerator, we can't come back empty-handed."

Crit pulled over in the breakdown lane and got out. He took the shovel and the tractor caught up and passed him, and the driver waved again. Crit walked up to what he could tell was a possum only because it still had its snake-like tail attached.

Then he saw a muddy brown Pontiac pull off the road fifty feet distant and park beside a new commercial building going up that was wrapped in white Tyvek. The driver's side window was dirt-streaked and he couldn't make her out much, but she had both hands on the wheel and was watching him. He decided not to look at her. He slid the shovel under the possum and carried it back to the truck. Hazard lights flashed and blinked. His ear sang. A muscle in his back twinged. He tossed the possum and turned toward her car and exhaled unsteadily. The Louvin Brothers sang high harmony over the rising hiss in his ear. He now walked back toward the Pontiac, carrying his shovel. Left foot. Right foot. There had been violence in the marriage, most of it his, but some hers. She could be carrying. When he was twenty feet away she put her car into reverse, but didn't let off the brake.

"Tire's going flat," Eldon yelled and honked the horn. "We gotta' go."

Her driver's side window was down. No makeup, careless hair, high cheekbones that said a few parts Cherokee. She was still good-looking but with deep lines in her face, like cracks in drywall. Two poison blue eyes drilled into the distant beyond.

"So what's the first fuckin' word yer gonna say to me?" Liddy finally said and every word was a harpoon.

Crit tried to speak. Nothing came out.

"You had fourteen years to figure it out and you got noth-ing?"

Now she looked at him and that dried up what he was about to say.

"You shoulda killed yourself in prison."

"I tried."

"Not hard enough."

Her foot lifted and she backed up and then shifted and U-turned into the northbound lane and drove off fast but not too fast. Crit heard the truck engine rev up behind him and he turned to see Eldon driving away in the opposite direction. The flatbed's hazard lights had been left on and they blinked and got smaller as the truck got smaller.

Crit stood there not moving until a customer pulled out of Hardee's and waited for him to move. Crit stepped out of the way and looked off to the western sky, where he saw an airplane va-por trail. It was side-lit by the setting sun and wafting outward from a slow-moving point spec. Crit marveled that such a small thing carried lives across this sky with troubles and joys he would never ever know.

Crit walked off the highway toward the Sunset Motel, drag-ging his shovel. He passed the Asian delivery man sitting on his haunches, attempting to reattach a bicycle chain. The delivery man looked up with oily hands and alarmed eyes. Their gazes met and ricocheted elsewhere.

Crit took the shortcut up the grass slope toward the motel and noticed the coupe from the Marathon was now parked be-hind the motel dumpster. Crit slowed and saw Rennie's red and blue hair rise and fall from the driver's lap. She sat up, coughed and spat. The driver and the man in the back brayed like mules. She climbed out.

Rennie said something angry to the driver and he smiled slick and offered her a small plastic baggie, then retracted his hand. She cursed and grabbed his hand and cursed again as he made her pry it from his closed fingers. She got what she wanted but fell over when she got it. The two men disparaged her cruelly and laughed and drove off.

She would have seen Crit if she was looking, but she wasn't looking at anything except what was in her hand. She picked herself up, stepped quickly to the door, took a key from her shoulder purse, unlocked and went in. The door closed slowly on its own weight because she hadn't bothered to close it. Her shadow passed across her curtain. And then it was just the red square of bright curtain he was looking at.

Crit wondered what to do with the scoop shovel. He decided to leave it around back behind the ice machine where it might not disappear. He went off that way.

"You got a phone call," Wild Bill called out.

Crit didn't see Bill at first. He was at the edge of the woods behind the motel, trying to attach a rainbow-colored nylon hammock between two trees.

"That gal that brought you here."

"What'd she say?"

"She said to tell you she might stop by Wednesday morning." Bill gave his hammock knot a tug. "So like she yer girlfriend?"

"She's married to Jesus."

"She can cheat on him, can't she?"

Bill gave a nasally laugh and then said, "I told her you were fixing up Momma's store. She got excited about that. Where'd you get the shovel?"

"Property of Breathitt County sanitation services."

"So they loan out shovels like a library now?"

"Did Sister Nikhael want me to call her back?"

"She didn't say anything about that."

Chapter 10

SCREENSHOT

Crit didn't have a clock but if he had, it would have said four in the morning. He held Tyler's softball in his hand. Turned it. Dug his thumb under a loose seam. He tried to hold it right there and keep it right there, not roll back the years. Not jiggle the nerve in his brain that shut everything down with an exorbitant fury. He focused on the way the overhead light exposed the convex top and ignored the rest. He set the ball on the coverlet and turned his gaze to the nearly finished drywall panel painting of a young boy throwing a softball, as seen from above. The softball was immense in the frame, like a glowing moon. Like the earth seen from the moon. The boy's hand, arm and body tapered down into eviscerated slashes of dark, as if he were standing waist-deep in dark earth.

Crit closed his eyes and ran his hands over the fresh wet of his work. It felt like the slime trail of a slug. He rubbed the muck-wet off on his pant leg.

There had been a constant creep of noise coming through his wall and now he heard her door slam. Footsteps pattered on concrete. A cough. A shadow flicked at his window. He looked at his door before he heard the timid knock. She knocked again.

"I know yer up. I can see you moving."

He had not moved at all but he rose on stiff knees and went to open the door. She stood barelegged in a baggy sweatshirt that barely covered her crotch. And she was barefoot. The reptile tattoo coiled up her right leg. She smirked out a smile and held out the bottle of Crown Royal that was down to a finger. In her other hand was her phone.

"I don't like to drink alone."

"You didn't seem to have much trouble with the rest of that bottle."

"You're like a cranky old cranky guy, aren't you?"

Their eyes squared off. It was like she had two different haircuts on one head and neither one of them was very becoming. He didn't like looking at her so close so he moved from the door and she followed him in. She said nothing for a minute or two and took in the charcoal sticks and pencils and watercolor set and dirty towels and drywall paintings and prison sketches, some intact and some crumpled.

"You draw all these?" She finally said.

Crit gave a nod, his back to her, she probably didn't see it.

"And here I thought you were an old perv watchin' porn all day." She unscrewed the top and took a sip from the bottle. "But you should open a window, it's kinda stale in here." Her words were slurred.

He sat down on the floor beside the bed.

"Fuck, is that me?" Rennie said now looking at the two-by-three-foot image on a drywall square of a frantic and stressed young woman clinging to a cellphone. "I don't look that bad, do I?" But she was not displeased. "So you been stalkin' me?"

Crit looked over at her.

She made a clucking sound like she'd caught him doing something bad and then offered him the bottle. He ignored her and thickened the outline of his softball sphere with a sharpie. She suddenly sat down hard on the foot of the bed and jounced his sharpie off line. She smiled coy when he frowned. She knew what she'd done.

Her cell phone dinged and she turned it over and looked at a text on the screen. "What phone company you with? I need to find a new one that don't suck." She typed a reply to someone with rapid thumb taps.

"I don't have a phone."

She sent the message. "For reals? Everybody got a phone. Unless they're a jailbird." She made her clucking sound again. "I know a few things about you."

"Know what?"

She turned back around to look at the image of herself. "Can I take a picture of my picture?"

"Why?"

She stood up and took three clicks of it from different angles with her phone. "My new screenshot."

Crit wet his thumb in a glass of dirty water and tried to rub out the errant sharpie line.

"I might let you paint me in my birthday suit, if you ask nice." She was looking at him with an unblinking, insolent stare.

Crit lowered his gaze and rubbed harder on the wet spot.

"When I have a bad day I paint my toes," she said and wiggled them. "And don't look a gift horse in the mouth. I'm about the best you'll get between here and the grave. And you know it."

She flopped back down on the bed with her head hanging over the edge and stretched up her arms, looking at the blue of her veins. "But even when I say yes, I might change my mind and say no, understand?"

"Less talk."

"Oh, am I disturbing you? So sorry." She reached out and picked up the softball and tossed it between her left and right hands.

Crit stopped painting.

"I used to play some baseball. I was better at it than my brothers."

He took the softball from her and put it back on the bed beside what he was painting.

"Mister Cranky."

She stood up to leave, changed her mind and sat back down in the chair next to the TV. Ten minutes or an hour passed. Crit looked up from his work; she had fallen asleep in the chair and was lightly snoring. She appeared younger and softer when she wasn't using her mouth as a weapon. Her hair was mushed against the wall, bare legs hugged in as if for protection or warmth. Her phone had fallen to the rug.

He worked until hints of morning leaked through the curtain. Then he stood up.

Crit struggled to get out his door under her weight. He wedged her against the mortar wall and twisted her doorknob. She moaned but didn't wake. He caught sight of Bill watching from his office window while eating a bowl of cereal. He thought Bill might come over to help but he didn't.

Inside her room, clothes were tossed everywhere. Fast-food bags, styrofoam cups, and pizza boxes littered the table and floor. He laid her down on the bare mattress. Her sheets were wadded in a corner. He took her phone out of his pocket and laid it on the dresser. Taped to her mirror was a small photograph of an infant. Next to that was a child's colored sketch of a stick-figure boy below a green tree with a bright yellow sun. There was a speech bubble above the boy.

Hi Mommy.

And below the sketch he saw a burnt piece of tinfoil and a butane lighter.

He looked at her. The bottoms of her feet were dirty. He could see the reptile crawling up her thigh was actually a dragon with wings and orange fire spitting from its mouth. She had on black thong underwear. She had taken out her belly button ring and there were two smallish red holes that looked slightly infected. Looking down at her he tried to remember the last time he had been with a woman. After Liddy, all he had were furtive, short exchanges of convenience. Mostly with young women who wanted what he and his brother sold, and looked a lot like this gal passed out on the bed. He picked a wadded blanket off the floor and covered her.

He closed her door after he made sure it locked from the inside.

He went back to his room. The Crown Royal bottle had barely a swallow left. He looked for the cap but couldn't find it. He even looked under the bed. He went to the sink and emptied it. He set the bottle back on the table next to the TV. He looked at his softball painting. Rubbed his face. Closed his eyes. And he remembered what Bill had said, that Sister Nikhael was coming. Wednesday. Fuck. Was today Monday? The thought of her visit filled him with unease. She expected him to be all those complimentary things she had said about him. He moved around his room and one by one he took out and looked at his newer paintings and sketches. Was there anything to them? Were they a map? He decided he had ruined good drywall. Made worthless good sketch paper. He had always anticipated the time when Sister Nikhael's warm affirming eyes would gaze on his work and harden like concrete. He fully expected that to happen on Wednesday.

Chapter 11

TUESDAY

Late Tuesday afternoon he was with Eldon, driving back toward Jackson. They were coming close to the junction where Upper Boone Fork Road merged into Lower Boone Fork. The low sun dappled sunspots across the windshield and exposed the dirt and bugs and grit. The cassette in Eldon's tape player had reached its end but Eldon hadn't bothered to turn it. He seemed to be dozing or praying with his eyes closed. But suddenly, after not saying anything for ten minutes, Eldon said, "How many rooms have you lived in?"

"Rooms?"

"Rooms. Like how many places you spent the night in or lived in yer whole life?"

"I couldn't say."

Eldon opened his eyes. "You were in prison, don't that make it easier to count?"

Crit shrugged. "They moved you around a lot."

"I'm forty-eight years old and I've lived in forty-two rooms so far," Eldon said. "Forty-three if you count the hospital I was born in. Does that sound like a lot?"

Crit said he didn't know.

"It's just something I keep track of and I've always thought a lot about."

Crit waited for Eldon to make a point or go into a sermon. But Eldon dropped his head into his hands and let out a sigh and closed his eyes and said nothing more about counting rooms. He seemed overtaken with a deep gray sadness. Crit decided there were peculiarities about Eldon that he didn't understand.

Crit drove on and watched the center stripes flicker beneath the hood and then said, "Can I ask you something?"

"Shoot." Eldon didn't bother to open his eyes.

"We're going past where I live. Do you mind if I pick up some things and take 'em downtown. If it's a problem, that's no problem."

"What things?"

"Some things I'm tryin' to sell at that store."

"Dope?"

"Nothing like that."

"You went in on a dope charge, right?"

"I did."

Eldon ejected his cassette tape and turned it over and listened to a bluegrass style intro to *Church in the Wildwood*. "Sure, why not," he finally said.

Crit pulled up the motel driveway. He went inside his room, retrieved his new paintings and sketches, came out and laid them face-up in the truck bed. He took care to keep them out of the wet patches of garbage water. Neither Rennie nor Bill showed themselves, and Crit was glad of that.

Then Crit drove downtown, unlocked his store, and made several trips back and forth to Eldon's truck. Eldon stayed in the cab and had no interest in the paintings and sketches that Crit carried in, or in anything else for that matter. His eyes stayed closed like he was nursing his dark mood. Then Crit drove the flatbed back to county sanitation and both men clocked out.

The sky was mottled and yellow with pink traces in the clouds and the overhead security lights had already come on when they stepped out of the office.

"My parents were dirt-poor and the state put me in foster care for awhile," Eldon said as he locked the two deadbolts. "I started counting rooms back then." He stepped away from the door and looked down at his steel-toe boots and then walked toward his Chevrolet Sonic that had a small American flag attached to the radio antenna.

Crit decided to call out, "See you Friday," as Eldon opened his car door. Eldon gave no reaction. He slumped into his seat, backed up, and drove away.

Of the dozens of times they had clocked out together, Eldon had never once offered Crit a ride home. It was as if Eldon had some innate rule that they could only be passengers in the same vehicle if they were getting paid for it. But Crit was okay with that. He'd known many behind bars who lived by arcane, self-imposed rules.

Crit walked back to his store. He passed a strip mall with a check-cashing/payday loan business and a Verizon outlet. A siren wailed in the far distance and about half of the passing cars now had their headlights on.

Two blocks from his shop he saw a man coming toward him on the opposite side of the street. The man was thin and hunched over and his clothes were soiled and dirty. He jerked when he walked like he had a bad foot or leg. In the darkening half-light, Crit still recognized him. His name was Pogue and he had been part of their crew, back when he and his brother had ten or more men working under them. His best earning years. Pogue had also played in a country-rock band with Wild Bill. He had rented out the convention hall at Natural Bridge State Park to get married in and then had gone on a honeymoon to a resort in Baja, Mexico. Crit had seen photographs of Pogue and his smiling, big-boned bride in sombreros, toasting with huge margaritas. From the look of it now, it appeared Pogue had lost all that.

Pogue limped past, head bent almost to his chest, not noticing Crit. And Crit was thankful for that small mercy.

Crit unlocked his store and went in and wondered if he was any better off than Pogue. He had a leaky roof over his head and an art teacher who believed in him. But given the severity of what he'd done, and had to live with, he decided he was worse off.

Tomorrow was Wednesday and Sister Nikhael was coming. Crit turned on his lights and hunted up a screwdriver and mounted his new works, one by one, on the walls and metal fencing. He then straightened up the place. He noticed the floor needed sweeping and swept it. When he ran out of things to do, he decided the place was as ready as it would ever be for his esteemed visitor. He moved to the counter, spun the globe and jabbed it with his finger. He'd landed on Bulgaria, another place he knew nothing about. He imagined that Sister Nikhael knew all sorts of things about all sorts of foreign and strange places.

He flipped through a sketchpad and looked at a drawing he had started of an Asian delivery man trying to attach a bicycle chain. The man had his head turned around and was staring wide-eyed at the viewer. His eyes gleamed with awkward distrust. Crit put the sketch on the counter and worked a bit at darkening the lines of the wheel sprockets.

"You open?"

A sixtiesh woman wearing a turquoise baseball cap stood in the doorway. She had on a bold-patterned blouse, almost Hawaiian, and tinted glasses with the ear temples attached at the bottoms of the lenses.

"My perm's gone flat as a pancake and I'm in town for an emergency rinse and set. But my hairdresser got backed up so I got time to kill. What kind of name is that on your sign?"

He wasn't sure he could remember exactly how Sister Nikhael had defined it, so he punted. "I don't know. Somebody else named it."

"Sounds like a Bible word."

"Maybe it is."

They stopped talking and she drifted around the place, even taking an interest in his paintings. He noticed that his ear seemed to vibrate differently when a strange set of eyes wandered the place. He tried to keep working on what he was working on, but the woman's presence distracted him.

"How much for that hand painting?"

He looked to where she was pointing.

"I haven't put a price on it."

She was looking at a sketch Crit had made in prison, rough hands holding a dirty miner's lunch pail. His momma had once dragged Crit and his brother up to live in Lost Creek with a man thirty years older who claimed to be dying from black lung. She had tried to marry him for his death benefits, but it turned out he had never divorced his last wife. Their stay in Lost Creek didn't last long. And on the day they moved out Crit and his brother had taken the old miner's lunch pail out and blasted it to bits for target practice. Momma had smiled at that.

"Looks like my husband's hands." The woman said. "He worked Eagle Creek thirty-nine years. He could never get that coal dust out of his fingernails. I'll give you ten dollars for it if you throw in that toaster oven."

The woman nodded at an appliance on the shelf that Bill's momma had already priced at ten dollars with a yellowed piece of masking tape.

"Sure," Crit said. "I can plug it in and make sure it works."

It did work and Crit took her ten dollars and placed the toaster on the counter and then reached up and took down the hand sketch and passed it to her.

"You look kinda familiar, where you from, Honey?"

"Here."

"Do I know you?"

"I just got out of prison."

She took him in and looked at him differently. Her glasses had a pink tint to them and he couldn't tell the true color of her eyes. But they looked like kind eyes.

"God loves you. He never stopped loving you. Do you believe that?"

"I'm sorry but I don't."

"But you do believe in Him?"

Crit read the model and serial number on the back of the toaster oven. "I'm not sure. People talk about him a lot and they ask all kinds of things of him. Favors. And some say he makes their lives better. But I think it's kind of selfish, maybe that's not the best word, but I think it's selfish to think he's got time for us as individuals. I want him to worry more about the important stuff. Not me. I done what I done. I don't know if there's a heaven after we're gone. If there is, I don't believe I'll ever see it. But I do believe there's hell on earth. And there's those that deserve that." He stopped talking and read the serial number again. "If you want your money back I understand."

She shook her head softly and leaned forward and gently touched his hand. "I'm gonna pray double hard for you."

"He needs it," a voice said.

Crit turned. His brother filled the doorway and smiled like his scratch-off had just come in. The woman put the framed hand sketch on top of her toaster oven and lifted both. She told Crit she'd be back to see him again soon. Chrome held the door open as she passed and she thanked him. He even politely tipped his sunglasses, which he was wearing like a rock star though it was dark outside.

"Bra, did you just sell a masterpiece?"

"More like I gave it away."

"Bill told me you do this now. I never woulda believed it. Prison turned my brother gay."

Crit ignored the comment and tried to figure out what he should do with the ten-dollar bill. Chrome moved around the store, checking out the sketches and paintings. His boots creaked the planking.

"I used to draw some. You weren't the only artist in the family. I'd be drawing my war stories in the back of Miss Hogsett's class. And I'd be making up sound effects. Wham. Bam. Kabam. Miss Hogsett smacked the back of my head for drawin' so loud."

Chrome chuckled and moved to the painting of a man practicing t'ai chi. "I got to say you got Bill's crazy just about right." Chrome then stepped in front of the image of Rennie screaming at her cell phone. "Hey, I recognize that cooch." He made a *huh* sound while studying it. "Bill said yer doin' her." Chrome's hand came up to the point of his chin. "We used to hang some." He stretched out the word *hang*. Packed it with meaning.

Crit found a drawer and stuck the ten dollars in the back of it.

"But I married a gal who don't like her. So these days I'm mostly hands off." Chrome tilted his forehead so Crit could see his blue-gray eyes over the rim of the sunglasses. "So ya can have at her while ya can, Bra. Drug whores got a short fuckable shelf life."

"What do you want?"

Chrome turned sideways, looked back toward the front window. "Your ex came down to the Breathitt County Sheriff's Department. Tommy Medlock's brother is sheriff now, if you don't know. Anyway, she had a big-time meltdown. Demanded that he charge you with murder. Said if he didn't make a move she's going to the state police."

Crit closed the drawer. His ear hummed like it was receiving signals from an alien planet.

"If she goes through with that. Not good. We don't need the state police down here asking questions about old crimes or new crimes."

"Stay away from her."

"Or what?" Chrome looked across the counter at Crit with a tight smile.

"Just leave her alone."

Chrome reached out and Crit flinched back a step. Chrome reached farther and patted Crit twice on the chest and grinned. "I like it when you talk salty." And he turned to leave.

"Where'd you bury him?"

Chrome stopped. He didn't turn around. He looked at the

world outside. "You should come out to my house sometime. Big wrap-around porch. Top of a mountain. We can go muddin' or fishin'. I got two kids and a former Miss Laurel Festival Beauty Queen frying my bacon. Life is good. I don't need you to unravel. Let it be. Wasn't that what John Lennon said?"

There was a thunderclap and a spur of light flared the window.

"Sounds like rain; you need a ride home?"

The wind whistled louder and Crit didn't answer.

Chrome pushed open the door. The wind gusted and looped a plastic bag past the door.

"Seeya' later, Alligator."

After Chrome left, Crit sat on the stool behind the counter and did nothing for twenty minutes. There was more lightning and wind, and two trash cans across the street toppled over and lost their lids. Then he headed home. Halfway there it started to drizzle. A thin spattering at first, driven by the wind, and then the heavens coughed a downpour. A hard, heavy rain. Runoff streams soon flowed in low places. A German shepherd mix mutt appeared wet and whimpering from behind the dumpster at Hardee's and followed Crit halfway down the hill. Until Crit turned on him in a fit of utter malevolence and chased him away.

After screaming at the dog, he turned his face up to the drizzling sky. He let the rain puddle his eye sockets. Felt it on his tongue. His wet hair mopped over his eyes and cheeks, and he could taste the dirtiness of it. He moved blindly into the middle of the highway and made cars honk and brake and circle around him.

He walked through puddles and didn't try to miss them and came in off the highway and went to his door and saw a small rifle leaning there. He took a step back to be sure of what he was seeing. He picked it up.

A Western Auto Daisy BB rifle.

It was wet from the rain and the stock had the owner's name carved where it should be.

T. Poppwell.

He turned, expecting to see Liddy's Pontiac. The highway was soaked and empty. Nothing moved except the blinking stoplight and the spattering rain. The downpour had eased but the gutters were overflowing, and cascading streams spigotted every few feet, all the way down to Bill's office.

Crit went inside and sat on his bed, holding the rifle. He drenched his sheets. His feet hurt. The earth rotated rusty and loud, and his ear filled with the drag and sift of hour-glass sand, ticking off poisonous seconds.

There had been a Christmas sometime, somewhere in a red-brick ranch house. The best home he had ever lived in by far. New trees in a sodded yard and tied by thin wires to stakes. Liddy had screamed and yelled that Taylor was too young for a BB rifle. As with all things, he hadn't listened. He might have smacked her. And she might have smacked him back.

There was a damp circle on the carpet beneath the drywall patch in the ceiling. He held the rifle on his lap and watched a water drop slowly gather on the new joint compound above him and then drip.

He had failed as a roofer, so it seemed.

He wondered if Liddy had left Taylor's room as it was. All these years. Door closed. Everything precious and gathering dust. Maybe Liddy's plan was to move everything Taylor had touched or owned from there to here, into this leaking, cell-like room, one item at a time, like a drip fills a bucket, until he drowned.

Tendrils of the past shivered his blood. So far away and so close. Taylor's death had been fast; now his was slow. He decided he couldn't live where he was anymore. He stood up. He could stuff a couple of plastic sacks with essentials. Grab his toothbrush. A change of underwear, canned meat, and go. As far away as possible. Where? To the other side of everything. Or he could walk away with absolutely nothing in his hands and keep walking into an infinite vanishing point.

He gave the Daisy rifle a tilt. Over the ringing tinnitus in his head he could hear the faint rattle of BBs, rolling in the loading chamber. He also heard the door next door quickly open and close. He heard Rennie enter as if in a hurry. He cocked the western-style pump, placed the barrel against his bare palm, and pulled the trigger. He jerked from the sting, then lowered the rifle and looked at his hand. The round copper pellet was half-buried under broken skin.

He barely felt it.

He sat back down. His hand eventually stopped oozing red and the blood drop turned dark. He listened to the sibilation in his bad ear. Like a scoop shovel pulling something dead across rough asphalt. Then he heard a vehicle gun up fast and brake. Footsteps. Someone was banging on Rennie's door.

Then everything happened very quickly.

"Open up. Open up now. You're dead-fucking-meat!" His brother yelled, followed by the brutal sound of wood splintering.

He heard Rennie scream, "Stay away from me! Get the fuck off me." Then she was shrieking a sustained high note, like a rabbit in the mouth of a fox. A thumping crash shook their shared wall.

Crit's eyes remained focused on the puckered welt in the center of his palm.

Suddenly his door burst wide and Rennie dashed in, bleeding from her lip and nose. She raced into the far corner of the small room and turned and cowered. Chrome entered with a merciless glare.

"Where the fuck is it?"

"I didn't do nothing, I swear."

Rennie ran for safety in the bathroom. Chrome advanced and jabbed his boot in before she could slam the door. He pushed through and smacked her hard, yanking her halfway across the room by her hair.

Crit watched as if watching a movie.

"Where the fuck is it?"

"Get the fuck off me!"

"I'm gonna kill you, you thieving piece of trash."

She crawled to Crit, and her panicked hand now locked onto

his ankle. "Help me. Please help me," she pleaded and tried to find Crit's eyes.

He didn't let her.

"Who the fuck you think taught me this business?" Chrome snarled, jerking her up and shaking her hard. "Poppwell's got no mercy for thieves and rats." And he put his legs into a full extension punch that bounced her off the wall.

She was unconscious before she hit the carpet.

"That's enough," Crit heard himself say as he rose to his feet.

"She stole from me, Bra. Take a step back." Chrome spat on her, hauled back and kicked her in the ribs.

Lightning quick, Crit raised the BB rifle over his head. His brother sensed the movement and started to turn just as Crit spun to gain velocity and cracked his brother in the head just above an ear. The Daisy rifle shattered. Chrome toppled like cord wood on top of Rennie's legs.

Silence overtook chaos. Crit stood there and didn't move for a moment. Then he sat back down in the wet spot of the bed, still holding the shattered muzzle. The noise in his ear whistled irregular and jagged.

Wild Bill's scraggy face edged through the door. His eyes were timid and wide. "Is he dead?"

They both looked down. Chrome lay there unmoving.

"I don't know."

"He's gonna kill you if he comes to."

As if on cue, Chrome moaned and rasped for air.

"I need to borrow your van."

"I can't do that, him alive and all."

They looked at Chrome again.

* * *

It had stopped raining. Crit staggered down the middle of highway 30, cradling Rennie. He'd carried her for nearly half a mile, and his arms were numb and his hamstrings had started to sting.

He tripped and splashed through a puddle and almost dropped her. He had to lean into a creosote utility pole to gain better leverage. He passed the open-all-night laundromat where in the over-bright interior he saw a short woman with bad teeth running several machines and trying to keep four young kids from destroying a gumball machine.

Rennie started to moan and revive, which made carrying her even harder. What the hell was he doing? He had no plan. He felt like someone else.

He carried her through his dark store into the back room and laid her on the sawhorse table atop a sketch he had half-started. Rennie moaned and hurt. Crit ran cold water and washed out a dirty paint rag. He wiped blood from her face. Her lip was busted and still bleeding. Her left eye was puffed and swelling. The other flitted open and closed.

"Aw, fuck. Where am I?"

"Downtown."

She turned to the door with sudden fear. "Where's Chrome?"

"Knocked out for now."

She coughed and wheezed out blood and snot. "You got anything? I'm hurting."

Crit shook his head and wiped her blood and snot.

"I'm fuckin' hurt bad. I need something. Where's my purse?"

"No idea."

"I need my fuckin' purse. You steal it?"

"I never saw your purse."

She thought for a moment, then said, "When Chrome pulled up, I tossed it out back."

"If its got his dope in it, better he finds it."

"Fuck no, that's not better, I'm going back for it."

She tried to slide off the table. He held her down. "Don't act dumb and crazy."

"Get off me!" she hissed.

"You've got a kid. How's he gonna feel if you go back and get crippled or killed."

"He'd be better off and you know it."

"No, I don't know it. All I know is I was minding my own damn business till you ran into my room."

"I need my fuckin' purse!"

She repeated the phrase several times like a machine gun. Crit couldn't hold her down. She kicked out at him, toppling the table, and both of them ended up on the floor. Crit managed to climb on top and use his weight until she finally stopped screaming. Her chest rose and fell against his at hyper speed, like a wild panicked bird trapped in a closed fist.

"I'll go back for it if you promise to stay here."

He repeated what he had said and she nodded like she understood.

"You better fuckin' hurry, Asshole."

Crit was disgusted with himself for what he was doing, but here he was, moving out of a stand of hackberry trees and climbing over a fence in the dark. He peered around the dumpster and caught sight of two Harleys parked behind Chrome's truck. Through the open door of the office he could make out someone wrapping his brother's head in gauze while his brother drank from a bottle. There was music playing inside and it was cranked up loud and fierce. Crit figured it even odds that Chrome would kill him on the spot. Probably better than even, since his brother burned hotter when there was an audience to play to. Crit knew to his own rotten core what Chrome was capable of. His brother had extinguished the lives of others twice that Crit knew of. Probably more since Crit had been in prison.

Crit crept around the tool room at the end and moved through the woods behind the motel. He stumbled into some kind of webbing that at first he thought was a net. Then he realized it was Bill's hammock. He backed up and went around and moved out of the trees and crossed the weeds and grass to where Rennie's small bathroom window glowed. He found it in the tall grass.

An Indian-beaded shoulder purse.

Inside was a cell phone, tic tacs, two tampons, and a rolled baggie with three fingers of white powder. At least half a kilo of premium skante. He turned to go and spotted Bill, who was holding an ice bucket and staring at him from the pass-through, which was twenty feet away.

"You need to get her out of town," Bill whispered.

Crit looked to the right of Bill, and his eyes found the scoop shovel, ten steps away if he needed it.

"He's plenty pissed. He needs time to cool down. Maybe you can borrow her mom's car. And just go away. If she stays around here, he'll find her."

Crit closed the purse.

Bill looked behind to make sure they were alone. "Sorry I can't help y'all any more than that. He'd put me in the ground." Bill said with something like a sob in this throat that said he'd developed a fondness for his tenant.

"Here, take this," Bill pulled a Walmart plastic bag out of a trash can and half-filled it with ice.

Crit took the bag. He turned and walked back into the woods. And as he walked he was thinking, *What the fuck am I doing?* But he shut down his thinking and was just a man in the dark moving, and climbing the fence, and then jogging through trees and wet brush back the way he'd come. He crossed the highway and cut behind the Hardee's parking lot and jogged down to the concrete bridge supports. He went under the bridge and followed the curving bank of the North Fork and followed it through weeds and river mist. His movement stopped bullfrogs from croaking. He paused when he heard a motorcycle gun past on the highway above. Then kept on. His shoes were muddy and his pants were soggy and wet. He had rubbed a blister and his arches ached. And he should have unlocked the back door before he left, but he hadn't, so now he had had no choice but to move out of the trees that flanked the river and up the hill to Court Street and then jog down an exposed half-block to the front entrance of his shop.

The sky had lost a good bit of dark and a new and uncertain

day was coming. He crossed the street and startled a starling that flew out of a shit-stained crack in the cap trim.

"We're fucked."

When she asked for a straw he had gone back into the front and pulled the ten-dollar bill from the sales drawer. When he told her she needed ice on her face, she told him she needed to get high first.

"We're fucked. And you know it. We might as well get mega-fucked," she said, and greedily vacuumed up a sparkling caterpillar of powder off the glass of a framed print of a group of dogs playing poker. She changed nostrils and snorted again, then leaned back, feeling the rush in her blood and swaying like a tree cut nearly through and about to topple.

"Chrome and you used to…date?"

A cold smile formed on her blood-caked lips. "You jealous?"

"Is Chrome the father of your boy?"

"Why you into all that now?"

"Is he the father of your boy?"

"Sometimes I say he is, and sometimes I say he ain't."

"Does he think he is?"

"Oh. I see where you're going. It won't stop him from killing us. Not for one second."

Crit knew that, even better than she did.

The phone in her purse chimed hip-hop beats. She took it out, looked at it, and showed Chrome's name on the screen as if proving a point. "He called five times since you went out." Then she reached into the baggie and pinched out a new line on the dog picture and offered it to Crit.

He took it and sat it on the table before him and looked down at what she offered.

"Use it or lose it," she said.

He picked up the ten-dollar bill. Tightened it.

"Go ahead, Mister Cranky. You know you want to. I heard you weren't no angel."

He was no angel. He was a shit stain. The map of his life was a toilet flush. He rolled the bill even tighter. He looked down at the promise of forgetting and the assurance of dropping into that infinite hole.

"Back in the day I heard you were worse than yer brother. Everybody was scared of you," Rennie said. "And I heard something else."

Crit was half-bent down to it. Alexander Hamilton up in his right nostril. "Heard what?"

"You killed yer own son and shit."

Her words eviscerated him. The life in his eyes evaporated. He straightened his spine one vertebra at a time and let the ten-dollar bill drop to the dogs. It unrolled slightly.

"Damn, that's cold-ass gangsta. I don't see my Tybo much but he's always with me in here." She thumped her chest with a closed fist and kissed it. "I'd never do him harm." Then she opened her hand and it was empty. "And I don't even know what the fuck he's doing right now. Maybe he's watching TV. Maybe he's playing a video game or maybe he's sleeping and drooling."

Her voice trailed off to a meaningless whisper and she grew angry and impatient and reached for the baggie.

But Crit took it first. "You get one last line, but that's all that you get. The rest goes back to Chrome."

"Like hell," she exploded.

"I'm trying to stop him from hurting you."

"Like I give a royal fuck!"

Something sounded wrong. Rennie was about to speak and he covered her mouth. Was that a squeak? A noise at the front door? They both heard it. A thumping knock. He released her and quietly unlocked the back exit for her to go out that way. She nodded like she understood but then she circled back and started to massage his hand that held the baggie and mouthed *please*. Crit shook her off. She wound up to scream and he clamped her mouth, then roughly pushed her hard toward the back door.

"Go. Get."

He pocketed the baggie and then he found a hammer. He edged

slowly and quietly up to the divider door with the hammer raised.

A woman had her back to him. She had dreadlocks and was checking out Wild Bill's t'ai chi painting near the sales desk. It was Wednesday morning. Crit lowered the hammer.

Sister Nikhael turned and when she did she smiled big and warm. "Morning stranger. I knocked and your door was unlocked. Sorry. Looks like I kinda freaked you out. "

"Naw, I was just doin' stuff. I didn't hear you."

"This place is like, wow! I like it." She nodded up and down vigorously. "I like it a lot."

Crit closed the divider door and put down the hammer.

Her eyes seemed more intense than usual, and she was smiling like she had sucked helium at a party. "I have some really good news. And here it is. I talked you up to this big art guy who curates shows at the Cincinnati Museum of Art, and he's putting together an awesome exhibit of regional outsider art at this ultra-cool new gallery in downtown Cincinnati called *Over the Rhine*."

She paused to catch her breath and grew more excited.

"Here's the kicker. I've mostly persuaded him to slide you in, sight unseen, as a fav to me. The show opens in two weeks so that's kinda unheard of. But I can seal the deal fer sure if I take a couple of pics of your new work and send them to him ASAP."

She raised her hand to high five him, but since he didn't move, she high-fived herself.

"Boom! It's an amazing opportunity to jump a couple of rungs up the ladder!"

Her dancing eyes looked around.

"This place is great, love the name on the sign by the way, I just about creamed my shorts when I saw that. And your new stuff is totally beyond amazing. Thumbs way up! You're adding more color to the equation. My art guy is gonna shit himself."

She returned to Wild Bill's t'ai chi painting and snapped it with her phone.

"Moving outside the prison experience has added a whole new vibrancy to your language. What is this on?" She felt the surface.

"Is that drywall?"

"Yep."

"I love that. Making use of found-object utilitarianism."

She turned to him finally drained of words. But both her hands were outstretched and open as if she wanted to physically catch his reaction. He was facing her but he wasn't seeing her and his good ear was tuned to the back door because he had just heard Rennie's phone chime beats. She hadn't left. And then he heard Rennie answer *hello*.

"I'm thrilled about this opportunity," Sister Nikhael continued and snapped the image of the Asian delivery man fixing his bicycle. "You should be, too. It could lead to a solo show! But why the long face? I'm like happy here." She raised her hand up high. "And you're like happy here." She lowered her hand down to her knees and fake-frowned. "What's wrong, Dude?"

Now Rennie was yelling. Sister Nikhael heard it and her eyes had questions.

"I'm sorry. There's just a lot going on right now."

"No worries. If it's a bad time we can talk later, I'll just take a couple more pics and get out of your hair," Sister Nikhael said.

Just then Rennie burst into the front room, looking like a battered and crazed rag doll. "Momma called. Chrome just took Tybo! I'm gonna kill the bastard."

"Took him where?" Crit asked.

She shook her head fiercely. "He threatened Momma with a pistol. Told her not to call the law. If he hurts Tybo I'll kill him. I swear to God!"

"Crit, what's going on?" Sister Nikhael asked in a thin voice.

Her question hung unanswered as Crit told Rennie to follow him and they dashed out the front door. Sister Nikhael moved to the window and watched Crit run faster than anyone over the age of fifty should run, followed by a young woman with red and blue hair and blood on her shirt.

***

They turned left on Main Street and ran four blocks to Miller's Branch. Eldon was most likely out with the regular morning trash pickup and that proved to be the case when they entered the sanitation yard and saw no one. The door to the office was locked but not a side window. Crit wormed through it and grabbed the truck keys out of Eldon's desk. A poster of Jesus with empathetic eyes stared at him reproachfully as he moved a chair to stand on and climb back out.

Tires spun as they roared out of the sanitation gate in the flatbed and turned South, continued farther South and turned onto 15. The maxed-out engine wined and groaned. Crit's plan, what there was of it, had evolved as Rennie explained that her momma lived at the top of a seven-mile-long gravel road up Big Branch Creek. If they moved fast they might cross paths with Chrome and Tyler at the bottom of the mountain. Then what? Trade the powder for the boy? Appeal to his brother's non-existent sense of decency? Crit didn't even have a weapon.

"Turn here," Rennie screamed, barely in control of herself.

Crit did and skidded close to sliding over a steel culvert. He straightened and roared up Kragon School Road and past Little Jerusalem Church. Trees and shrubs whipped past.

"This the only way in or out?"

She nodded, clenching the dashboard and leaning forward to get there faster. They reached a curve, and Crit pointed.

"I think that's him."

The side of the mountain above them had been clear-cut and they could see a fast-moving pickup descending a series of switchbacks. Crit turned while braking and fishtailed the truck into a roadblock. Chrome was on them fast and skidded to a halt. Rennie jumped out, screaming her son's name. She banged on the tinted driver window, then immediately dashed around to the passenger door.

Crit tried to get in front of her.

The passenger door now cracked open two inches and a .38

Colt poked out. Chrome had slid over. Rennie stopped howling and Crit was able to hold her back. Above the dark barrel his brother's face sneered malignantly, and behind him Tyler's young face trembled and watched. Chrome had a bandage of gauze circling his ears, like a short-order cook. His spikey peroxided hair stuck up above it like bristles on a paintbrush.

"Let him go," Rennie said, her voice hoarse and husky.

"Bitch, you'll be lucky to see sundown."

Crit knew from his brother's tone that sundown was wishful thinking. He stepped in front of Rennie.

"I'm 'bout to blow your brains to Kingdom Come, Bra."

Crit stepped closer into the nothingness of the barrel gape.

"You want to pull it. Pull it. Do us both a favor. I like the idea of you finally catchin' a capital bid," Crit said. "They shoulda thrown the key away on you and me a long-ass time ago. So pull it. Fucking pull it!" Spittle flecked Crit's lips and he pressed hard into the dark hole of the barrel.

"You're crazy," his brother said, his eyes like railroad spikes.

"You're damn right."

Crit snatched at Chrome's gun hand and the pistol exploded. A .38 hollow point missed Crit's stomach by an inch and puckered metal exiting the truck door. Crit smashed his brother's fist into the side of the door and yanked the weapon free. Chrome lurched out of the door and tackled Crit to the asphalt. The pistol sailed clear as Chrome crawled on top. Crit kicked upward into his brother's groin and they grappled and gasped and rolled and clawed with a bottomless rage. The brothers rolled across the road and tumbled down the bank to Big Branch Creek. They flattened shrubs and small trees and plunged in the creek, flailing and splashing.

Chrome flung Crit off and charged through the knee-deep water. Crit was on his back but scissor-kicked and toppled his brother. Chrome spat out creek and curses and splashed. They pounded on each and then separated, circled, breathing hard. Chrome's expensive haircut had flattened like wet dog fur.

A shot rang out and a tree branch beside Chrome's head shattered. Both men turned to where Rennie stood, gripping the Colt. She tilted her head and adjusted her shaky one-eyed aim.

"Baby, I was never gonna hurt Tyler," Chrome pleaded and he raised a hand with painted fingernails. He moved toward her and she fired again. The bullet creased though the gauze on the right side of Chrome's head and nicked off the lobe of an ear. What came off pendulummed by a thread. Chrome felt at the wound and his hand came back wet and red. He exhaled a *fuck* and throttled back his anger. He looked around, inched closer to a sycamore tree, and Rennie told him to stay where he was.

Now Tyler came into view on the road above. He watched with big eyes as his mother re-gripped the pistol and aimed it squarely at Chrome's chest.

Crit looked from the boy to his mother. "Don't do it," Crit said, as calmly as he could. But he couldn't hear his own words above the shot reverberations pounding. "Your boy's watchin."

She didn't seem to have heard him, either. He waded across the creek, then climbed up to her. He slipped, regained his footing, and then reached her. Her eyes were wild and she now pointed the pistol into the meat of him alone. His hand eased down and met some resistance, but he was able to take the gun. She finally saw him and their eyes held. "Get yer boy back to the truck and I'll take care of this."

"He threatened my son."

"I'll fix it."

"Bury him in a hole."

Crit nodded and stared deep into her, and she left him with the pistol and climbed up to her son.

When she and Tyler were gone from sight Chrome sat down on a high-water flood log and spat blood into the creek. "You still pack a punch," Chrome said.

This was his chance; now if ever. Now. What he had vowed to do in sleepless nights in his dark mud. Just step forward and double tap the son of a bitch. And be done with it. He could drive the woman and boy back to Jackson, then come back and deal with the body after sundown.

Chrome watched Crit as if reading his mind. And his smile seemed to say *come on*.

Crit waded into the middle of the creek, halted, and ejected three .38 shells and three spent casings one by one. They plopped and sank like tadpoles.

"If she hadn't showed up I woulda kicked yer ass."

"In your dreams."

Crit sat down on the log beside his brother and set the Colt between them.

"You think there's anything to sew back on?" Chrome turned his face to show a small piece of red mush dangling from his ear.

"Probably not. Leave her alone and you get yer dope back."

Chrome didn't answer right off. He took off his gauze bandage, wet it in the creek, wiped at the missing part of his ear, and winced. "Bitch came within a half-inch of killing me. She stole from me. And you broke my skull. I can't keep my people in line if I don't hurt her good. And probably hurt you some, too. You know how it goes."

Crit stood up. He pulled out the thick plastic baggie of white powder from his front pocket and opened the sealed top to dump it in the fast water.

"Hold up," Chrome said.

A dragonfly landed on the part of the log Crit had vacated. Both brothers looked at it until it flew away.

"I might leave her, and you, alone if you give me that." He considered what he had said and then added, "And something else. And then something else."

"What?"

"You paint a picture of me. You done Bill and her. Even some damn China bike guy. Everybody but me," Chrome said and tossed his bloody gauze into the current. It floated off and got stuck on a rock.

"Are you kidding me?"

"I'm stone cold serious." His eyes said that he was.

"What else?"

"You come work for me."

The words punched. The water flowed and got louder. Crit shook no.

"Well then, no deal. Catch yer wind, Bra, cause we're going round two." Chrome picked up the pistol like a cudgel. "And after I bury you, I'm gonna bury that crazy bitch and her boy."

Chrome smiled like a black snake crawling through warm milk and waded out and away from the log, and started rotating his head and flexing the bands of muscles in his shoulder and neck. "Come on," he said.

* * *

Crit drove back down Kragon School Road. He hated himself more with each mile and turn of the wheel. He was weak. He was getting old. He was tired and sore and bruised and bleeding and mush-headed, and his clothes were wet and he was headed back to prison if Eldon got back to the sanitation yard before him. And Eldon surely would. And on top of it all, he had foolishly started to half-believe some of what the good sister had buzzed on about, that his scratching and scrawling meant something. Meant what? The essence of bullshit and bluffing. If there was a fire at his store he doubted he would bother to save one picture. You can't clean shit with piss. He could not be repaired. The only thing keeping him from flooring the flatbed straight through the galvanized guard rail into the North Fork ravine was the dumpster fire of an unfit mother sitting beside him, and her child, who was scrunched in beside him and sucking his thumb, even though he was of an age well past that. Mostly it was that damn thumb sucker that kept Crit's tires on the road.

They came off the mountain and drove through an elongated depression in the topography where the river valley flattened out. Rennie kissed the back of Tyler's head as they passed the *Welcome to Jackson* sign that was planted in a triangle of brightly colored petunias. She started singing in a husky lullaby whisper.

We got married in a fever.
Hotter than a pepper sprout.

Crit recognized what she sang. He seemed to remember having seen and heard Johnny Cash sing it alongside his wife June Carter Cash on a black-and-white TV somewhere back when he was young. Before the TV was hocked or sold. Or had he just imagined that?

We been talking bout Jackson.
Ever since the fire went out.

"What fire?" Tyler asked and took his wet thumb out of his mouth.

She tickled him under his armpits. "A big campfire. We're gonna go camping one of these days," Rennie said.

Tyler giggled and laughed and asked, "will we see any bears?"

"We'll see plenty of bears, Sweetie. We'll see Smokey Bear and he'll tell us to put our fire out." She hugged her son tightly and started to shake and tear up.

"This truck smells bad," Tyler said and wrinkled up his nose.

Crit eased up to the red light below the Courthouse just as Sister Nikhael's Prius curled through the four-way and crossed in front of him. Headed out of town. Headed to Little Sandy, no doubt. He didn't think she had seen him. But maybe she had and was done with him. He switched his gaze to his outside mirror. In seconds she was small and a hundred yards away from where she had been.

They drove two more miles to the motel. The sun was a third of the way up and hidden in a mostly overcast sky. Crit pulled over at the bottom of the grassy slope and kept the engine running. Rennie and Tyler climbed out.

"My door's all busted up."

"You can hang in my room." Crit said and fished for his key. "Lock the door." He gave her his key.

"Like lockin' the door did my door any good." She looked behind her to make sure Tyler was far enough away then turned back to him with accusing eyes. "Why didn't you kill him?"

"I wasn't sure I could."

"Well next time make sure. You comin' back?"

It was more likely he was headed off in handcuffs straight to the county lockup and then to Little Sandy.

"After I drop the truck," he said looking ahead so he didn't have to look at her. "I'll be back."

She shut the door, walked away and joined Tyler without thanking him. Only Tyler watched him drive off.

Crit entered the county sanitation yard and motored up to the office. And Eldon was right there. Sitting outside on a milk crate at the end of morning with his tape player praising Jesus. There was a closed Bible in his lap. Crit looked around the yard, all seemed as it should be. No cop cars visible. But maybe they were hidden. Crit parked next to the stack of steel piping, the space where he had taken the truck less than an hour before. He cut the engine and stepped out, wary and alert, and walked up to Eldon, who didn't even glance up.

"Keys?"

"In the truck."

"Well go get 'em," Eldon said with an edge of boss-like frustration.

Crit walked back to the truck, got the keys and handed them to Eldon.

"I give an inch and you take a mile."

"A personal emergency came up."

"I believe you used county gas on non-county business."
"I can pay for the gas."
"I'm missing a scoop shovel."
"Well, that was when I had to walk home from Hardee's. I'll bring it back."
"Two hundred dollars for the gas or I tell your P.O."
Crit's ears blinked. "Two hundred dollars for gas?"
"Did I stutter? Consider it a donation to start my church."
Eldon closed his eyes to let the gospel move in. Crit counted out all he had from his wallet and pockets.
"I can give you twenty-seven dollars now. And the rest later."
"One hour. And bring the shovel."

Chapter 12

PINE TREES

Crit walked out of the sanitation yard and down Millers Branch Road and then turned onto 30. He passed where the old building had been bulldozed down and his throat constricted like a noose from his past was tightening his breathing. He felt it tighten even more as he gazed on his brother's used car lot. Chrome's F-Series pick-up was back and parked. So were two Harleys, and one of the bikers was watching his approach.

Crit let tens and twenties drop into his bloody-knuckled hand. Chrome was doing the counting and his head had a fresh, red-stained bandage. His mood was surprisingly cheerful, given that he was missing an ear lobe and his face was beat to shit.

"One hundred seventy-one, seventy-two, one seventy-three." Chrome capped off the stack of bills with four quarters and a bouncy grin. They were standing outside the garage door. "I don't usually give advances before services rendered, but I know where you live."

Chrome hadn't wasted any time binding their agreement. His brother had always been impatient that way. When Crit had showed up and asked for an advance on wages, he had been informed that there was a job that needed doing right then. Chrome's impatience and eagerness was a business advantage that no doubt had gotten him his big wrap-around-porch house on a mountaintop and a Miss Laurel Festival beauty queen in his bed.

Chrome popped the trunk on a five-year-old Honda Accord. One of the ugly bikers who hung around Chrome like a bad smell came out of the service bay, cradling a small red toolbox. There it was. The cheese. And here he was, the rat, crawling back into the trap. At this moment he no longer felt hatred and anger toward Chrome. This was a trap that he had constructed for himself, and he alone was in his self-loathing crosshairs.

The biker set the toolbox behind the spare tire in the trunk. And closed it. Chrome dangled the car keys with a shimmy shake.

"Good, to have you back, Bra."

Crit took the keys and opened the door and it felt like stomach acid was eating through his intestines.

* * *

Fifteen minutes later he had paid off Eldon. Forty minutes later he was driving to Hazard on a narrow county road pot-holed by coal trucks. Drug haulers and coal operators with over-the-max axle weight always steered clear of the big roads and interstates. Up ahead parts of the Cumberland Plateau had been crushed into nothing by strip mining. Then for the next ten miles he got stuck behind a slow-moving school bus that stopped every quarter-mile to drop ragamuffin kids off at shotgun shacks and singlewides. He tried listening to the radio, but that didn't make him feel any better.

Taylor had driven these same back roads. Liddy had complained when he came home with his pockets full of green cash. Enough to buy her a dishwasher and his first car at sixteen. A baby blue 1968 Camaro with fat tires. Liddy hadn't been living under Crit's roof then, but she'd shown up to throw a fit. And to curse out his girlfriend of the moment. Crit had told Liddy the only other job prospect for Taylor was joining the Army and going off and getting killed in Iraq. Did she want that? He'd pounded a finger into her chest and told her the poor man was fucked by the coal companies and the government. The only way to rise above your raising was to make and bake. There was cheese in these mountains and all they had to do was bring crackers. Those stupid and boastful claims now haunted him. If only Taylor had taken his chances with land mines and snipers. And run like a scalded dog from his father.

Crit turned off the highway where he had been told and bumped down a seldom-used mining road. Tall weeds in the middle mound scraped his undercarriage. Trees and kudzu vines crawled in on both sides and blocked out the sun.

Farther ahead the road opened into a broom sage clearing with an abandoned coal tipple and hulking steel chutes. A pair of headlights flashed from beside a rusty truck container. Crit steered there.

A slender woman leaned against a muddy and dented Chevy Blazer. She had a sharp nose, camo pants tucked into cowboy boots, and a neck tattoo. Crit pulled over beside her. She tossed a cigarette and walked slowly toward him. She stopped at his back window like a cop. He had to strain around to see her. Her neck tattoo said *Mercy*. She had a big metal ring hole in her ear lobe that he could have put his finger through.

"If you try anything funny, my man will shoot," she said.

Crit looked out and imagined a gun sight on him from the pine trees up the ridge, or maybe from the shadows of the coal tipple.

"Pop yer trunk."

He did and she took out the red tool kit and knelt. His eyes drifted to his rearview. She was mostly hidden but he could see enough to know she took out a knife and pierced something in the tool kit and tasted the contents. Then she closed his trunk. She stepped back to just behind him and handed over a wrinkled envelope with green cash peeking out. "My man knew you from Roederer. You and him got into a rumble."

Crit had no idea who she meant and didn't try to remember. He took her money.

"He kinda holds a grudge. He wanted to cap yer ass and throw you down that tipple."

"Well, what the hell stopped him?"

"I told him yer brother wouldn't like it. Killin' you would be more trouble than it's worth." She half-smiled and rubbed a runny nose. "See ya next time."

Her left eye either twitched or winked.

***

Crit crossed back into Breathitt County at Ned, driving fifteen miles over the speed limit. He was on the main road now with a clean trunk. Up and over the ridge-tops, back down snaking creek beds, his tires crying on the turns. The sun was almost gone and the western sky celebrated its leaving.

He saw too late a one-hundred-and-eighty-degree switchback sign and drifted wide into the oncoming lane. There was no other vehicle in the blind turn but by the time he got back into his own lane his heart was galloping and his head was trying to figure out why was he driving fast enough to get himself killed? Was it because he wanted to get back to see how Rennie and Tyler were doing? Or was his recklessness a crawl toward the dark abyss?

He passed the post office at Quicksand. It was closed but a Breathitt County Sheriff's Department SUV cruiser was resting in the parking lot, nose to the cars going by. Crit didn't worry a whit until two miles later when the cruiser was right behind him, twenty feet off his bumper. It had black and white stenciled markings on the side but didn't have a bubble top so it could sneak up on the unsuspecting. Crit checked his speedometer. Seven miles over the limit. He pulled it back. His eyes flicked to his rearview. The dark-tinted window behind him gave no hint as to the identity of the driver. But then he hadn't been on a name-knowing basis with any Breathitt County law in fourteen years. He bent into a curve and slid his left arm into the seat-belt strap and drove with one hand and clicked the buckle. He fully expected the siren to whelp any second. The road straightened and he passed Walmart and the clogged business strip just South of Jackson, which had seen a lot more development since the Walmart had gone in. Gas stations, pawn shops, and tanning salons lined both sides of the highway. He stopped at a red light and the cruiser rolled up right behind him. He clicked on his blinker late and turned North onto the bypass. The cruiser didn't bother to use a blinker but also turned and stayed on his tail.

If he had been a younger man he might be sweating bullets right now, but he wasn't younger, and the only thing he had on him was money. And it wasn't his. And it was wedged into a cut in the foam under his seat. What he also had was no license and a bloody, red, and broken past, and no future, so he told himself he was fine and dandy with the cause and effect of getting pulled over. Let it be, as his brother had said.

Up ahead Chrome's used car lot came into view. He was tempted to pull on in with the heat hot on his tail. But at the last minute, maybe some hard-wired outlaw code made him drive on past. One of the Harley bikers was outside next to Chrome's truck and tracked him with watchful eyes as Crit and the cruiser drove past.

By the time he decided to pull into the Marathon Gas and Go the cruiser had been on him for eight miles. And that's what he did. Turn signal. Pulled on in, motored past the dual pumps and parked just left of the entrance door. The cruiser pulled in right beside him. Crit cut his engine. The cruiser didn't. Crit sat for a moment and thought about heading inside and buying something. Maybe it was his last chance at a Teriyaki Beef Jerky on the free side of the mud. He unclicked his seat belt, cracked his door, and slide out without looking over. He stepped up to the Marathon door. His reflection met him at the glass. Then he suddenly pivoted, walked around the front of the cruiser, and stepped straight to the tinted driver's window.

The unseen lawman was a barely visible shadow and made Crit wait as the six-cylinder engine hummed and a coolant condensation drip-dripped the asphalt. Ten seconds passed. Crit reckoned the wait was a ploy to knock him off balance. Over his left shoulder he saw that the Pakistani clerk was stacking produce boxes near the big window and watching.

Crit was about to walk.

But then the window rolled down.

A fleshy officer with buzz-cut reddish hair, a bald spot and green uniform was talking on his cell phone. Mid-thirties. He stuck a finger in the air to tell Crit *just a second* while he finished his conversation. "I gotta go now, Babe, I'll call you later, love you."

The officer hung up and turned to Crit with a smile like he was selling something. "You're Crit Poppwell."

Crit barely nodded.

The officer stuck out a hand. "I'm Tommy Medlock's brother, Aaron."

The handshake felt soft and clammy-wet. Aaron's brother had been Breathitt County's Sheriff back when. The Poppwell brothers had paid Tommy Medlock enough under the table to put his kids through college. A heart attack had done Tommy in eight years or so back, Crit had heard.

"Chrome wanted me to give you this." Aaron handed over a booklet with a circled wire spine.

A Kentucky Driver's Manual.

"There's no way around not taking the written test. But the written ain't that hard, mostly common sense, and you won't have to take the driving part. Just call me after you pass the written. I wrote my number on the cover there."

Crit looked down at the manual.

"They give the test at the county clerk's Monday through

Friday, no reservation needed, just walk in. Got it?"

Crit gave a small nod.

"You can't be driving around without no license," Tommy Medlock's brother said like it was the punch line of a joke. He reached above his sun visor and took down a pair of aviator shades and slid them on. "Get it done soon, okay?"

Crit nodded for the third time and the cruiser backed up and drove away. Crit looked down at the condensation wet spot and thought, *so I'm back on the name-knowing basis with the Breathitt County law.*

He bought a small bag of beef jerky and finished it off while parked outside, then he drove to the used car lot where Chrome met him with a beaming smile and had two beers in his hands. Crit declined the beer, pulled the money out of the foam cut under the seat and gave it to his brother. He stepped out and left the empty jerky bag on the seat. He glanced at the driver's manual and thought about leaving it, too. But he decided if he wasn't getting his parole revoked any time soon he might need a valid license. So he took the booklet.

"What you doin' for dinner? I can put some steaks on the grill."

Crit pretended not to have heard his brother and walked toward the setting sun.

"I'll call Bill when I need ya."

Crit walked back to the motel like an ant crawling toward its mounded hole. He passed the Asian delivery man gliding down a hill. They noticed each other but gave no indication that they had. And he suddenly stopped and stood on the highway shoulder for ten minutes without moving as the blinking red stoplight blinked. He went inside himself. Thoughts throbbed into a headache that felt like someone was beating the back of his neck with a hammer. He doubted if he wanted to paint his silly pictures anymore. He thought about walking to the south side of town and lying down on the railroad tracks. Or jumping from a bridge, but there were none in the county high enough.

A couple of teenagers on a moped scootered past. A memory flickered to when he and Chrome had stolen a Briggs and Stratton mini-bike and had come to blows over whose turn it was to ride it. God to fuck he had lived too long.

He reached the motel. Rennie's room was completely dark. There was light glowing from behind the curtain in his room. The muffled wail of Wild Bill's electric guitar seeped from the office. Crit moved to his door and it wasn't locked. He pushed through and Tyler was standing on the other side of the bed, drawing a sun ball and clouds on the far wall with a set of Crit's colored sharpies. Several pages of Crit's sketchbook had been ripped out and filled with stick figure doodles of dogs and kids and trees. He looked some more and saw that Tyler had even colored over one of his prison sketches. Tyler reacted as if he were caught doing something wrong and corkscrewed into the wall. Crit dropped the driver's manual on the dresser. The bathroom door was open and Rennie wasn't there. That wasn't good.

Crit noticed Taylor's softball on the bed. He picked it up. It had a smiley face sharpied on. Tyler watched him fearfully.

"That's nice. Is that a nose?" Crit put his finger on a squiggle below the eye circles.

"Must-ash."

"Oh, a mustache. That's real nice. Here, catch." Crit tossed it to the boy and he caught it. "Good catch. You know where yer momma's at?"

Tyler shook his head.

Crit walked outside and followed the electric guitar wail to the office. He stopped just outside and peeked through a curtain crack and caught sight of Rennie and Wild Bill laughing and dancing. Bill was wearing only boxer shorts, but still had on his miss-matched crocs and his guitar. Rennie danced wearing only her black bra and panties, arms out, head back.

Crit moved in. Bill stopped his playing and Rennie turned her bruised face to him and gave him a split-lip smile and put Vs over her eyes and moved them sideways and undulated her body like he vaguely remembered an actress doing in some movie. Crit could see where Chrome's boot had left a large purple bruise mark above her stomach.

"Can we talk?" Crit said.

"Talk, talk, talk," Rennie chirped.

"We're playin' strip poker without the cards," Bill said and bent a blues note.

Crit noticed there was a charred glass pipe on Bill's desk and a small plastic baggie with the corner ripped out.

"Your kid needs to go back to your momma's."

"You need to go back to yer momma's," she said and farted. Bill laughed like that was the funniest thing ever.

Crit gave her a don't bullshit me look and Rennie switched into furious.

"Who the fuck are you to judge me. Tell me what to do? You don't own me. Go away. We're having a party."

Bill strummed a power chord, but he immediately stopped when Crit's eyes drilled him. Crit then turned to Rennie. "He's not stayin' here with you usin'. I'll take him back before I let that happen."

"Yeah, and I'll call the cops and amber alert yer ass." She punched devil-horn hands at him like exclamation points. She would have said more but she caught sight of her son standing just outside the open door. His eyes were big, and he was hold-ing the softball. She hissed out air in surprise. Then she moved out the door. Tyler stepped back and threw the softball. It bounced off Rennie's shoulder and rolled to the gravel. She staggered in place, trying to find her balance on rubbery legs.

"What'd you do that for, Baby?"

"You said you'd come back," Tyler said.

"I was coming back."

She knelt and opened her arms for him and tried to smile. He stepped farther away. Her mouth puckered into a circle of hurt and she gurgled a sob and collapsed onto the ground.

Crit looked back at Bill, who was pulling his pants on.

"What? What'd I do?" Bill asked.

Crit stepped forward fast and kicked his boot through the ten-inch speaker of Bill's Marshall amp. He had trouble pulling his boot out. "Give me the keys to your van."

Bill turned over the keys without hesitation or complaint.

Crit stepped outside. Rennie was gulping air and rocking back and forth. The boy was peeking out from behind one of the broken-down cars. Crit picked up the softball out of the weeds and tossed it to Tyler. The boy juggled it but made the catch.

"That's yours. You can keep it for good. Now we're gonna take a ride and go visit your Granny, how's that sound?"

The Boy didn't answer, but didn't show alarm.

Crit cracked open the side door to the Econoline. He lifted Tyler into the back seat and looked at Rennie, who was twitching on the ground. He went over and stood over her. She refused to look up at him.

"You comin' or stayin'?

She blubbered inaudibly. He put his hands under her shoulders and lifted her up, told her to put more clothes on.

They drove South out of Jackson and turned up Long Branch Creek. Rennie was lost into herself. Tyler rode on the long back seat and tossed the softball up and down. He dropped it and it rolled out of view to the back of the van, and he climbed over his seat to retrieve it. Crit watched the boy in the rear view mirror and guessed that if they were pulled over, or had a wreck, he would be headed back to prison for not having a child seat. And no license. But he kept driving.

It was almost dark. A few stars peeked out from behind stippled clouds. He turned on his headlights and passed the place where Chrome and he had bitterly fought. He drove overtop the black skid marks where he had turned the truck sideways. There were many places he and his brother had come to blows, spread out high and wide over the whole damn county. Crit climbed up the mountain all the way to the top and dropped over the other side into shadowed darkness.

Rennie told him to turn up a river gravel drive and he did and he stayed in his seat clasping and re-clasping the steering wheel and listening to the lawnmower whir in his head while Rennie and Tyler climbed out and walked up a paving-stone path to the front door of a well-kept singlewide. Rennie knocked and meekly stood on a small patio porch lined with potted ferns. A porch light flicked on. Chickens clucked and scampered about the pine needles in the twilight. Someone had planted a half-dozen pine trees on the property years ago and they stood tall and impressive. Crit leaned forward in his seat to see how far up into the purple sky they went.

The trailer door opened and Rennie's mother came out, wearing a flowered apron and a worried face. She grew more worried when she saw Rennie's bruises. She put both her hands on Tyler's shoulders. Tyler showed off the softball and she smiled and guided him inside. Then Rennie and her mother spat hot words at each other. Crit heard most of it. The mother demanded to know who beat her up. Rennie didn't want to discuss it. The older woman then pointed in Crit's direction, saying she knew who he was and that he was just as bad as his brother. And they went around on that for several minutes until Crit impatiently honked. Tyler's face appeared at a back window. The boy raised the softball to the glass and smiled just a little bit.

Crit's fingers lifted into a goodbye wave.

Rennie climbed in fast and sat stewing. She bit at a fingernail, then changed hands and bit a nail on the other hand. On the porch her mother shook her head one last time and went back inside. The porch light clicked off. Rennie lifted up her knees and hugged them into herself and put her sandaled feet on the dash. "I need to fucking paint my toenails."

A cackling rooster chased a hen around the base of one of the pine trees.

"What are you waiting for? Let's get the fuck out of here," she said.

Crit turned the ignition. The engine didn't start at first. He pumped the gas and tried again. The starter ground, then caught.

Crit drove back down the mountain. The van's headlamps needed cleaning and barely made a dent in the draping darkness. Rennie's eyes stayed closed. He thought he heard a despondent moan. He drove and looked over at her several times before he finally spoke. "A lot of folks were born in a shit river. And a lot of 'em drown. I know something about that."

"Do you now?"

She didn't say anything else for several bleak and bumpy miles. Then she said, "You were a user?"

He nodded. "Since I was fourteen."

"How'd you stop?"

"I got locked up."

She opened her eyes and started to rock back and forth. Her tongue came out and felt the split of her lip. "I'm ready to quit. For Tyler's sake. But I've said that before." She started to cry. Deep sorrowful sobs. Wet rivulets streamed down her battered face. "And I always fuck up."

"It's not easy. I started a lot of fights. Getting beat up helped me."

"Will you beat me up if I need you to?" She choked back a sob, then coughed.

"I won't do that. But I'll help you."

Crit found a couple of take-out napkins on the dash and handed them to her. She blew her runny nose as he pulled up to the stop sign at 15. He could smell pulverized brake lining. Her wet eyes found his and held for a moment. But even as he was looking at her doubts and recriminations rolled through his head. Why had he offered what he did, and why was he getting tangled up in the troubled mess beside him. A good part of him wanted to drop her off in the ditch, like chucking a beer can, and floor it for the state line.

* * *

The sky had lost all hints of the sunset and it was dark and fireflies twinkled. Crit walked to the ice machine with a plastic bag. Maybe she was broken beyond repair, he thought, like he was. Piss cleaning shit. That never comes clean. He filled the bag with ice as a couple of moths suicide-banged into the florescent fixture above his head. Eldon's shovel was still there. He had to get that back. He closed the ice machine door.

"So she shot Chrome's ear off?"

Crit turned and Bill was standing outside his office, holding a carton of take-out Chinese in one hand and chopsticks in the other.

"Who told you that?"

"Dude who rides that hardtail with the sunrise tank."

"What else did he say?"

"That you're workin' off her debt. Nobody will hurt her as long as you come through."

Come through.

Crit looked up at the distant half-moon emerging through parting clouds.

Come through.

It sounded like he was an indentured mule tied to his brother's plow.

"I appreciate you standin' up for her. She's a good kid at heart," Bill said, and his downcast eyes looked at the limp noodles dripping over the sides of the carton. He turned his boot sideways. It appeared he wanted to say something more, and he did. "There's nothing to it. *Us.* She likes her dope. And I'm just a guy, I guess." Bill didn't like the way that sounded. "So, if y'all are hungry I can order more Chinese. Anything to help."

"No, thanks. But I guess you can get that scoop shovel back to Eldon at sanitation for me. I'm gonna have to call in sick."

"Sure." Bill said quickly, to be helpful.

"And I need you to keep any and all glass pipes and any other kind of shit away from her. All of it. Even when she comes crawlin' and beggin' to blow you. Keep it away. Or it won't be a speaker I put my boot through next time."

Bill said he understood and they nodded at each other and said goodnight.

* * *

When Crit entered Rennie's room she was jumping up and down on her bed like a trampoline. She had changed into the same outfit he had first seen her in: Baggie UK shorts and a cut-off tee that advertised the Smoky Mountains.

"This ain't so bad. I got it licked," she said, and threw a couple of boxer uppercuts. "I used to pick fights with boys before I got tits. What's in the bag?"

"Ice. Your body temperature will rise before you throw up and shit yourself."

"Gross. Are you gonna be here for that?"

"I'll be here."

"Pervert."

She stuck out her tongue. Crit set the ice in the bathroom sink. Rennie started to sing again. Johnny Cash again.

We got married in a fever.
Hotter than a pepper sprout.

Rennie's voice wasn't bad and she was only half-trying. She sang a few more lines and then she stopped. "I used to think that song was written about this shitburg. Did ya ever think that?"

"I guess I did, a time or two."

"That song makes it sound like Jackson's some awesome fuckin' place. That ain't exactly my impression of our local surroundings."

"I reckon not," Crit said, and looked over at her broken door latch.

"There's a Jacksonville, Florida. Maybe that's where they meant. I've never been to Florida. But I did go down to Myrtle Beach for my seventeenth B-day. Chrome took me. But we never saw the beach, just stayed in a motel near an airport. I could hear those big planes zoomin' in." She made the vroom sound of a jet engine.

They were both quiet for a while until she said, "Does it bother you that I used to be with your brother?"

Crit looked at the scabs on his knuckles. "I guess everything about him bothers me."

"Sometimes I think I'm a really bad person. Like the worst."

Crit wanted to tell her that she wasn't even close to being the worst person in the room, by a long shot. He stood up and checked out where the metal plate on her door jamb had splintered out. The screws had pulled out big chunks of wood.

Rennie dropped down on the bed and bounced on her butt a few times before lying on her back, staring up at a stinkbug on the ceiling.

"Why didn't you kill him?"

"Chrome?"

She nodded and held up her hands and lined up the bug through the cracks of her fingers.

He shrugged. "Maybe I'm trying to cut back on the bad stuff I used to do."

"You and me both. I wanna take Tyler someplace nice. Maybe Florida. Maybe Hawaii. Someplace with sand and a beach and palm trees and a warm ocean. Maybe I can get a job singing in some nightclub in some exotic place. I'm gonna do that when I kick my bad habits to the curb. You wanna come?"

"We'll see," he said. But what he thought was that she was still young enough to imagine being pleasantly surprised by life.

She pointed a forefinger at the stinkbug and pretended to pull a trigger. She chattered on for a while longer about a school trip she had once taken to Mammoth Cave and how she still remembered the differences between stalactites and stalagmites.

And then she talked less, and three hours into it, her dope comedown set in. She started breathing faster and her mood soured like bad milk. She paced and re-paced a U-shaped pattern around her bed. To deal with the grimness of the hours, Crit took the driver's manual from his room and started to read it. The first page had a photo and message from Kentucky's smiling governor. *We are privileged each time we get behind the wheel of a vehicle and drive down one of Kentucky's scenic back roads or expansive highways. Along with this privilege comes a great responsibility— something we should keep in the forefront of our minds as we traverse the Commonwealth.*

Rennie flipped on the TV. A Cincinnati Reds baseball game was in progress. The fuzzy reception made picking out the ball impossible. She tried to dial in another channel but found only static. She turned the TV off hard enough to break the dial. She paced some more. Opened the curtains. Closed them. Bit a nail. Then turned the TV back on and tried messing with the rabbit ears, but that didn't help.

"People around here pay good money for their damn rooms. Seems like Bill would spring for cable."

Crit doubted she had ever paid rent money in her life. He put down the driver's manual and told her he was going to fix her door. She didn't react like she had heard him. He went out and walked down to the tool room to find the drill and some screws.

He came back and she was peeing on the toilet with the door open. "We're out of toilet paper," she said.

He went out again and got extra paper towels and toilet paper from Bill. Then he started work working on the door. He sank the screws slow and careful so as not to split the wood.

"Do you have to make that noise?" she said.

The first time the lock didn't line up correctly. He had to re-adjust and re-screw it. He got it right and closed the door, tried the dead bolt. It held firm.

Rennie looked at herself in the bathroom mirror and itched at her hairline. Felt her legs to see how badly she needed to shave. Looked at her bitten nails. "I'm a fucking mess," she said.

She came out of the bathroom and turned the TV off. She tried to look out the window but had trouble with the curtain, so she went to her door and seemed pissed that it was now locked.

She unlocked it and opened it and looked out into the darkness and seemed disappointed with that too.

Crit watched her. She might head off somewhere. To Bill's or somewhere else. He wasn't sure he could or would stop her if she bolted. She took a step farther outside and stood there for a moment with a hand on a cocked hip and turned her head one way then the other.

"You're letting bugs in," Crit said.

She stepped back in, closed the door and locked it. She flipped the lock back and forth several times to make sure it worked. "Tell me something funny," she said in a hostile tone.

Crit shrugged and looked back at her with a blank expression.

* * *

Time moved very slowly to a couple of hours after midnight and Crit hated every disquieted and exasperating second of it. She was listless. She was up and down and twisting and fidgeting and yelling for no reason. He sat and closed his eyes but all that was there was dark and the rending of his ear. He picked up the driver's manual again. *A flashing yellow light means you must slow down and watch for others. It is found at intersections, construction areas, and on some vehicles, like tow trucks. A flashing red light means you must come to a full stop and proceed only when the way is clear.*

Rennie rolled over and coughed and hacked up yellowish phlegm. He wiped it off her bed sheet and made her drink a cup of water. She drank half and tossed the cup to the floor. She kicked at her wadded bed coverings and moaned. Her face was red and sweat-hazed. Crit picked up the cup off its wet spot and loaded it with ice. He brought it to her and tried to drop ice chunks into her mouth.

"Suck on this."

"Is that a proposal?"

"Chewing helps. Open."

She opened and took the ice on her tongue.

"I don't feel so good."

Her words were garbled. She spat out the ice and coughed up snot that trickled out her nose. Crit wiped her. He tried to dab perspiration off her forehead but she shrank from him.

"You know what your problem is? You're too damn quiet. You're starting to creep me out."

Crit ignored her.

"That fuckin' wall talks more that you do."

Crit went to the dresser and picked up her phone that had ear buds twined around it. "You can listen to music."

She looked at her phone. "Every song on there I heard a zillion times already and I hate every one of 'em."

Crit put the phone back and she tried for ten minutes to pick a fight with him, but he wasn't having it, and eventually she gave up and drifted off to sleep.

Crit managed to doze a few hours in the chair. He had a dream about finding a hole in the ground that led to a dark passage in a cave. He went down a long ladder into it. He was deep in the ground but somehow moonlight glistened off the stalactites and stalagmites. The cavern split into different tunnel passages and he had to decide which passage to take. He decided to retreat instead and went back to get out the way he had come in, but the ladder was gone and he was trapped in the cavern.

When he opened his eyes the room was dim but there was a bluish blush of morning in the curtained window. Traffic sounds from the highway trickled in. He looked over at Rennie and didn't know if she was asleep or awake. He looked closer. She was grinding her teeth and making a soft moaning sound. He rose on stiff joints and moved to the window and pulled back the curtain. He saw Wild Bill in a swirl of morning mist, moving through his gyrations. Crit's bowels rumbled and he decided to go back to his own room to use his toilet.

Wild Bill was barefoot in dew-heavy grass and bent over at the waist. He peered under his armpit and saw Crit unlocking his room and shot him a peace sign.

When Crit came back out he caught Bill peeking through Rennie's window.

Bill stepped away and said, "You need anything, Bro? I'm goin' to Walmart." His wet footprints dotted the cracked concrete.

Crit shook his head no.

"How's she doin'?"

"Shaky. But she's hangin' in there. So far."

Both men watched a large tanker truck pass. It braked and released compressed air.

"You know what the kids are doin' these days?"

"Not really."

"Wasp spray. They snort that shit."

Crit nodded but didn't say anything.

"I guess we were just as bad, with the gasoline and glue. Remember all that shit we did? And we survived, mostly." Bill looked down at the blades of grass stuck to his dew-wet feet. He seemed to be waiting for Crit to say something to answer what he had said. "I took that shovel back to Eldon. I talked him into not firing you."

"How'd you manage that?"

"I told him when he gets his church I'll play in his choir band."

"That sounds more like a threat than a favor."

"I'm a spiritual being. I most def believe in a higher power."

Crit thanked him, opened the door and slipped inside. His movements seemed to wake her. She turned over writhing and rasping, and rolled off her bed and landed on the floor. She pulled over her coverlet and pillows, and tried crawling to the bathroom while wadded all up in a sheet. She moaned curses and he helped her and held her hair out of the way so she could toss her guts into the toilet. She retched and then dry-heaved and when it seemed like she was done, she heaved some more and he wiped her mouth. She collapsed on the floor and her legs rippled with tremors. She had soiled herself.

"I'm not gonna make it."

Crit spooled out toilet paper and tried to hand it to her. "If you can, you might want to clean yourself." Crit moved to the door and turned away to give her privacy.

She squirmed around to face him and moaned something.

"I didn't hear what you said."

"I think I got my fucking period."

"When it rains, it pours," he said.

She raised her middle finger.

Crit tossed and flushed the toilet paper. He took off her basketball shorts and wet a towel and wiped her. She was too weak to complain. He found a pair of boy's brief underwear on the floor in a corner. He slipped a washcloth into them and pulled them up on her. While he did that her cheek stayed flat on the linoleum with her rump in the air. Her eyes stayed fixed on the cobwebs under the claw-foot tub.

Crit stepped outside and it was dark again. A full day had come and gone. He dropped soiled towels on the concrete walk next to the door. He would deal with them later. He felt like smoking a cigarette but he didn't have any. He thought about bumming one off Bill but the Econoline was gone. Then he heard Rennie call out his name. It was the first time she had done that. Called him by name. He stepped back inside.

She was on the bed on her side looking away from him toward the wall. She said his name again like she hadn't heard him come in.

"I'm here."

"I opened my eyes and you were gone."

"I'm here."

"This is damn hard."

Crit nodded but she was still facing the wall and didn't see it.

"You ready for some water?"

"No."

"I may have to leave for a bit, to get things at the store."

"Don't go."

Her voice rasped like a rusty file. She turned over and her eyes swallowed the shape of him crossing in front of the window. He sat close to her in a chair. She calmed a bit and breathed in wheezes and gasps. "It hurts."

"Uh-huh."

"I don't know what hurts worse. Chrome beatin' me up. Or my dope sick."

Crit didn't say anything and she didn't say anything more for a while. He was unclear what he wanted to do next, but he picked up the sketchpad that Tyler had torn pages out of and found a blank page. Then he picked up a sharpie and scratched out a few lines. Soon he had the outline of a woman locked in an open-mouthed stare, with eyeholes staring up at a stinkbug or heaven.

Rennie turned over and looked at him with one eye open and one eye shut. "Once, when I was little I played in this fiberglass insulation in my Granny's attic. That shit bout ate me alive. I was red and raw and itchin' for days. That's how I feel now. What are you doin'?"

He shrugged.

She managed to elevate herself onto an elbow, and raised her voice. "Don't you dare draw me like this. You promise?"

He closed the sketchpad. "I think you're over the hump. You're getting your bossy back."

"Damn right. Somebody has to be boss around here."

He thought about reading more from the driver's manual and picked it up. The cover had the Sheriff's phone number on it. He put it down.

Rennie rolled her neck and winced as if stretching the muscles made them worse. She looked at his sketchpad on his lap. "What do you feel when you make up that stuff?"

He told her he couldn't hear what she said. That his hearing was not what it used to be. She repeated herself.

"I forget who I am for a minute."

"How do you decide what to draw?"

A car with a blast muffler accelerated outside, squealing its tires for no good reason.

"I start working with my hands. I may not even have an idea in my head, but my hands get busy and my mind relaxes."

"You know what I like about the picture you did of me?"

"No clue."

"You kinda really saw me." She blew her nose on her sheet. "The me behind the me." Her eyelids started to tremble and she closed them, and they still trembled but eventually stopped, and she drifted off to sleep.

Crit rolled the sharpie between his finger and thumb. Had he really seen her? What had he seen? Her image had been born of random slashes with a mind of their own. He'd listened to nothing but the aimless scratch and scrape of his pen point—serenaded by the abated buzzsaw grumble in his ear. *You saw what?* Swirling apparitions in a crepuscular dream. An awakening in the dark. Lines without a plan. Running helter-skelter. Like a needle stitching his shroud. Flicker and flare. Witnessed by cold eyes, blood-veined to an ice-cold heart.

Chapter 13

ASHMED

Ashmed Farooqui's parents had moved from Rawalpindi, Pakistan, to Zanesville, Ohio, when he was five going on six. He remembered how big the earth looked, and how flat and wide and far below the 747 airplane's window. It took hours to cross the dark blue of the Atlantic Ocean. He and his father, mother, and older brother had landed at Cleveland's International Airport because his uncle owned a forty-nine-dollar-a-night motel off of I-70. Ashmed and his parents settled into living there and managed the motel. He and his older brother and younger sister, who was born shortly after they arrived, grew up cleaning the rooms, washing dirty sheets and emptying the trash. Ashmed's English had been very poor and he was bullied mercilessly when he entered the Muskingum County public school system. He at first had no friends outside his family and cousins. He improved his English by watching American TV shows. He took summer courses, and his parents hired a tutor. He had a good head for science and numbers, and by his senior year in high school, he was able to excel and had become a National Merit Scholar runner-up. Known as Ash to his American friends, he also played drums and cymbals in the school's marching band. He navigated the strange dance between his family's immigrant traditions and

American pop-culture. After graduating, he put off college and toured Ohio and Pennsylvania with a Muslim punk band called Four Dead. The band had gotten its name from a Neil Young song, but they played hard and loud, mostly Iggy Pop and MC 5 covers. Ashmed ran the band's soundboard and became its only roadie, driver, and social media marketer.

Two weeks into the tour, his parents grew increasingly alarmed at his life choices and had sent his older brother Taz to intervene. Barely out of his twenties, Taz had two young children from his arranged marriage and owned a string of convenience stores in small Kentucky and Tennessee towns. Thus, he was a superstar at every extended family gathering.

Taz had shown up at a Four Dead show in a Harrisburg dive bar called The Hub Cap. Only three Central Penn students and a couple of local drunks had turned out. At the sound check Taz and Ashmed argued. Ashmed told his brother that his family needed to back off. Taz said that what his brother did with his life reflected back on his family and community, that what Ashmed needed to fully become a man was a beautiful wife and his own business. Taz promised to help Ashmed attain both of those things if he gave up the band.

Ahmed didn't jump right away. It took blowing a head gasket seventeen miles South of College Station. The band had to sell the van to the local gas-station mechanic for barely enough to pay for Greyhound tickets back to Ohio.

On the ride home, an elderly female passenger became alarmed that the Four Dead were up to no good and called 9-1-1. The band and Ashmed were then taken off the bus in Wheeling, West Virginia, where they were questioned by local police, who also searched their instruments. They would have probably talked their way out of it had not the lead singer taken umbrage and blurted out that he just might run off and join the Islamic State because of the Wheeling Police Department's practice of illegal profiling. Ashmed spent a night in jail and his parents had to drive the three hours to Wheeling to vouch for him.

Ashmed was given the choice of working for his brother or being disowned by his family forever. He didn't have a plan B, so three weeks after his night in jail he was living in a shitty one-bedroom apartment in a six-unit complex on the south side of Jackson, Kentucky, and managing his brother's convenience store and gas station. Ashmed worked long hours, seven days a week. He was seven months in and his brother had yet to mention the "beautiful wife" aspect of their deal. He wasn't sure just how much more he could take. He had no friends in this backward mountain town and his store was overrun with toothless hillbillies who spoke with an almost indecipherable lockjaw drawl. Any free time he had, he face-timed with members of the Four Dead, watched big-budget action and comic hero movies, and looked at naked women on Chauterbate. And lately he had taken up video poker.

And so it was an hour before closing when a shirtless man with belly fat hanging over his cargo shorts came up to the Plexiglas barrier that thankfully separated Ashmed from his customers. His brother had admitted it was *bullet resistant,* not the more expensive *bulletproof.* A heavy caliber shot would surely crack it, but the rednecks didn't know that.

"Hey, you know me, right?"

Ashmed wasn't sure. His customers tended to look alike. But he nodded anyway.

"I need fifteen dollars' gas to get to West Virginia. My kid's sick, right? And I wanna pay ya, but all I got is twenty dollars in stamps."

The man's eyes were wild. Ashmed was fairly certain he was wired on something. The man pushed a SNAPS food stamp booklet through the sales window.

"We can't take those for gas."

"You think I'm dumb. I know that. But I'm like offerin' ya a five dollar tip here, if you can find it in yer heart to help me out this one time."

"What you're asking me to do is a crime."

"How about you front me the gas and hold onto these stamps and I'll pay you back cash tomorrow. Hell, you can keep the stamps as well."

Ashmed reached up and tapped on the back of a handwritten note scotch-taped to the bullet-resistant glass.

Absolutely no credit.

The man pushed his red and sputtering face closer and his breath fogged the Plexi. "Hey asshole, my brother fought in the desert to save yer camel-jockey ass."

Ashmed looked around. He was thankful the store wasn't entirely empty. There was an older man moving down the paper goods aisle toward the counter. And Ashmed remembered this man's unsmiling face. He had given him cardboard boxes a week or so ago.

A percussive bang made Ashmed jump. The shirtless man had smacked his palm onto the counter and knocked over a Bic lighter display. The multi-colored lighters clattered and spread out on the tile floor.

"Sir, you are on surveillance." Ashmed said as calmly as he could and pointed up at a camera on the ceiling. "I don't make the rules. I don't own this store. I work here. I am on surveillance too. So I cannot do what you ask. And if you don't leave, I will call the police."

The shirtless man spewed out a stream of curses and threats and coiled both fists. Ashmed noticed the older man had moved up and stood just behind the angry man.

"Maybe you should go back to wherever the fuck ya come from," the shirtless man snarled. Then he picked up a can of Red Bull and cocked it like a hammer to smash the bullet-resistant glass.

"You heard him," the older man said in a steady voice. "He's got rules to follow. And you're on camera."

The shirtless man turned and fixed his wild eyes on the older man. "Mind yer own fuckin' business."

The older man said nothing in reply but he stared back with

eyes like two lethal and cocked .45s. The shirtless man spewed out more curses and threats and gripped and re-gripped his Red Bull and moved back and forth in a half-circle around the older man and the older man didn't move an inch and didn't seem to be breathing at all.

Ashmed picked up his mobile to dial 9-1-1.

Then, surprisingly, the shirtless man backed down under the gaze of the older man, lowered the Red Bull, scraped up his food stamps, and retreated toward the door. "I'm just trying to see my kids," he said in a defeated tone and walked out.

The older man placed his items on the counter—a twenty-ounce Pepsi, a roll of paper towels, canned meat, crackers and a box of plastic picnic spoons. And then he squatted and started picking up the plastic lighters off the floor.

"You don't have to do that," Ashmed said. "I can do that. But thank you."

The older man picked up all of the lighters. He set them on the counter in a pile. "I'm lookin' for adult diapers," he said. "But I didn't see any out there with the regular diapers."

"If you didn't see any in the aisle, we must be out."

"There's none in the back?"

"Sorry, no."

The older man nodded. "Do you have any duct tape?"

Chapter 14

WINGS OF A DOVE

Crit unlocked and walked back in carrying two plastic sacks from the Marathon. Rennie woke up with a sudden coughing fit. He set down his purchases and brought the trash can closer. He placed it under her head but nothing came out except a swaying cord of saliva. He wiped her face and went to the sink and brought her a glass of water. Put it to her lips. She pushed it away.

"Would you stop fighting me and just let it happen."

Her eyes held onto him like a caged prisoner looking through death-row bars. He gently brought the water back to her lips, tilted the glass, and she gulped down a swallow. She settled down a bit. Crit felt her forehead. Didn't seem as hot. He went to the plastic sacks and pulled out a package of infant diapers and broke open the wrapping. He then pulled out a roll of duct tape.

"What's that for?" Rennie asked.

The sun came up, passed across the sky, and eventually dropped below the horizon as it had done the day before. Crit squeezed toothpaste onto the spangled bristles of a well-used toothbrush. Rennie sat on the toilet wearing diapers held up with duct tape. She didn't open her mouth at first. He tapped the toothbrush against her crusted lips. Then she opened with an exaggerated grimace. Crit moved the toothbrush back and forth. Teeth and gums. He had her spit in a coffee cup.

"You know, you have a lot of nose hair," she said.

He nodded.

"And out yer ears, too."

"Maybe I'm a werewolf."

He had her drink more water. And she swallowed down two spoonfuls of canned meat. She refused the third. Her hands were on his shoulders. He picked her up and laid her back on the bed. He sat on the edge of the mattress as she closed her eyes with her hand circling his wrist. He looked down at her fingers. Liddy used to sleep something like that, holding onto his penis. Rennie's nails were bitten and raw. He compared their skin. Hers was pale and smooth. His bulged with veins, scars, age marks, dry patches, and more scars. Some of the hairs on his arm were gray. He could smell himself.

Crit slipped back to his room. He stood naked in his tub, wrapped like a cocoon in circular yellow vinyl gummed with grime. He stood long enough for the hot water to turn warm and then cold. And he stood longer. His chin tilted up into the icy spray. He turned off the water and stood cold and dripping. He looked at the tattoos of crosses on his knuckles, which he had cut into his flesh with a razor blade back in juvenile detention. Age fourteen. Baby oil and burnt charcoal rubbed in. Now blue-tinged and faded. He looked at his wrist and imagined her fingers encircling it. What were they to each other? He had answered to no one in prison. Not even to himself. And before that he had put food on the table for Liddy and Taylor but hardly ever showed up to eat it. His mother had been untrustworthy. She had left him and his brother for days and weeks at a time. They had begged food from neighbors and shoplifted from grocery stores. He tried to remember the last time he had seen his mother. She had come to him to ask for money, claiming she wanted to move to Tennessee. She wouldn't tell him where or why. But there was usually some stubble-faced chain-smoking boyfriend around that she'd pull into her tumultuous orbit and then ditch. Those last few years before she died he only saw her when she came asking for money or pain pills or both. He usually gave her some, but not all she asked for. That last time he only gave her a twenty and no pills, and she'd left cursing his name. And then she was dead in a trailer fire down in Jellico, Tennessee. Chrome had driven down. His brother said they found her six feet from her door, burned to the bone on an incinerated couch. It could have been foul play, or drugs, or a heart attack with a hot plate or candle left on. No one knew for sure and no one was ever charged. Chrome had gone down and had what was left of her cremated. Crit didn't even know where her ashes were. Spread, kept, buried, he didn't know. And had never asked.

Crit shaved and cut his chin. He lowered his face to the basin and ran cold water on it until it stopped bleeding. He slipped on his cleanest stale shirt. He came outside into twilight. It was comfortable weather. A couple of degrees above cool. Summer was closer now. He noticed how the fading evening light brought out the colors in things. The green of the trees and grass seemed more saturated. A robin glowed iridescent. Crit watched two more robins land and peck and hop contentedly on the grass patch below the motel sign. Across the highway the unyielding mountain peaks rose to meet the darkening sky. He had been out of prison going on five weeks. April had turned into May. Wild Bill pulled the cord on a push mower and scared off the robins.

* * *

The next afternoon Crit placed two chairs outside. Rennie no longer needed diapers and she wore pink *Hello Kitty* shorts and a low cut sweatshirt that drooped off one shoulder. They sat and shared a bag of Lay's sour cream and onion chips and watched the birds and hills and the cars pass. Felt the good weather. They watched the old couple work in slow tandem from the top of the hill all the way down and through the blinking stoplight.

"Fourteen."

"What?"

"That's how many cans they picked up." Rennie licked her salty fingers. "How much you think they get for a bag of cans?"

"Can't be much."

"Maybe that's my new job. We can go in as partners."

"I don't know about that."

"We can set our own hours."

The old couple worked their way out of sight and Rennie stretched out her legs and toes. They watched cars pass and ate more chips.

"You wanna play car poker?"

"I don't know what that is."

"I used to go visit my Granny up in Saldee, way back in the hills. She didn't have a TV. Or teeth. Bitch made her own soap. We used to sit on her porch and guess what color the next car that came over the top of the rise would be. It was a one-lane county road and be like twenty minutes between cars. We'd keep score. She'd get wasp-mad if I won. I remember I always felt so lonesome up there. Waiting for the next damn car. Waiting for something to happen. Like I was living at the end of the world."

Rennie started to guess car colors out loud. She called out red, switched to blue, missed on five cars in a row. Crit didn't join in but he did notice that there were a lot more neutral color cars on the road than cars with primary colors. If he stuck to white or gray he'd probably clean up. She said he was a spoilsport, then reached out and circled his wrist with her fingers. The strange sensation of her touch changed his breathing.

"You think I'll go back to it?"

"Your old ways?"

She nodded. Crit thought yes but said no.

"I hope yer right." She tilted her head back to feel the sun. "My momma said she remembered you from Wolverine."

She gave his wrist a slight squeeze. The ringing in his ear warbled off-key.

"She used to live across the creek from y'all."

"Couldn't have been for long. We moved around a lot. My momma didn't like to pay rent."

"Did you know yer daddy growing up?"

Crit let the question hang for a moment before speaking. "My brother and me had different—I guess you'd call 'em dads. Mine left before I was born. He went up to Ohio to find work, started a new family up there. I've seen him only twice in my life."

"What was your momma like?"

"Crazy, tough, poor, angry, sad, unreliable."

"Sounds like me. She still live around here?"

Crit shook his head and pulled his arm away. He squirmed out of his chair and stood up abruptly.

"Where you goin'?"

Crit's ear squalled. "Someplace they don't ask so many damn questions."

Just then the county half-ton turned in and clunked up the drive. Eldon was driving and singing. The truck chased off the birds pecking at the grass. The engine coughed to a stop as Eldon belted out the closing line of "The Old Rugged Cross" and clicked off his tape player. His window was half-down. "You wanna work?"

"When?"

"Now. I got a call."

"I'm kinda busy."

"You don't look busy?"

"Can I come?" Rennie asked.

Eldon hiked up his short frame to get a better look at the young woman. "You like gospel music, Darlin'?"

"Hell, yes," Rennie blurted. "Do you like sour cream chips?"

She stepped up to Eldon and offered him the bag. Eldon looked at her with a bemused smile, took a couple of chips and chewed them, and looked at her some more. "Come on."

"I'll be back shortly," Crit said loud enough to dissuade her. Her coming wasn't a good idea.

"He said I could come," Rennie said, tossing the empty *Lays* bag into the dumpster and then joining Crit at the truck. "If I have to look at those damn four walls another minute, you might as well shoot me."

She told Eldon her name and he told her his and he climbed down and went around to the passenger door and opened it for her. She thanked him but then said she had to get her sunglasses and ran back inside.

The half-ton climbed switchbacks East into the mountains as the late-afternoon sun winked through serrated treetops. Crit drove and Rennie rode sandwiched between the two older men. She wore big oval sunglasses and held onto a plastic Pepsi bottle that Crit had bought her when they stopped at the Marathon. Eldon talked non-stop about how the county needed to fix more potholes, how liberals in Washington were trying to take away guns, and how most people who read the Bible didn't understand it. Crit could tell Eldon was a lot more talkative with a young woman around. Rennie commented on how she loved Eldon's gospel tunes. And Eldon seemed happy about that and said how he had liked all kinds of music growing up but what he had grown to cherish most, now that he had less time on this temporal earth, were songs that praised the eternal life he aspired to. But sometimes he still listened to straight country. She said she liked old country like Waylon and Willie and the Boys. Eldon said he liked Willie too, but not all that marijuana smoking. They both agreed that Carrie Underwood had an amazing voice. The half-ton rolled through the one-stoplight town of Noctor. Past the Dollar Tree store. Past a closed and abandoned gas station. And Rennie joined in and sang word for word and note for note with Eldon.

When troubles surround us
When evils come
The body grows weak
The spirit grows numb.
When these things beset us

He doesn't forget us
He sends us his love
On the wings of a dove.

Eldon's right hand drifted up into the air as he sang, as if the notes were being shaped and lifted by his palm. When the song finished he started preaching. "God made me, heals me, loves me, defends me, forgives me."

Rennie echoed his amens.

"He raises me up, mends my wounds, heals my soul. Leads me to gentle water."

"Amen."

Crit couldn't tell if Rennie was buying in or just going along. But he figured either was a good thing if it took her mind off her want. Crit braked and stopped where he was told and climbed out and tossed three garbage bags and a broken child's stroller into the truck bed. Then climbed back in.

"You sing like an angel." Eldon said to Rennie. "You saved?"

Rennie drummed her fingers on the dash. "I'm baptized. I used to go to church regular. But I may have back-slid a bit."

"If nobody sinned, Jesus woulda been out a job. I'm starting up a new church and we sure could use a ringer in our choir."

"Well, you just hit me in my happy place, Mister, if you think I can sing, 'cause I sure like to sing."

Eldon started up an old Carter Family tune. Rennie knew most, but not all the words. And where she didn't know, she harmonized. Crit even found himself humming along. The road ahead cut through uneven terrain beneath a vast sky, all clear except for a couple of straggling cotton ball clouds. Crit down-shifted and climbed a ridge to the peak and crested and drove down and up to the next. Less than a week ago he'd believed Eldon would send him back to prison. He'd fully expected it. Maybe he had even wanted it. There was a lot less coming at you when you're buried in your own mud. Crit stuck his arm out and caught a stream of air in his palm. He tilted it like an airplane flap and let it sail up and down on the current. There was that. You can't stick your hand out a moving vehicle in a dark hole, he thought.

Crit picked up a soiled mattress that was lying half-on and half-off the road and managed to single-handedly hoist it up and toss the wobbly bulk of it onto the flatbed. He climbed back into the cab and Eldon told him to turn around and he did and they drove back the way they'd come. On a downward incline, Rennie reached over and circled Crit's wrist with her fingers. It was getting to be a habit. And if Eldon thought that strange he didn't say anything. The preacher flipped his cassette tape and sang to the Statler Brothers. The sun was now lower and Rennie seemed tuckered out. She closed her eyes and didn't sing any more, but she hummed occasionally.

***

The next morning Crit woke in his own bed from a deep sleep without the usual wrenching separation from some unpleasant dream. He blinked and the ceiling was opaque and softly blurred. He wiped at the crust in the corners of his eyes. He rose in his underwear and washed his face and shaved and slipped on his pants and shirt. Music with a pedal steel guitar was seeping from Rennie's room like smooth syrup. Not her usual frenetic beats. He listened. It sounded like Willie Nelson but he wasn't sure.

He walked outside into the morning. Daylight had found a seam between two dark bilious clouds. His hair was still damp and he looked at the clouds and hills and decided to take his driver's test.

Rennie's door was locked. He tented fingers and peeked through her window and she was curled up with a pillow over her head. Her phone was plugged in and now seemed to be playing *Blue Eyes Crying in the Rain*. He went back into his room and wrote a note about where he was going and wedged it under the crack beneath her door.

Walking toward town he passed a Little Caesar's Pizza and two chopped Harleys came roaring down the road straight at him. The riders were helmet-less with long, wind-whipped hair, and he immediately recognized them as Chrome's posse. The pair didn't slow and passed him with loud exhausts punching the air. Both had stuck their left hands palm-down below their gas tanks in a recognition wave that bikers always gave to fellow bikers.

He was back in it.

At the courthouse, Crit placed his driver's manual and keys, wallet and change, in a plastic tray and walked through a metal detector while being indifferently watched by a prematurely bald young deputy propped in a folding chair with a newspaper in his lap. Crit inched through. Prison experience had taught him fast movements tended to trigger a response. As it was, his belt buckle set if off and the deputy had to wand him.

After collecting his personal items he walked down a short hallway that had gray walls and red carpet and turned right. He remembered where he was supposed to go—past the double-doors to the courtroom. Past the office of the judge who had sentenced him. Up ahead a plastic sign stuck out at ninety degrees to the wall above a door and said *County Clerk*. There were a handful of folks waiting in line and the last two—a pregnant young woman in gray sweats with her wizened grandfather, leaning on a twisted hickory walking stick—were out the door into the hallway. After ten minutes he was next in line. There was a six-foot tall wooden divider with ornate molding that ran the length of the room. Two windows had been cut into it for serving customers. Off to the right was a door with a sign that said *Vault Entrance, Deeds, Mortgages, Marriage licenses, etc.* A young man in a greasy mechanic's jumpsuit was arguing with the clerk on the left about a lien that had been placed on the car he had just purchased, making it impossible to get the title transferred until the lien was lifted. As he stomped off, the jumpsuit man stated loudly that the seller had never mentioned the lien and that there would be hell to pay. His place was taken by a blonde woman in a pink top and black leggings who was picking up a vanity plate that said, *Miss 45*. Crit didn't know if that reflected her age, the current president, or her preferred caliber of firearm.

The pregnant teenager and her grandfather peeled off to the window on the right. When called, Crit stepped up to the window on the left where the jumpsuit man had left a tang of oil, and gasoline and body odor. Crit took out his probation letter and was surprised to see that the clerk was an African-American male, about thirty, wearing a blue bow tie and glasses. Two reasons for being surprised: there were only a handful of members of his race in the whole county, and it usually took family connections to land a county job.

"Can I help you?"

There was something pleasant, almost feminine about the man's voice. The nameplate in front of the clerk said *Robert Bridgewater*.

"Ah. I was told I needed to take a driver's test to get my license back. And I should show up here." Crit unfolded his probation letter.

"When you say *get it back*, do you mean your last license expired? Or was it taken away due to a court judgment?" Robert flipped his hand expressively when he spoke. That affectation took a lot of balls to pull off in a redneck town.

"Expired, I think?"

"When did it expire? If it was less than ninety days, you don't have to retake the test."

"It was more than that. I'm not sure when it expired. I was locked up."

Was your last license issued in this county?

"Yep."

"I need your name and some form of I-D."

"I've got a parole letter with my name and address, will that work?"

"That's all you got?"

"All I got."

Crit handed the creased letter across the transom and noticed that a heavy middle-aged woman with curly black hair and heavily rouged red cheeks was watching him from a desk against the far wall. Something about her seemed familiar. Her desk was the largest in the room, so she was probably *the* county clerk. He wouldn't have recognized her except for the nameplate on her desk said *Hazel Ings*. He had known her as Hazel Sizmore back when they used to screw like mad bunnies in the back of one his stolen cars.

Hazel cast Crit another glance and then got up and moved to where the clerk was looking up Crit's previous license on a computer. She and Robert conferred for a moment, then she walked up to Crit, holding his parole letter. Robert retreated to the coffee machine corner to refill a turquoise mug that had a yellow daisy on it.

"You don't remember me, do you?" A hesitant smile formed on bright red lips. Her heavy makeup seemed pancaked on.

"Hazel."

His saying her name seemed to bring a spark to her green eyes.

"I'm afraid to even count the years."

Crit shook his head and waffled out air instead of saying anything.

"You look pretty good, for an old guy."

"You look good, too."

"You said that, cause you had to say that. I got fat. Maybe I should go on a prison diet."

He looked at her and tried to figure out whether he should be on the defensive.

She smiled without malice and dropped both of her fleshy arms onto the transom. "Look at that, bigger than ham hocks."

"Yeah, well they do tend to underfeed you behind bars. But I wouldn't recommend it."

What he said seemed to tickle her and she giggled. "How long were you in?"

"Fourteen years, nearly, this time."

She made a tisk-tisk sound with her tongue while sizing him up. "I was real lucky not to get knocked up by you. You were bad to the bone. I bet you woulda been a terrible husband."

"No doubt." Crit remembered she had liked to say outrageous things, even back then.

"But we woulda had a few fun times, right? And now here we are, almost dead. You're not still married to Liddy, are you?"

Crit shook his head no. Liddy had sent him one letter in fourteen years. Stuffed with divorce papers.

"I'm between husbands at the moment. A lot of the dating now is all on the computer. Like Facebook, the kids started it all, but we're taking it over. I'm aspiring to be a cougar. You get on there, looking like a sexy old badass pirate, a lot of old cows would be mooing all over that."

Crit found himself smiling. The bow tie clerk was gossiping with another office worker and both were watching Hazel and Crit like they were putting on a show. No doubt Hazel was a fun boss to work for.

Crit rubbed the top of his eyebrow with one finger. "So I need to take the test again, right?"

"I guess so, unless I get a million dollars or comparable favors."

"I was never that good."

Hazel snorted a laugh. "You weren't bad, as I remember it." She took a legal form out of a drawer and set it on the transom. "You normally need an alternative photo I-D, but...I've seen you naked."

The bow tie clerk let out a whooping laugh and Crit heard him say, "No she didn't."

Hazel handed Crit the test form. "Fill this in and take it to room three-oh-four. Use the stairs. That's where they give the test. Have you studied for it?"

"A bit. Not much."

"Well, they say it's like riding a bicycle." And the way she said it made riding a bicycle sound like a carnal act.

Crit finished the test in thirty-seven minutes and the officer who monitored the room then had him sit in a folding chair in front of his desk and go over all of his wrong answers. He had failed six. He had missed what to do when you enter a roundabout island. Crit wasn't sure what that was. And what to do if you have a blowout—the right answer seemed to defy common sense. But he had scored thirty-four out of forty. Two above failing. And that was good enough.

He came out of the courthouse and the sun was directly above his head. Two old-timers were perched on the bench near the sidewalk. One of them had a rolling oxygen tank that made a metallic noise. Both men watched him. Crit stepped to the sidewalk and saw an SUV with the Sheriff's Department insignia double-parked on the other side of the street. He crossed to it and Aaron Medlock was waiting. Crit didn't like owing the sheriff any favors. If he had managed to pass the written part on his own, he could have most likely passed the driving part. Crit went up to the open window. The sheriff wore a thin smile and was drinking from a can of Ale81. Shades on. There was a radar gun on the seat beside him.

"How'd you do?"

"Good enough."

"You got your paper?"

Crit handed it to the sheriff and he took a clipboard off his dash and put the paper on it and signed it. And held onto it.

"Your brother wants to see you."

"What about?"

"Your wife calls our office every day or two now."

"We're not married and I can't stop what she does."

"You can try."

He handed Crit back the driver's form. "She's tying up our phone lines."

***

It was the first time he'd seen the place in a week, and when he turned on the lights the space jumped out at him as if something were different. Something had changed. He moved around slowly and carefully and looked over all the items and stuck his face down close to each of his paintings and determined that everything was as he had left it. Or so it seemed. The only difference he could tell was that several pieces of junk mail and a magazine had been pushed through the mail slot into a pile on the floor. Crit sorted through it—mostly bills—all addressed to Wild Bill's mom. The magazine was a *Cosmopolitan* and had a sexy model on the cover in a skin-tight latex top and bold letters about learning new sex positions. Crit was surprised that Bill's mom was a subscriber.

A man about fifty with bushy red sideburns, a bald head, and painter whites came in and told Crit that somebody had stolen his tools out of his truck and he was looking for paint gear and hand tools. He told Crit he had left his truck parked at a work site and gone to lunch with a co-worker. The thieves had even taken his twenty-foot extension ladder.

"I'm damn surprised anyone wants to steal tools anymore because nobody wants to work." The man said. "I can't get nobody to show up two days in a row for fifteen an hour."

"I don't got much but most of what I got is on that shelf." Crit said and pointed him to what he had.

The man bought a hammer, a crescent wrench, a set of screwdrivers, a skill saw without a blade, and a set of sockets that were missing a 7/8 inch and an 11/16 inch. The total came to twenty dollars. The man took out a folded ten and a five clasped under a paper clip and Crit said that was good enough.

After the painter left, Crit cleaned the bathroom with Comet. There was a drip in the rusted basin he would have to fix later. He went and sat behind the counter and didn't move for ten minutes. He figured he should probably head back to check on

Rennie. He moved his sketchpad closer. He turned the globe and read the names of countries in Africa and the Middle East. Then he grabbed a nub of charcoal. Opened his sketchpad to a blank page. He started thinking of drawing a palm catching air. He scratched out a couple of aimless lines and his brother walked in, talking loud on his mobile and moving about as if he owned the place.

Crit didn't try to listen in, but he couldn't help but hear that the conversation was about Chrome's wife complaining about landscapers who had done a shoddy job. They'd left splotchy piles of mulch all over the lawn. Chrome told her he would make sure they came back and did it right. And then he told her that he loved her and he clicked off.

Chrome moved over to the counter. Crit didn't look up and kept drawing. Chrome glanced at the indistinct lines Crit had incised on the white paper and his jaunty smile suddenly dropped off his face like it was cut off with a butcher knife. "You think I was kidding?"

"About what?"

"About my painting."

"What painting?"

"Painting my damn fucking picture."

Crit laid down his charcoal and looked. The half-formed hand looked more like the comb of a rooster. "I thought you were joking."

"Why'd you think that?"

"Because I thought it was a joke to ask what you asked."

"Does this look like a joke?" Chrome pointed at the missing part of his ear. The wound had crusted over badly and was barely closed. "I want you to paint me with a good ear. The way God made it. Or would that be cheating? Crossing some fucking moral code you artists don't wanna cross?" Chrome's eyes burned and he gained another notch of angry for no reason. "And you know what else is a fucking joke? Tryin' to catch some drug whore slut from hittin' rock bottom. How fucking dumb can you be?" Chrome reached across the counter. He picked up Crit's charcoal nub. And he ate it. His eyes stayed on Crit and he chewed and crunched down on it until his teeth were black and his smile was black. He spat black saliva onto the floor and rubbed it in with his boot toe and paced to the front window. Then he worked his head back and forth like his neck hurt and calmed down a bit. "But who knows. Hope springs a turtle and Jesus walked on the water. I just wonder if I set up this whole damsel-in-distress thing just to get yer stubborn ass to find out who you really are?" He came back to the counter, his lips were charcoal-black. "But I'm not that smart, am I?"

Crit looked up at his brother and his brain fired up an idea that he would indeed paint his portrait. With a festering ear wound that would dominate and infect his whole rancid face with boiling corruption.

Chrome went over to a wall mirror and pushed a tuft of his bleached blond hair into place with a finger. He picked up a placemat and rubbed some of the black off his teeth and lips. "You know the story bout the frog and the scorpion? Well, this scorpion needs to get to the other side of the river and so he comes up to the frog and says…"

"I know the story."

"I know you do. You told it to me after you stole my favorite bicycle. Once a chicken-killing dog, always a chicken-killing dog." Chrome then wadded up the placemat and tossed it over his shoulder. He went back to Crit and moved the globe so he could lean in closer. "I know who you really are, even if you don't."

Their eyes locked like coiled and swaying snakeheads. Shared DNA heated and boiled.

"What?" Chrome asked. "You got somethin' to say?"

Crit said nothing and imagined the sick yellows and reds needed to paint his brother's pustulant face like a deformed leper.

Chrome found a box of Kleenex and blew his nose. Then he wiped his lips some more. And the front door opened and Sister Nikhael came in.

"Guess who's included in the big Cincinnati group show!"

Chrome took in the beaming dread-locked woman in the rainbow-colored top like she was the majorette in an alien parade. She bounced forward and reached into her low-slung macramé bag and pulled out a printed flyer.

Crit had thought he would never see her ever again. Never hear her voice. Never see her braids jangle or her eyes smile. And she'd come back with all those things and more, and he was happy for it. He took what she handed him.

"And guess who's work they put on the front of their brochure to advertise the whole damn thing?"

Crit looked down at what he held—a glossy three-color brochure with his sketched and colored-in image of Rennie on the cover—*South of the Ohio: New Visions in Outsider Art* was printed atop her anguished face.

"I got more." Sister Nikhael dug into her bag and pulled out a dozen more brochures and dropped them in a pile on the counter.

"How many of these they print?"

"I don't really know, lots, hundreds, maybe thousands." She said in a child-like voice and the end of her sentence climbed two octaves.

Crit fanned out the brochures like playing cards while Sister Nikhael beat-boxed hip-hop beats. He looked at the multiples of Rennie spread out and tried to roll back what Sister Nikhael had already said. There was some kind of show. His work was going to be put up in it. In front of people he didn't even know. Was that really true?

"You're that gal that taught art in prison," Chrome said creeping up to the counter.

"That would be me."

"I heard about you. I'm his better-looking younger brother."

"I see. I see. Everything's a matter of opinion. Did you hurt your ear?"

"Somebody did." He gave Crit a look. "I was just talkin' to

my brother about his next masterpiece. It's gonna be his best ever."

"I hear that. I bet it will be."

Crit looked at Rennie's face on the brochures. He turned and checked out the original on the wall. The smaller versions were different. The red and blue was more saturated, sprang out at the viewer more. Crit decided that somehow the smaller looked better.

"The curator needed a title fast so I gave them 'Girl With a Phone.' Was that kosher?"

Crit nodded, his ear sounding like a sputtering airplane engine.

"He liked your work so much he put it on the cover to represent the whole damn show. Gives your contribution more weight and presence. I should have called to tell you, but last time I saw you, you were otherwise engaged. I wanted to show up in person and ask if you're doing okay?" She peered at him closely.

He gave her a quick nod and looked away. "I'm good."

Chrome took a flyer and read out loud what was printed on the back. "*Creative environments built by intuitive and self-taught artists reflect art at its purist and most uninhibited form.*" He lowered it. "What the fuck does that mean?"

"Kind of a bogus statement. But what's way cool is the last show in this space was written up in *Art Forum*," Sister Nikhael crossed herself. "It was a miracle to get your brother into this thing. I paint and I'm jealous. Major win!"

She pumped her arms and moved her feet in a kind of victory dance. Crit leaned back against the metal fencing and scratched his nose.

"Can I keep one of these?" Chrome asked.

"There not mine. They're all his."

"In that case." Chrome pocketed three brochures. "Where's this thing at?"

"Downtown Cincinnati. The opening's next Friday."

"Opening?"

"That's like the big kick-off party for the exhibit."

"Can he make money off this?"

"Well, exhibited works are usually offered for sale. Crit would have to set his price. And I need to take these two back with me." She pointed at the Rennie and Wild Bill paintings.

"I know some heavy peeps in Cincy. They'd buy my brother's shit if I twist an arm or two."

"His paintings are really strong. And I'm kind of hoping they'll get purchased by an established collector."

"I like yer hair by the way. I used to date this gal said she was from Jamaica, but it turned out she was from Puerto Rico." A rakish smile purred across Chrome's lips. "She had that sexy dread thing going like you do."

Sister Nikhael didn't seem to be offended. "My family was originally from Haiti."

Crit heard their voices chirp and laugh. But he didn't listen and the conversation dissipated into a dry otic hiss. He slowly and closely read every letter of his name on the flyer. Small black letters embedded onto a shiny surface that felt baby smooth between his rough fingers. He wasn't sure what he was feeling. Pride. Worry. Suspicion. Sister Nikhael was certainly giddy about it. But Crit fully expected another shoe to drop. Something bad to slither out of the good. And when it did, that's what he would understand better.

Crit helped Sister Nikhael take down and wrap the two paintings she needed for the show in large plastic garbage bags. Then he propped open his door and helped carry them to her Prius. He placed the images of Rennie and Wild Bill side by side on her back seat. She had him put a protective layer of cardboard over them and then buckled them in with seat belts.

"So, you're gonna make the opening party, right? I know it's coming up quick, but this whole thing was amazing—that we could slide you in after he'd already basically picked the show," she said.

"I don't know if I can."

"It would mean a lot to me if you could."

"I can't even leave the county."

"Unless your P.O. signs off. I could talk to them."

"What am I supposed to do up there? Stand next to my stuff and say, *Hey, look at me. Ain't I special?*"

She moved closer to him and her kind eyes took him in. "Yep, pretty much. You are special. Give yourself some props."

Crit detached from her gaze and looked back at his store. Chrome was pacing the sidewalk, talking on his phone. The call seemed to piss him off. Crit figured his brother was talking to his wife's landscapers.

"You have a talent that needs to come out from under your rock." She said. "Don't be an emotional miser. It's okay to share something of yourself. Dare to be vulnerable."

Now his brother was walking fast toward them.

"Can I at least talk to your P.O. about the show?"

Chrome interrupted, "Hey, Bra, we got to get somewhere. There's a thing."

Chrome was smiling but Crit knew there was nothing good behind it.

***

Chrome drove and pumped *Iron Maiden*. They crossed the viaduct over the North Fork and headed out of town. Chrome shouted out some questions about Sister Nikhael and the art show over the throb and thrash from his speakers. Instead of answering Crit reached over and turned the throb louder until it pounded his head and sinuses. He thought about Rennie. His note had said he would be back in a couple of hours. Four hours had already passed. Now he didn't know where he was going or when he'd return. He asked to make a quick stop at the motel on the way out of town but Chrome had stared ahead and nodded but didn't stop.

South on 15 and almost to Lost Creek. Turn left. County

road. Turn left again. Up a skinny logging road. Chrome switched into four-wheel to navigate a series of rutted erosion ditches. There were fresh vehicle tracks in the mud they drove over. They climbed higher up the ridge and plateaued, and Chrome stopped at a metal cattle gate. Crit got out. The air smelled fragrant and damp. He heard crickets or maybe it was just his bad ear. Some kind of rusted old farm implement was partly hidden in blackberry bushes. Two slender redbud trees blossomed bold crimson. The gate had no hinges. Barbed wire held it to a locust post. Crit had to drag it to open it. Chrome motored through and told him to leave it open. Crit climbed in. They went ahead another quarter-mile.

A singlewide with vertical rust stains stood in a clearing next to a farm pond. There was an old wood-framed tenant house with a caved-in roof moldering behind the pond. A muddy ATV was parked next to a concrete pump cistern with dozens of red gas cans and blue buckets scattered around, along with more than a dozen butane tanks. The buckets and cans and tanks suggested this was much more than a fly-by-night shake'n bake operation. The best-looking thing on the place by far was a fairly new Ford 150 with nice wheels and turbo up-pipes.

A barking Rottweiler ran at them across a bare patch of feces-littered dirt but was yanked back by a chain. He barked and foamed and fought the chain.

"So what are we doing here?"

Chrome shrugged and honked his horn.

A shirtless teenager came out of the trailer, holding a shotgun. Chrome climbed out and stepped ahead and raised his hand in greeting. The kid nodded, lowered his weapon and walked forward on his toes. He was pale and skinny like an anemic Johnny Winter.

"What up, Gary?"

"I thought for a minute you was them comin' back," Gary spoke fast and jittery like he was plugged into an electric current. He then yelled at his dog to shut up. It didn't. He went over and kicked at it, and the dog whimpered and retreated beneath two pieces of particleboard that had been tented together as a piss-poor doghouse. Gary then placed his shotgun on top of a fifty-five gallon drum, clasped hands with Chrome and soul-hugged.

"Road got worse since that last rain. I may have to send out a front-end loader," Chrome said.

"Yeah Man, it's gettin' rough."

The kid glanced over at Crit with wired eyes. Hadn't-slept-in-a-week eyes.

"My brother. He just got out. He's a famous artist. Con-artist, that is."

Chrome laughed and Gary nodded with a mix of confusion and agreement.

Chrome then looked around and over the place. "Tell me again how it went down."

"Ah...sure. First thing this morning, my dog was barkin' loud and crazy, and I come out and I thought it was some raccoon or possum or something wild and then these two dudes step out from behind me. Right there." He pointed a trembling finger. "They had a gun on me. Two guns. Pistols."

"You didn't know 'em?"

The kid quickly shook his head. "They had masks. Bandanas pulled up. One dude was tall and the other had an accent. Maybe Mexican."

"A Mexican all the way from Mexico?"

"Maybe, I don't know."

"How'd they get up here?"

"Whatever they drove they musta' parked it below the pond," Gary said, and pointed beyond the pond. "I didn't see no car."

"What time was this?"

"It was early. Maybe eight or nine. There was still some mist and shit."

"Why'd you wait to call me?"

"I couldn't find my phone. It was under the seat in my truck but I thought it was in my trailer. I was scared shitless. My head wasn't on straight."

"I hate when that happens. They take anything else or just my shit?"

"Two kilos, what I was holdin' for you."

Chrome nodded and cocked his head. "I see they left yer shotgun."

"That was hid. In a hiding place."

"You coulda pulled it out and gave chase."

"Look, Man, I'm a cook, not a killer. That's yer job. And I was major freaked, okay, after they pointed guns at me. And now they like fuckin' know where I live." The kid shook his head hard and his whole body started to shake.

Chrome picked up the kid's shotgun off the drum barrel, cracked it open and saw a shiny ten-gauge shell seated snug.

Crit saw it all play out before it played.

Chrome snapped back the barrel, smiled, and tilted up the business end in the kid's alarmed face.

"Watch it, that thing's loaded, Man."

"I know it is."

Chrome jutted his forehead at the kid's truck. The barrel stayed where it was. "Those Verde Kaos rims?"

The kid's eyes bulged and he sucked air fast and his words jumbled out in a high-pitched rush. "I got 'em, I...I...bought em off a *Craig's List* guy in Knoxville."

"I was up here Friday and you had shit rims."

"I bought 'em Saturday, Man, I didn't do nothing. They stole from me. I swear to God."

Chrome turned to Crit. "Do me a favor. See if there's any gas in that jug over there." He said it like asking for the salt and pepper for his potatoes.

Crit hesitated.

Chrome leaned into Crit's hissing ear. "I either teach him a lesson or bury him. Up to you. No difference to me."

Crit didn't look at his brother. He climbed out and walked

over to the ATV as if on autopilot, as if reliving some home movie that got stuck in the sprockets. His stomach felt sick. The Rottweiler started up again. Crit picked up the gas can. Half full. He didn't look at the Kid. But he could hear him whimpering. He brought it back to his brother who cast his cold eyes at the kid's truck. Crit unscrewed and dowsed the cab and hood. Gas fumes scorched his nostrils. He tossed the empty jug away. He didn't have a match or lighter so he went and sat in his brother's truck and closed his heavy eyes. The Rottweiler's barking jackhammered into his head.

The kid stuttered out pleas for mercy and pissed himself as Chrome pressed the shotgun harder into his forehead. "Listen to me you piece of shit. I'm not gonna burn yer trailer cause that's where you make my sunshine. But don't you never sell to nobody but me, you hear? Or I'll burn you alive and bury the ashes."

The kid nodded fast and furious.

Chrome lowered the weapon, leaving an indented flesh circle like a third eye. He stepped back to Crit. "There's a lighter on the console."

Crit reached over and found it. An expensive polished chrome cigar lighter with the initials $C.P.$ Probably a Christmas present from a loving wife. Or kids. He gave it to his brother. Chrome pulled something out of his back pocket—the three art gallery flyers—he lit them and let the flame build. Flickering yellow tendrils ashed through the glossy three-color printing. It burned and Chrome's eyes burned and stayed fixed on Crit.

Then Chrome walked over to the kid's pick-up and tossed the flyers.

Whoosh.

They drove out the way they came. Behind them the Ford 150 with its shiny wheels and up-pipes blazed and burned. They passed the pond and lost sight of the flames but Crit could still hear the dog barking. They drove through the cattle gate by the blackberry patch and Chrome stopped and Crit climbed out and dragged it closed.

The sun had inched below the mountains by the time they got back to Jackson. Chrome tried to strike up a conversation about U.K. basketball but Crit had sunk like a stone into a dark place. And he didn't talk and barely breathed. Chrome let him out in front of the motel and Crit walked up the driveway with hands smelling of gasoline.

Rennie's window was dark. He moved to her door. It wasn't locked and she wasn't inside. He flicked her light switch. Her sheets had been pulled off and the mattress was bare. Towels gone. On the floor was his crumpled note. The low rumble of an approaching car drew his attention outside.

The Celica notchback coupe with the same rough-looking crew pulled up. Crit bent down to see inside. He fully expected Rennie to stumble out glassy-eyed and half-naked and spitting. But she didn't. The window rolled down, revealing the sneering face of the ugly driver. Up close, Crit could see that he had a broken and poorly reset nose that gave his face an off-kilter disagreeableness.

"Where's Rennie?"

"What do you want with her?"

"I wanna get my dick sucked, you wanna suck it?" The driver said and sniggered a laugh.

Crit walked thirty feet to the end of the motel rooms. He picked up a two-by-four he'd remembered and walked back to the Celica. The passenger turned around and yelled a warning. The driver couldn't find a gear fast enough, and Crit was up on them, swinging and smashing the front windshield into a cratered spider web of cracks. The passenger pawed under the front seat for some kind of weapon that he couldn't find, and Crit lanced the two-by-four straight through the window and cracked him in the side of his head. The passenger screamed in pain and the driver gunned into reverse. Crit managed to dent the hood then sling the two-by-four at the fleeing car. The Celica bottomed out on the dip to the road and almost collided with a speeding panel truck. The driver shifted and accelerated and almost hit another car at the stoplight.

Crit screamed out that if they came back he'd kill them. And screamed it again.

Wild Bill heard the noise and stepped out of his office, wearing only pajama bottoms. There was a purple snooze mask dangling from his neck. His curiosity turned to fear as Crit moved toward him.

"Where is she?"

＊

Wild Bill drove him in the Econoline and dropped him off in front of the all-night laundromat. Crit stepped closer to the glowing front window.

"You want me to wait?" Bill shouted.

Crit didn't answer and he walked closer and stopped and stood outside in the dark and watched Rennie inside. She was wearing gray sweats and was struggling to load an armful of sheets and towels into a dryer. A washcloth dropped and she stooped to pick it up and shook it off. She closed the dryer lid with her butt and hunted her beaded purse for coins.

"I'll wait right here," Bill yelled and turned off his ignition.

Crit walked across cracked asphalt and stepped inside. Rennie saw him and her face lit with a luminous smile.

"I got tired of smelling my shit," she said.

Crit nodded. "You need any change?"

"I'm good. I bummed some off Bill already."

They sat in molded plastic chairs that were linked together and she held onto his wrist and drew her knees into herself. They watched her laundry spin and turn through the fogged oval while Wild Bill waited in the parking lot. There was a dryer beside hers that didn't work and management had taped an "X" over its door. Crit noticed somebody had lost a sock on the floor. Rennie closed her eyes and started to hum the old Carter Family song she had sung with Eldon.

"How do you feel?" Crit asked.

She shrugged but didn't open her eyes. Crit sensed she didn't feel like talking. And that suited him fine. The dryer clanked and turned.

"I don't know," she finally said.

"Don't know what?"

She didn't answer and hugged her knees tighter.

He watched a heavy woman with a heavy son roll in a grocery shopping cart overflowing with dirty clothes and proceed to stuff a washer to the brim. The change machine didn't take her wrinkled bill right away and the woman cursed and slapped the machine with her meaty fist. And that didn't work at all.

Chapter 15

HALF UNDER

The next morning Crit borrowed Bill's van and drove for the third time up Long Branch Road. There was a state crew up ahead repainting the center lines and funneling two-way traffic into one lane. They had to wait for a flagman's signal to proceed. They drove slowly past the work crew. Rennie was on edge and nervous but tried not to be. She sang a song about a fire on the mountain as they climbed higher. It took Crit a moment to remember who had recorded it. Marshall Tucker. It had been popular way back when Crit was stealing bicycles and huffing glue. He wondered how it was that Rennie knew so many different kinds of songs.

They parked under the tall and straight pine trees.

Five minutes later they sat on a faded plaid sofa with frayed arms. Rennie's mother sat across from them on a kitchen chair at her dining table and she scratched at a ketchup stain on the plastic tablecloth with her thumb. They could hear Tyler chasing chickens outside.

"You don't have a job."

"I'll get a job," Rennie answered.

"Where?"

"There's a sign at Hardee's that they're hiring."

Crit wondered if that was true. He hadn't seen such a sign.

"What will you do with Tyler when you're working?"

Rennie looked over at Crit. "He can watch him."

The older woman's face scrunched up like someone had farted sulfur.

"Are you two together?"

"He's my friend. He's helping me to get through this, giving up drugs and all that."

"He'll be a great help. You know I know who he is? What he's done."

"He's turned over a new leaf. And me, too."

The older woman looked at Crit in a way that said she would never like or trust him ever. Crit shifted his weight. He knew he should say something solid to affirm what Rennie was selling. Help the cause. Had he changed? He was back with his brother hauling methshine and burning trucks. He couldn't find any helpful words.

"How do you even sleep at night?" Rennie's Mom asked, her eyes like pepper spray.

"Not very good," Crit said and looked at the back of his hands. Thick veins snaked through saggy flesh. On the carpet next to his boot were several pieces of a log cabin erector set.

"Rennie, I think yer fallin' out of the frying pan into the fire. I really do. Your life is in such disorder," the older woman said and teared up a gusher and went to the sink to get a rag to wipe her face and then clean her table of ketchup flakes.

* * *

Sunspots dappled the twisting mountain trail. Rennie and Tyler ran on ahead. Crit walked steady and behind them. The wooded path wove through rhododendron and laurel thickets. The air was thick and fecund and insects buzzed. Crit followed their laughing voices as they climbed stairs of spiked logs cut by the forestry service. One hot summer he and his brother had worked minimum wage digging back-burn lines for the forestry service near here. The work had been heavy and hot, and they were let go for slacking off and showing up late or not at all. They had retaliated by stealing picks and shovels from their employer and selling them for next to nothing. Crit reached the top of the pinnacle. A massive thrust of rock pushed out and away from the trees, incised with deep crevices where one could break a leg or twist an ankle. At the edge was a sheer drop-off—four hundred feet down—into a bowl-shaped valley. Crit carefully stepped to the edge and could see twenty miles out into wide-open sky where tattered clouds and sawtooth peaks crested to the horizon. He had lost sight of Rennie and Tyler and couldn't hear them.

Then there they were. Tyler was peeing behind a fallen pine tree and Rennie was beside him waving off a buzzing horse fly. She skipped over to Crit. Tyler followed, zipping up.

"Is that a waterfall?" Rennie asked and pointed at a slew of fast water dropping over a cut in the rocks below.

"Yep, Broke Leg Falls."

"Can we go down there."

"If you want yer leg broke."

"If I was a bird, I'd fly." She said and closed her eyes and started to sing a song about birds and flying that Crit didn't know. Maybe it was a newer song that came out after he was locked up. Katie Perry or Taylor Swift or somebody like that. Or maybe she was making the song up as she sang it. And then Rennie started to turn in circles with her arms outstretched, head back, eyes closed. Still singing. Tyler watched his momma turn and then he started to execute his own wobbly smaller circles.

Crit moved around the spinning dervishes to the edge of the drop and turned back with raised arms just in case they got too close. A tree stump with visible roots clung to the cliff edge like a giant dead spider. He looked up and squinted to avoid sun-blindness. Two turkey vultures floated into the far distance. Just specs. Almost gone. Already over the next county.

* * *

They drove back to Jackson and on the way back to the motel Tyler said he was hungry. He couldn't decide what he wanted to eat. He started to reel off his favorite things he liked to order at his favorite places: Hardee's, McDonald's, and Sonic. They passed Hardee's and Tyler still couldn't make up his mind. The golden arches approached and Crit pulled in, which ended the debate. Crit started to pull up to the drive-through but Rennie said the van was too hot and she wanted to eat inside instead. So they went in and waited five minutes behind a boisterous pack of Little Leaguers with black smear marks under their eyes and clattering cleats. Tyler watched the older boys with awe and said he didn't want to order off the kid's menu. He asked for a double quarter pounder with cheese and Rennie went for the bacon clubhouse and fries. Crit wondered if he had enough to cover and ordered only fries and a cup of water for himself. He placed their orders with a teen girl with freckles and braces and a ginger ponytail sticking out of the size reducer at the back of her cap. She seemed to not understand Crit's language and had him repeat each item twice.

Rennie picked up two *Color Us McDonalds* placemats and a fist full of crayons, and she and Tyler found a table beside the side window. When Crit brought over their food Tyler had already colored in Ronald McDonald and was working on his fast-food pals.

"Why'd you color those French fries black?" Rennie asked.

"They're scary French fries."

"Oh, they be like vampire fries?"

"Uh-huh."

"Well, they need vampire teeth."

She picked up a yellow crayon and started to add yellow fangs but Tyler told her to stop in a shrill voice and pulled his placemat away.

"Okay, you can draw yours and I'll draw mine." And she went

to work on her own placemat.

Crit chewed a salty fry into paste and felt an uneasy shiver. His prison radar. Someone was watching.

He glanced across at the Little Leaguers chattering away and eating with their red-faced coach. Beyond them an older couple didn't pay him any mind. A road construction crew with florescent vests had come in and were ordering at the counter with their backs to him. Probably the paint crew they had passed earlier. He turned around to the window and saw it.

A brown Pontiac at the take-out window.

He couldn't see her clearly but knew he was seen. Just then the driver door cracked open and banged into the take-out extension. Liddy couldn't get out that way so she crawled out the passenger door. She stepped around the front of her car and headed inside.

Tyler and Rennie colored their placemats and had no idea. Crit rose and moved toward the entrance, hoping to take it outside, but Liddy had already pushed through and he met her near the cash register. She glanced over at Rennie and Tyler, who hadn't looked up yet.

"So, you have a new family now," Liddy said. "Ain't that nice."

She said it calm and even-toned. She had on work jeans and a paint-stained T-shirt and her uncombed hair spilled over her shoulders. She was a good-looking woman who never did care a whit how she looked. And she liked to repaint and refurbish antiques. Most likely what she had just come from. Her hands were stained, too.

"They're just friends."

"Oh, so you have new friends now? What's the boy's name?"

Rennie and Tyler stopped coloring and looked up.

"You don't need to know his name."

Liddy's face twitched and she raised her voice over the divider. "Hey, what's yer boy's name, Honey?"

Rennie knew enough not to answer but Tyler said his name out loud.

"Tyler. Ain't that nice." She turned to Crit and her smile evaporated. "Sounds a lot like Taylor don't it?"

Crit stopped breathing.

Now the car behind her Pontiac started honking. A twenty-five year-old assistant manager with bad skin and a thin tie came up and told Liddy she would have to move her vehicle. Liddy turned to the assistant manager like she wanted to slap him. "Do I? Do I really have to move it? Will this world fall off its fucking axle and come to the end of times?"

The assistant manger's mouth moved like a fish sucking air.

"Do you see that man right there?" Liddy slung a finger at Crit like a whip. "Do you know that man right there used to be Breathitt County's biggest Ox and Meth dealer? He even pulled his son into it. One day Taylor was swinging at baseballs like them boys over there." Her hand flapped at the little leaguers who were now watching her. "A couple of years later he's runnin' dope for his daddy."

More honking. The assistant manager braved up and told her for the second time to move her vehicle. She didn't bother to hear him.

"But Taylor wasn't one hundred percent asshole like his daddy. No. There was a softness, a human being-ness to him. But he had a rotten last name. When he got arrested, the state law threatened to throw the book at him because of who his daddy and uncle was. So I told him..." She stepped up to Crit with eyes that could weld metal. "I told him to do anything, tell them everything they wanted, about anybody. Tell the truth."

There was a pearl of saliva on her lips. She backed away from Crit to the counter. Her body shook and stuttered like a car driving too fast. "And that was his death sentence."

"Ma'am, please," the manager said.

She turned back to face the manager. "And you know what happened to my baby? You know what happened next?" A single tear descended her cheekbone, like a water sluice down a sandstone pinnacle, a wet, twining trickle.

The manager shook his head because the fierceness of her eyes demanded an answer.

"I don't either, because his body was never found."

Nobody moved. The McDonald's workers and landscaping crew looked at Crit like he was Hitler. Even the old couple's bifocaled stares judged him as vermin.

A wave of self-loathing surged up from deep inside. Toxic bile he could taste. The other shoe had always been there on the edge. And it had dropped. He could never get clean. Never get clear. He winced his eyes closed and his bad ear grated and hissed. Why was he even breathing? He should be skinned alive and salved with hot tar. Dropped down a mine. Dragged up a bad road with a chain. He felt something hit his face. He opened his eyes and it took him a moment to realize Liddy was pelting him with French fries from a tray the road construction crew had ordered. Then she bounced a wrapped grilled fish sandwich off his chest.

The Little League team now started to punch each other and giggle.

Liddy seemed to have trouble standing and she started to collapse like a broken ladder, rung by rung. Crit stepped forward and put both hands on her arm to hold her up.

"Get the fuck away from me," she said, faint and falling.

He let her go and she collapsed on the tiled floor, which was now littered with fries.

Crit moved to the exit door. He pushed but it didn't open. He pushed twice more before he realized he had to pull it. He went out and walked across the parking lot without stopping at Bill's van. He crossed the street fast in a straight line and only changed course when he was about to bang into a brick wall.

The assistant manager came out and offered to help Liddy up. She raised a hand and clamped it like a claw onto the counter and got up on her own. He asked if she needed anything. The teen worker with braces came out with a broom but hesitated sweeping up. Liddy grabbed a napkin from a chrome dispenser and blew her nose and walked to a trash can to toss it. She glanced over the divider and gave Rennie a shredded look.

Rennie looked back square and hard. Liddy started to say something but didn't; she turned and went out.

"What was that woman so mad about?" Tyler asked.

"Some people just wake up mad," Rennie said, and bit into a fry.

***

Crit walked. North. Past a payday check cashing business and a secondhand tire store. He cut diagonally through a blinking red light intersection and forced a rusty beater to swerve to miss him. A dog barked. A man with soiled clothes was limping and approaching on the other side of the street. The man called out to Crit by name. Crit saw it was Pogue, the man he'd seen on the street before. He ignored the greeting and kept on walking until he reached where the asphalt stopped at the edge of the North Fork of the Kentucky River. Crit didn't stop. He kicked through snarling weeds, slipped and slid down the mud bank, and waded out into the dark water until he felt the frigid cold in his ball sack. He stood there. Submerged to his waist. Minutes passed. Fireflies blinked. Ripples rippled. A bullfrog croaked and then ceased croaking. Across the river headlights streamed and flickered on the bypass. Beyond that a dark slab of mountain rose up and blocked out most of the sky.

The grinding in his ear grated and pulsed with each pulse breath. He sat down and exhaled air from his lungs and let the cold water climb over. Chest, neck, ears, the top of his head submerged in the frigid dark. Icy cold wrapped his face. Taylor was under the dark somewhere. Unmarked. Dirt filling eyes and nose and mouth. Worms crawling. There were so many gone. His momma dead. Incinerated. Forgotten dust. Maybe his father, too. Untold ancestors going back to when man was barely human, gone and forgotten. On this pitiful sphere the moldered souls from the past must surely outnumber the living. And the barely living. His lungs ached. Crit forced his eyes open while under water and they stung and saw nothing. He opened his mouth. The frigid wet came on inside. And he gasped and choked.

He came up gasping and choking and spitting and wiping his eyes.

Coward. Fucking worthless coward.

He climbed the grade and stumbled and slipped up the mud and dirtied his pants. His left shoe got sucked off. He stumbled ahead.

He limped down Court Street. Dripping. His sock flapped half-off so he kicked it all the way off.

There was a figure in the shadows beside his shop door. He thought it might be Rennie but then he saw the bicycle. The Asian delivery man had parked on the sidewalk and was peering at something through Crit's shop window.

The man jumped two feet back, startled at Crit's approach, and knocked over a metal trash can. He froze as if ashamed of the noise he'd made and looked at Crit, then raised his hands in servile apology, and bent to pick up the trash he had spilled. Crit had thought this man was younger, but up close, he could be over fifty.

"It's okay, don't worry, leave it," Crit said.

The delivery man nodded, happy to leave fast and scurried to his bicycle and peddled away. Crit moved to where the man had stood. On the other side of the window was the painting Crit had done of the delivery man, squatting down and fixing the chain on his bicycle.

River water puddled under his foot.

He unlocked and went inside without bothering to pick up the trash and he left wet footprints on the planking. He made no effort to turn on the light. He didn't want to look at anything, see anything, least of all not his so-called *works of art*. He kept his eyes low and slumped into a chair. He sat for a moment and then opened his lips and emitted a low guttural phlegmic growl. He adjusted the tone to match the endless grinding in his auditory nerve.

He heard voices outside.

"Never be a litterbug," Rennie said unseen.

He looked out toward the street and now saw Rennie picking up the trash with Tyler. They put what they gathered back in the can.

"Now you stay here. Don't go nowhere," she said to her son.

The boy gave her a piece of paper. She took it. The door was open and she came in and stood in the doorway.

He couldn't see her face in the dark.

She took another step and pawed for a light switch and found it. The overhead fluorescent buzzed on sickly green. Crit turned away like an insect looking for a scurry place. She came up to him. His eyes moved off her and found a place on the wall that didn't have one of his stupid-ass paintings on it and he stared there. At a nail hole.

"The van's still over at McDonald's. Somebody walked off with the keys."

He gave no response.

"What happened to you, you take a bath?"

No answer.

"Tyler wanted you to have this."

She held out a McDonald's placemat and he didn't take it so she dropped it onto his lap. He looked down and saw crayoned dark vampire fries with fangs. There was a word bubble above the fries that said *boo*.

Rennie sat down on the floor cross-legged beside him. "He's already thinking about his Halloween outfit. Guess what he wants to be?"

"I put a gun to his head."

Rennie reached out and made a fist and tapped Crit's bare toes twice. "You don't have to tell me. I know you're sad about what happened and you wish whatever happened never happened." She said and put her hand around his wet ankle.

Crit had never told anyone what he was about to tell her. His eyes stayed on the puckered nail hole and he told her that it happened during a time when he had stopped using and was moving more product so he didn't even have a fucked-up druggie's excuse. He and Chrome had gone down to Somerset where Taylor was visiting his girlfriend for the weekend. The intent was to scare him off testifying. They took him up some road, out into some woods, and he put a gun to his own son's head. At first Taylor was scared. Then he got pissed and started yelling. He grabbed at the pistol and it went off. There was a red spray and Taylor fell over. One second he had been standing there alive and then he wasn't. Somehow Crit made it home and never saw daylight sober again until he went to prison. Chrome dealt with the body. Crit never knew what happened to it. Liddy raised a stink about the disappearance but with no body or witness willing to talk, the Poppwell brothers walked away from it, and got away with just about the worst thing anyone could get away with.

He finished talking. Outside a car whooshed in the silence.

She squeezed his ankle and said, "Okay. That's the worst fucking story I've heard in my life, and I could tell you my own shit that would scorch yer hair follicles. But if you and me walked into a rehab meeting right now they'd say you win."

She looked down.

"So what happened to yer shoe?"

Crit shook his head.

Tyler entered and stood back a bit and watched them. "Did he like my painting?"

Crit looked at the boy. There was no poison there. Just wide sinless eyes. He forced his fingers and then his hands to move and he touched the corners of the placemat. His wet knees had made two wet spots on it.

"He loves it," Rennie said to Tyler. "He thinks he can sell it for a million bucks to his gallery lady."

"Sick," Tyler said, stretching the small word out like a tire leaking air.

Crit stood up and walked with a one-shoe limp to the empty

place on the wall. He took a roll of Scotch tape and taped Tyler's vampire fry placement over the nail hole. "It's really good," he said, and looked at it some more.

"Give me your keys, I'll go get the van."

Crit hesitated.

"Tyler can't stay out all night."

Crit turned and handed them off. She went to her son and told him to wait with Crit and she'd be back soon. The boy started to complain but she told him that he'd be all right with Crit and that there were plenty of toys in the place to play with.

After she left Crit and Tyler didn't talk much. The boy moved around the store, looking at things. He turned the globe a few times and then looked at his vampire fries on the wall. Crit put the Scotch tape away. They only spoke when Tyler asked what happened to his shoe.

"Lost it in a river, I guess," Crit said.

Tyler kicked at a Nerf ball that had fallen off a shelf and then he found a red fire truck. He spun the top ladder around and around like a windmill.

Rennie pulled up and honked out front. Crit went to Tyler and asked if he wanted to take the fire truck home with him.

"You mean back to my Granny-Mom. "

"I think you're gonna be stayin' with Motel-Mom tonight."

Tyler didn't say anything but he took the truck and they went out. Crit locked up and Tyler waited for him to do that, and they walked together to the curb and climbed into the van. Tyler sat in the back. Rennie drove. They came up to a stoplight that flashed from yellow to red and Rennie braked. She hummed a familiar melody while they were stopped, then when the light turned green, she gave full voice to it. and got through the first verse of *Amazing Grace* and then went on into the hard-to-remember other verses.

Through many dangers
toils and snares

we have already come through
'twas grace hath brought
us safe thus far
and grace will lead us home.
'Twas grace that taught my heart to fear
and grace my fears relieved.
how precious did that grace appear
the hour I first believed.

They got back to the motel and parked in the usual place. Rennie climbed out and unlocked her room. Rennie's mother had packed a suitcase for Tyler and Crit got it out of the back of the van and carried it in and sat it on a chair. Tyler brought his new fire truck to the doorway but didn't go inside. Rennie started pulling out T-shirts and lacy bras from her dresser drawers and she told Tyler he could have his own drawer. The boy's mood suddenly changed. He told Rennie the room was too small and that he didn't like the wall color. Rennie told him they could paint it any color he liked and asked him what color he would like it to be. He didn't answer and made a pouting face as Wild Bill's guitar squall kicked in from the office. Bill was riffing on the Duane Allman/Dickie Betts song, *One Way Out*, and not too badly.

Rennie toppled over and bounced on the bed. "When you lay on the bed and close your eyes this room can get as big as a ship on an ocean." She patted the space beside her and smiled at Tyler. "Come on, be my shipmate."

"That's dumb," Tyler said.

She said a few more things to coax him into a better mood and Crit moved past Tyler and out the door.

"You don't have to go, Mister Cranky, we can have a make-believe party."

But Crit didn't stop and he stepped out and across the driveway and felt a big piece of gravel poke his bare foot. He looked up at the stars and didn't see any. Clouds must have rolled in.

Bill paused his guitar playing. Crit could now hear Rennie raising her voice with her son, telling him that she was doing the best she could and that that would have to be good enough. Wild Bill started up a new riff that Crit didn't recognize.

He heard other voices and a dog barked nearby. On the far side of Bill's office an open motel room door was spilling light out onto a muddy minivan with a crunched-in side and missing rear bumper. He hadn't seen it before. Beside it there were two shirtless kids playing with a pit bull puppy. The boy was about seven and the girl a bit younger. They were struggling to pull a squeaking rubber bone out of the pit bull's stubborn jaws. Crit moved up to the office and slid Bill's van keys into the mail slot. A heavy woman with black leggings and thick hair in a loose braid came out of the open door and leaned against a roof support. She smoked a cigarette and watched her kids. The boy and girl finally snatched the bone from their dog and ran with the barking pit bull in pursuit. Maybe these kids would become playmates of Tyler. Or maybe the boy and girl and mother would be gone in the morning. He wanted to ask the woman for a cigarette but she had noticed him watching and was now looking at him like he was a one-shoed child-predator.

Crit turned, limped back to his room, unlocked and shut his door.

He undressed to his underwear. He spent five minutes running water from the sink through the dirt stains on his pants and then hung them over the shower rod. He looked at his scattered clothes and thought about the fact that he did not own one piece of clothing beyond three or four years. What little he had was either prison issue or recent purchases from Walmart or the dollar store. Nothing of the past. Not even a favorite pair of jeans or boots.

He must have fallen asleep because he was dreaming about throwing a rubber bone to Black Eye, a mixed-breed mutt with a black circle of fur under one eye. He and Chrome had found the dog abandoned on the highway. Their momma at first had said they couldn't keep him, but they had hollered so loud and long that she had relented and allowed them to keep the dog outside, tied to a tree. A few weeks later they woke up and Black Eye was gone, his rope leash chewed through. In Crit's dream he was playing with Black Eye at the edge of Broke Leg Falls. He pulled the bone out of the dog's snapping jaws and tossed it far out over the cliff edge. The bone sailed and fell like a dead bird into the rushing waterfall below. Black Eye looked up at Crit with accusing eyes, like he had lost everything that mattered, and then started barking and foaming.

A knock at the door drew Crit out of his dream and into fuzzy half-consciousness. It took a moment for him to realize where he was. The window was dark. He didn't know if it was the middle of the night or close to morning. Another knock. He leaned up onto an elbow. "Who's there?" His voice was thick and he coughed to clear it.

The unlocked door pushed open and Rennie came in and she didn't bother to turn on a light. She moved to his bed and said shit quietly when she banged her shin on the bedpost and then she lay down in the dark shadows beside him. "Tyler said he can't sleep with me tossing and snoring."

Crit took a moment before he said, "Maybe I can't either."

"Well, we all have to make sacrifices for the next generation."

Her hand found his wrist and circled it and squeezed. Several minutes passed with Crit now very awake. She rolled over on her side and her sudden movement jostled him and he knew she was looking at him. But he didn't turn to her.

"Do you still work, down there?"

"I don't know."

"If we mess around does it mess up stuff?"

He could smell her slightly sour breath. "You mean does it mess up you being a drug addict and me being a killer?"

She punched him in the arm. "I'm a former drug addict. And your story actually sounded like a couple of notches below murder. It's horrible, but it's like what do they charge you with when you're drunk and hit somebody with a car?

"Manslaughter."

"Yep, but the *slaughter* part always makes it sound worse. Like a horror movie. Like *Texas Chain Saw*. And everyone just assumes anyway?"

"Assumes what?"

"That we're doing it. My mom, Bill, your brother, everybody."

"Making love to you would be like a skeleton making love to a peach."

She laughed. "Somebody thinks I'm peachy." And she beat a drum riff on her tummy and the mattress shook. "You are funny. I didn't think you were when I first met ya. But you can be real funny."

She chattered on for five more minutes. About Tyler. About looking for a job. About missing out on seeing the ocean when she was in Myrtle Beach. Eventually her words slurred and the spaces between them grew until she inhaled more softly and she was asleep with her fingers circling his wrist.

Crit lay beside her for an hour. Then he separated himself from her hand and got up and moved quietly to the bathroom. He checked if his pants were drying. He closed the door and peed against the mineral-stained side porcelain so as not to be loud. He sipped water from the faucet. He wet his face and eyes. Then he went to the window and looked out. No cars. No moon. No stars. Nothing moved except the blinking stoplight. But the darkness in the air sounded different. His ear seemed less angry. Or did it? He listened hard. He cupped a hand to the side of his head. The ringing was distant, more hushed. Or was he only imagining that? Had he gotten used to his tinnitus so that he didn't hear it? He snapped his fingers beside his ear. He heard the crisp *thwick*. There were other things he heard. The rise and fall of crickets outside, like sad notes on a mountain fiddle. The low hum of a train, far away, and going farther. He could hear Rennie's abrading inhales. He could even hear the drip in the toilet that never stopped trickling. His pupils adjusted and he could see the outline of the sunball and clouds that Tyler had drawn on his wall. He moved closer to the bed and stood over her and listened to her sleep.

Chapter 16

PEA LUMP

Brenda Cowan rarely cursed. But she just had. Her car was dead in the driveway of her modest red-brick ranch house a mile West of Jackson. A thermos of Maxwell House and a zippered Naugahyde pouch stuffed with probationer cases was on the molded plastic console beside her. And her first appointment was in fifteen minutes. *Dammit to hell.* Five weeks ago she had traded in her reliable fourteen-year-old Ford Fiesta at a large-volume dealership in Winchester for a charcoal gray, nearly new Hyundai Elantra with too many gizmo lights on the dash. It even had a keyless smart fob that she had yet to get used to. Given her recent run of luck, she had no doubt that she'd bought a lemon. She punched the fob again and got nothing. Not even a contact click. She gritted her teeth and thwacked the steering wheel with both palms. And cursed again.

She had texted *car dead need help* to Deputy Sherriff Corky Hibchen, the man she was seeing part-time. He was separated but still married and hadn't even moved out of his wife's house yet. He had even hinted that they should stop seeing each other if she didn't like the arrangement. And he hadn't bothered to text back.

Her grown son knew about cars but he was currently warehoused in the Kentucky corrections system. She had written him off as beyond saving. And as far as asking her closest neighbor Wilma Brown for a ride, they hadn't been on speaking terms since the crazy bitch brought home a garden gnome sculpture of an elf boy with his pants down, peeing on a tree trunk. The sculpture was vile and she had told Wilma so.

She'd been nursing a foul mood for two weeks, since last Monday when she had felt a pea-sized lump in her right breast while lathering up in the shower. The thin-lipped doctor with a shaved head at the clinic had felt her up, and instead of telling her it was nothing to be worried about, had taken copious X-rays and then told her she had to see a specialist in Lexington. That dreaded appointment was coming up soon. And she hadn't even told Corky squat about it. As if he cared. And now her fancy, low-millage Hyundai was dead as roadkill.

Dammit to fucking hell.

Her daddy lived five miles away in Noctor and knew about cars, but she hadn't spoken to him since last Christmas and he would no doubt tell her she had bought a foreign piece of shit when she should have bought American. Maybe she could shame the big Winchester dealer into taking it back. But she was pretty sure that would be a hard row as they had been very clear about her thirty-day limited warranty.

She tried the fob again and got nothing. But this time she held the *on* button down and turned on the headlights. She couldn't tell if her lights had come on or not, so she turned on the windshield wipers. They didn't work. Neither did the radio. Okay. Not the starter or the alternator. She had learned a thing of two holding work lights for her daddy while he slide up under the chassis of countless junkers that filled her childhood driveway. And more than once she had gotten slapped when she handed him a box wrench instead of the regular wrench. He had sometimes worked the mines but mostly fixed cars and drank and terrorized his wife and kids. At fifteen she had started sleeping with every boy in the East side of Breathitt County just to piss him off. She had married the first one she could rope into marriage and left home the day after she graduated high school. She had five kids by three husbands by the time she was twenty-five and then had the good sense to have her tubes tied. Her wildness abated and she juggled husbands and ex-husbands and kids and managed to somehow get a B.A. in criminal Justice from EKU in Richmond. Her two oldest had inherited some of her smarts and drive, and had good enough jobs and had done all right for themselves. They both lived South of Lexington in Nicholasville. The middle one was the jailbird. The youngest could still go either way.

And here she was in a fancy Korean car that she didn't even know how to jump-start and dating a man who wasn't even separated and wouldn't even text her back. She was twenty-two years into a state job with a good pension that she might never see a dime of because of the pea lump in her breast.

And where the hell was the hood release on this damn thing? She tapped around by her left knee and found it. She climbed out and moved around to the front bumper, and it took another minute to wiggle her finger under the hood and pop the latch.

Her fingernail now had a nick in its salon-lacquered finish. She fumed and glared at the belts and wires and battery and noticed a blue-green mold-looking growth of corrosion sprouting on the negative battery terminal.

There was a hammer and an adjustable wrench inside her mudroom somewhere, but instead, she impatiently picked up a landscaping brick from beside her azaleas and banged on her battery terminal five times. Hard.

She got back into her car and punched her fob and the Hyundai started right up. Then she made it to work five minutes late and found a three-time repeat offender leaning against the wall outside her door with a mixed-race hippie mama wearing a large wooden cross and sitting cross-legged on the floor.

"Oh boy," Brenda Cowan thought. "And so it begins."

"It's an amazing opportunity for personal growth and redemption," the woman with dreadlocks said three minutes into the meeting. She had introduced herself as some kind of nun and art teacher. "This gallery is very well known and only displays art of serious cultural value."

Brenda thought this woman certainly didn't look like Sally Fields in that flying nun movie. Or any other Catholic she had seen in real or on TV. She looked down at the exhibit flyer through half-glasses. And then her eyes invariably shifted to the ragged notch in her salon nail. A thirty dollar fix at least. But at least her new air conditioner hummed and chilled. She looked back up at the woman still speaking and then she looked at Crit Poppwell and thought somehow this habitual low-life had conned a bleeding heart libtard into caring about him. Her own incarcerated son had gotten a do-gooder state doctor to sign off on a bogus diagnosis that he was bi-polar. He'd sent her a handwritten five-page letter claiming all his transgressions were due to his newly defined illness. So he wasn't responsible for stealing her blind? Knocking out her tooth? But just watch—her son and this unsmiling convict would probably outlive her.

"What's outsider art?" Brenda asked when Sister Nikhael finished speaking.

"It's a term for art created outside the mainstream, or outside of the big cities and away from academic influences. It's grass-roots populist art."

Brenda nodded like she understood. She peered over at Crit who hadn't said a word and didn't seem all that interested in this art show thing. "What do you gotta say about it?"

"It's an amazing opportunity for personal growth and redemption."

Brenda checked the time on her phone. No text. "You can't stay overnight. You'd have to check in with me at eight am Saturday morning. And I'm gonna piss you."

"You work Saturdays?" Sister Nikhael asked.

"I will this Saturday."

Hippie Mama thanked her and Brenda stood up and shook hands and asked the woman how long she'd been teaching art in the Kentucky corrections system. The nun went into a drawn-out answer and Brenda spaced out and nodded nice and then told her she was doing admirable work. But all the while Brenda was thinking that it was more than likely this old jailbird wouldn't show Saturday and she'd have to put in a weekend emergency call to Corky Hibchen and get his coward-ass out of his wife's house to go hunt down a felon who had crossed state lines.

And she hoped to hell to make that call.

Chapter 17

CROSSING THE OHIO

"Wow, that went better than I thought," Sister Nikhael said as she walked outside into the sunshine. "Your P.O. seems like a straight-shooter."

Crit followed her out. The Breathitt County Courthouse rose above them, capped with a green-roofed clock tower. The two old-timers Crit had seen before were there lounging on a bench. The thinner one whittled on a piece of wood while the masked one rasped out metallic wheezes through his portable air tank and watched Crit and Sister Nikhael pass.

"I can pick you up Friday, but we'd have to leave early. I volunteered to host the reception."

"Don't worry about me. I can get there on my own."

"Okay. It's happening." Sister Nikhael said and jiggled two thumbs up. "I have a good feeling about this. I have faith this is gonna lead to a ton more victories for you."

Crit looked back at the old men and thought that when they were gone, there would be none coming behind them. "Can I bring a friend?"

"Ah. So he has a friend." Her eyes grinned.

"And my friend has a son who might want to come."

She smiled, but a wrinkle of concern crept into it. "Oh, you mean that gal who said her son was in trouble? Isn't she a bit young for you?"

"We're not together that way."

"What about her troubles?"

"She's okay now."

"Well good." Sister Nikhael said and nodded several times. "Okay, well then absolutely. Bring them. It's open to the public. Did you ever imagine when you walked into my class at Big Sandy that your work might end up in a Cincinnati art show?"

He said no.

"I didn't either. And it's all on you. The amazing work you've done. I've got some time to kill. Can we go see some of your new stuff? If that's okay?"

"There ain't."

"Ain't?"

"Nothing new." He looked down at the sidewalk.

"Okay."

"Busy with other stuff."

"No worries," she said. "You want to grab a coffee at Speedway and feed the ducks or something? If there's any ducks anywhere to feed."

He said he had things to do and she acted like she wasn't disappointed and gave him the gallery flyer and pointed out its location on the map on the back. Then she got out a pen and a packet of yellow sticky notes from her glove box and wrote out several lines of directions.

She handed him the note. "Or if you're with somebody with a phone they can Googlemap *Over the Rhine Gallery, Cincinnati, Ohio.*"

He took what she gave him and held it and looked at it. Sister Nikhael started talking about her admiration for the curator of the show, but he drifted off into remembering another time crossing the Ohio. He had been seeing Liddy only a week and he had talked her into a spur-of-the-moment road trip. Teenagers with no destination in mind. They somehow found themselves crossing the Ohio and made their way to King's Island. They rode *The Beast*, *The Orion* and *The Diamondback*. He actually remembered the names of those rides. Liddy had worn a bikini top and cut-offs and had screamed and giggled and gorged on cotton candy. Their last ride of the day had been on an ordinary Ferris wheel. Liddy said she felt sorry for it because it had no crowd waiting and they should ride it because it was lonely. They rode it hands all over each other and gliding lazy circles up into a sunset sky. At the apex they could see the blood-red sun ball sliding down over Cincinnati's western outlying suburbs. They drove back in the dark and got lost somewhere around Big Bone Lick and made jokes about the name and pulled over and went at it in the back seat until dawn. They woke cold and shivering. They didn't have any coats or blankets and had to cling to each other for warmth.

"See you Friday," Sister Nikhael said as she climbed into her Prius and waved and smiled again and silently drove away.

Crit watched her leave and wondered if he'd ever again pick up a brush, pick up a pencil, pick up a sketchpad. It felt like another person had done all that. But if he did, he might like to draw a lonely Ferris wheel.

* * *

"I don't know if I wanna go," Rennie said, while cutting the edges off a slice of Wonderbread. She was making a bologna sandwich for Tyler, who was laid out on the carpet with his head propped on his hands and staring at wavy static patterns on the TV.

"I want mustard on mine," Tyler said.

"I know you do, Baby." She squeezed out a fast-food packet of mustard onto his sandwich. "It sounds like a bunch of fancy people tryin' to be all fancy."

Crit shook potato chips onto three paper plates from one bag. Rennie placed a sandwich onto each plate. Tyler's was the only one with no crust. The way he liked it. "Come on," she said. "We're eating on the patio."

They moved outside and settled down into lawn chairs and ate their sandwiches and watched cars pass. The sky shredded red and gold above the mountains. A new pickup honked at a slow-moving beater and swung out and passed it on the double line.

"Who are the people?"

"What people?"

The people who will be there."

"I don't know."

"What will they be wearing?"

"You're asking the wrong person."

"Well, who else should I ask?"

"Sister Nikhael, I guess."

"Well, she's not here, is she?"

"Can I go play with Trey and Brittany?" Tyler asked. He had finished his sandwich and was watching the new neighbor boy and girl try to pull a red ski cap down over the head of their pit bull.

"Sure, don't get all dirty."

Tyler jogged off toward the barking dog. Rennie picked up his empty plate and put the rest of his chips onto her plate. "What're you gonna wear?"

Crit shrugged. "What I'm wearing, I guess."

"Don't folks get dressed up like the CMAs? And arrive all in limos?"

"I don't think it's that fancy."

The pit bull shook off the cap and barked. The neighbor boy and girl offered the cap to Tyler and he put it on.

Rennie got up abruptly and went into her room. Crit stayed outside and he looked up at the telephone lines and utility lines and transformers and saw how those things were attached to each other and to the utility poles. He then looked to the other side of the office and saw that the minivan with the missing bumper was gone. Trey and Brittany had been left on their own.

"Come in here," Rennie called out.

He got up and went in. Rennie pulled out every dress she owned and laid them out on her bed. Low cut and scrunchy cocktail dresses, a red leather mini with a wide black belt, a leopard-print skirt with a slit up the side. She told him to choose a dress for the show. Before he said a word, she said it didn't matter what he chose and paced around her bed. "None of these will do."

"Well, I'm not a fashion designer so you're on your own."

"Any idiot can have an opinion."

"I'm gonna go watch the kids."

She told him he was no help and he went back outside. Tyler and the neighbor kids were rolling like logs down the grassy hill and nearly onto the highway. Crit yelled for them to stop before they got run over. The older boy stood up and cursed Crit and told him he wasn't his daddy. Then he tied his barking dog to a piece of rope and led his sister and Tyler off to play on Bill's hammock in the woods behind the motel. Rennie turned up her rap music. Crit sat and couldn't decide what to look at or what to do or think. He noticed a red spot on the hillside. It was the ski cap the kids had left behind.

Chapter 18

COAL TIPPLE

Wild Bill's mother was waiting for him in an open doorway. He recognized it as the rough-plank-and-batten-sided farmhouse they'd lived in up in Lost Creek. Gone were her breathing tubes and drips and bedpans. She was younger and standing tall and handsome in a nice dress and her hair was wavy dark and she rang a dinner bell and called out his name.

Billy.

He tried to reach her. Her voice echoed and receded. He was mired in something that restricted movement. The colors in the landscape changed and he was now crawling across the motel driveway like an infant or a cripple. The Chinese delivery man bicycled past. He didn't want that food. He wanted his momma's home cooking. He struggled to crawl to her. Struggled to speak. When he looked up she was gone and the farmhouse was gone. Then he was in a green hallway, some kind of wing in a hospital or assisted living facility. He moved past open doors. Pale old people sat on cots and stared at him with sullen eyes.

Wild Bill gasped awake. He was sweating and his pulse was up. His mother's dinner bell rang again and he turned over and tried to sit up. Morning light bled through thin curtains. He knocked an ashtray off the armrest as he swung his legs off the

166

couch to the floor. Cigarette butts and empty beer cans dotted the carpet. The ringing was coming from his phone on the desk. He felt a surge of intense dread. Maybe the dream was an omen. He stood up wobbly and grabbed his mobile and saw the name on the screen. His shoulders sagged and he cleared his throat.

"Hey."

"Hey B," Chrome said.

"Yeah, Man."

"Is Crit up?"

"I don't know."

"Asshole needs to get a phone."

Bill yawned and rubbed the blur from his eyes and glanced at the NASCAR wall clock and saw that it was just after eight in the morning.

"Get him up, I got an errand for y'all."

Wild Bill hung up and immediately dialed the assisted living number he had stored in his contacts. He demanded to speak to the floor nurse in his momma's wing and she came on and told him that his momma was good. She had even eaten some corn pudding the night before.

An hour and half later he was eight miles East of Hazard, listening to *Judas Priest* in his Econoline.

"Turn here," Crit said.

Bill turned and drove up the seldom-used mining road. His window was down and "Breaking the Law" banged off passing trees. The scant two tracks of gravel soon disappeared under leaves, vines, and mud. They climbed higher.

"Not much of a road, is it?

"Not much."

The undergrowth scraped and the shocks compressed over erosion ditches. They lost traction in a wet rut and Bill spun his tires until white-hot smoke clouded behind and they barely fish-tailed out. They came out into the broom sage clearing where Crit had been before and scared off four or five deer that were feeding. Then they parked in the shadows of the abandoned coal tipple. Before he cut his engine, Bill turned off the music and gunned it and asked Crit if he thought the muffler sounded louder than before. Crit wasn't sure. Bill climbed out and knelt and pulled a broken tree branch from under his chassis. The slender woman with the *Mercy* tattoo on her neck stepped out of the same dented Chevy Blazer and opened her hatchback and showed Crit seventeen gallons of Acetone and two factory-sealed cardboard crates of DayQuil Cold and Flu Relief medicine. Crit handed over money that his brother had given him. She took her time counting it and licked her finger between every other bill.

"Don't try anything funny. My man's got a bead on you." She said it matter-of-factly and jutted her sharp nose up the ridgeline. "He's still holding that grudge from Little Sandy."

Last time the woman had said *Roederer*. The change of the prison location made Crit doubt that what she was saying about her man was true. She was probably alone. On her own. Living the outlaw life, unprotected.

"Later." The woman said after Crit and Eldon loaded the acetone and DayQuil into Bill's van. She said it with comfortable familiarity and a half-smile, like Crit and she would indeed be seeing each other again and again.

Driving back down the mountain Bill clipped a dangling tree limb. His outside rearview mirror was smacked flat and they heard an angry scraping the entire length of the van.

"Chrome needs to buy me new wheels if he's gonna send me up bullshit roads like this."

Bill didn't bother to fix the mirror until they reached the state highway. They reached it and Bill braked and came to a stop. Several of the acetone tins flipped over. Bill climbed out and yanked his mirror straight. He then felt the depth of the new scratch. It had cut through three layers of paint to the factory steel.

"Damn, gonna need some Bondo." Bill climbed back in. "Main road or back roads?"

Crit shrugged.

"Yesterday Rennie had me drive her to Goodwill and then

Walmart. She bought you some fancy stuff to wear. We had to guess yer size."

Crit shook his head. The whole of everything was getting to be too much. The errands for Chrome. The show tomorrow. The trees. The hills. The kudzu. The sky. The clouds. His mouth and throat were parched and irritated. He rolled down the window and worked up some saliva, and spat.

Wild Bill pulled onto the highway and gassed it and about half of the acetone tins slid backward in unison with a loud clunk.

"You think they're okay?"

"I expect so," Crit said. "But I wouldn't smoke a cigarette."

Wild Bill slotted in Twisted Sister.

Chapter 19

THE DARKEST HOUR

Crit secretly wished the boots wouldn't fit. He was perched on the edge of her bed, wearing thin brown socks. Rennie hovered above him with playful eyes. He placed his right foot into the boot mouth and pushed down. With some effort he wormed and worked his foot deeper into the stiff faux-reptile pattern. He had to pull up on the back of the heel to get it on.

"You better try the other one. Sometimes they don't make 'em so they match."

He grunted and pushed into the left and got it on. They were tight. They were made in China. And they looked like something a city slicker might wear to a dude ranch. He stood up and walked around the bed to the window to loosen them. His feet felt constricted. He felt foolish. "Where'd you get the money?"

"Bill loaned me."

"I'll pay him back."

She acted like she hadn't heard him say that and reached into a plastic Walmart sack and pulled out a black denim button-up shirt with gold lariat trim. "I got you a large," she said and shimmied the shirt. "You should see what I bought for me, myself and I."

An hour later he was back in his regular work boots and Rennie nuked three TV dinners in a microwave that Crit had brought back from his store. Crit and Rennie had Salisbury steak and Tyler had a mac and cheese. As they ate, Tyler told them how Trey had thrown a rock and hit his sister in the face. She had a Band-Aid over her eye. Rennie asked if he'd meant to do it and Tyler said he swore he hadn't, but he believed he had. Rennie said it was never nice to knowingly hurt someone. They finished their TV dinners and Rennie washed their utensils in the bathroom sink. Crit took their dinner trash out to the dumpster in the Walmart bag his boots came in.

The temperature had dropped and it was dark and cold and not quite summer. He slid back the lid and tossed what he had. He turned and looked back at Tyler's small silhouette, moving across the curtains toward the TV. Then Rennie's shadow appeared and grew larger as she moved away from the window. His mind went back a couple of months to when Rennie had picked his bottle of Crown Royal out of the trash. Now they were sharing meals. He tried to imagine what lay ahead. Rennie and Tyler had drifted into his riptide. So it seemed. Would they swirl down with him? Or was a different fate possible? Sister Nikhael had promised big things. What kind of big? He might have to leave Jackson if he was to turn a page. He'd have to finish out his parole first. And he would have to separate from Chrome. Had to happen. Hell or high water. Either through an act of life or an act of death. He pinched his nose and blew mucus between his finger and thumb and wiped it on his jeans. He looked out toward the highway. Headlights glowed and engines hummed. The hills were night-colored. The ski cap was still there, a red dot in wet grass. Taylor was somewhere down near Somerset. Decaying in unknown ground. Taylor's teenage girlfriend was most likely married to someone else by now. He couldn't remember her name. Liddy probably did. He'd met her twice and she had seemed like a nice cheerleader type. Probably had a pack of kids. He rubbed his tongue against his teeth and loosened and swallowed a sliver of Salisbury steak gristle. Here he was, somewhere between what he'd done and the final days of his life. This time tomorrow he would be in Cincinnati. And who knew what might happen after that. He sucked air through stained teeth and walked back toward Rennie's room having reached no conclusion about anything.

***

He woke up feeling the pressure of her caressing him hard. Without a word, she climbed on top, hands on his chest, and he was inside her and she rested for moment then incrementally moved her lower self and ground down and against him. At first he thought this might be a dream. His ear *zizzed*. The ceiling was gun-metal dark and her chin was up and her eyes were closed and she moaned short, rhythmic breaths. The bed frame squeaked and slid as she pumped harder. It was happening. Sort of. Now fully conscious he knew it was real and he was deflating. At first she ground on with wishful intensity as if she could will him into doing better. But he was out of her and she stopped.

"That almost worked," she said and slid off.

"Sorry."

She lay down beside him on her back and he couldn't tell what her mood was. It had finally happened and had ended awkward and premature. Neither of them spoke for a good while until he finally said *it's not you.*

"Hell's, Darlin', I know that. I've never had no complaints."

"I'm just...old and..."

"Out of practice."

"Probably."

"There's always a medical cure for being out of practice. Even younger guys are taking pills these days. I think it's all that virtual pussy on the internet. Guys don't value the real thing."

He lay still for a moment and then he rose up over her. Kissed her neck and breasts. She started to laugh and said it tickled. He started to slide down toward her real thing. She took his head in her hands and pulled him back up and kissed his forehead and said he didn't have to do anything. She had wanted him to get off because it was his big day tomorrow.

"You don't owe me any favors," he said.

"And you don't owe me any," she answered. She lay on her back and didn't say anything else and then when she did speak she said something that stayed with him long after she said it. "If I hadn't met up with you, I might be dead in a ditch by now, or close to it."

He mumbled something about not doing much.

"Anyway. I wanted you to know how I felt. If I get hit by a car tomorrow, I wanted you to know I love you."

She kissed his forehead and got up and went to the bathroom and ran water and he figured she was washing herself. In Crit's dysfunctional relationship history when someone said they loved him it was usually screamed in anger or as leverage for something else. Rennie hadn't said it that way. She had just said it plain— no chaser. She came back out and lay down beside him. She circled his wrist with her hand and gave a squeeze and turned onto her side with her naked back against him.

"You don't like your boots much, do you?"

"They're all right."

Her breathing slowed and changed timber. She had a knack for falling asleep that he envied. Her inhales grew louder than her exhales. A body knows its purpose, he thought, to breathe, even when the mind is blacked out.

"I lost a good part of my hearing in prison."

She was beyond hearing.

"Somebody hit me in the head."

For a while he watched a rippling shadow of a tree branch shimmer the wall. Then he finally drifted off but woke several times in the night. Once when a dog barked far away. Again when he thought he heard a hoot owl. And just before dawn a large truck came in off the highway and its headlights swept the curtain. It came to a stop and there was a repetitive beeping sound as it backed up. He listened in anticipation and heard every part of it. The whine of hydraulics extending. The bang and clank as the motel dumpster was lifted. The rattling trundle of garbage emptied and then the dumpster returned to the ground. The truck pulled away and Crit listened to the same symphony repeat a quarter mile distant.

He reached down and felt his deflated self. He was no longer wet from her.

Chapter 20

CHILD'S SEAT

At the end of the next morning Crit sat on the edge of his bed alone and stared at his new boots. The mottled reptile pattern irked him. His Walmart shirt felt stiff and unnatural. But then maybe this was how things were supposed to feel in a new world. He scratched a blemish on his neck. He reached down and touched where Rennie had slept. Where he had failed at making love. He remembered his ineptitude with a curious, detached disappointment. He stood up and told himself he wasn't the person he had been. He was someone new. And this was a day of new things. And then there was a knock at the door.

"I'm gonna check the oil," Wild Bill called out. "And I put a jug of water behind yer seat. When you get where you're goin' you ought to top off the overflow tank."

"Okay."

Crit bent over and pulled his black jeans down over the top of his boots. He moved unsteadily to the other side of the bed. The heels made him taller by an inch. He went into the bathroom and stood at the basin mirror and gave himself a final look. He had shaved yesterday. That would have to do. He ran cold water into his hands and splashed his face. Wiped off on a towel. He then ran water again and slicked back his hair. Winced a graveyard smile. He looked like a grifter or a pimp. He peed and listened to Rennie's hip-hop beats seeping through the wall.

Today was the day of new things.

He came out squinting into the brightness. The sky was blue and the sun was already below directly overhead and Wild Bill had the hood up and was wiping the van's dipstick with a rag. The traffic on the highway was loud and normal. Crit stepped to the driver's door. The long scratch cut on the DayQuil run reminded him that things had to change. He opened the door and pressed his thumb down on the glue part of Sister Nikhael's sticky note to make sure it adhered to the dash. *North on I-75.*

"Seems bout a half quart low."

"Well, when it gets a full quart low, I'll put a quart in," Crit said. "What time is it?"

"Two-twenty."

He turned to Rennie's door. It was twenty minutes past when they'd agreed to leave and her music was still thumping.

Then the music suddenly died and her door opened. Both Crit and Bill looked that way. Tyler came out in a new polo sport shirt and khaki pants. His hair had some kind of gel in it.

"Is she ready?"

Tyler shrugged. "She told me to get out. I wanna ride shotgun."

"You can work that out with your momma."

It was another fifteen minutes before she teetered out on three-inch stiletto heels, wearing a low-cut, single lady black mini dress with shredded peekaboo detailing that exposed the dragon climbing up her hip. Her lips were ruby red and she had somehow added sparkly glitter to them. Her eye shadow was dark blue and she had extended her eyelashes with dark lines and covered up the last hints of her face bruises with heavy makeup.

Wild Bill wolf-whistled. "Hot Mama."

"Do I look too slutty?"

"Never such a thing."

"Tyler, put that gas cap back on and get in here," Rennie demanded.

Tyler was at the back of the van and had the gas cap off. and was sniffing at the tube to the gas tank. He put the cap back and Wild Bill walked over to make sure it was on tight. Rennie slid open the side door.

"I wanna ride in the front." Tyler protested.

"We can trade off, but I'll ride up front first—is that okay?"

Tyler grumbled and climbed into the back seat.

"Don't this seat even have a seatbelt?" She asked Bill, searching for it.

"Ain't sure."

She dug into the gritty seam and pulled out a seat belt strap, a beer cap, and some change. Tyler happily picked up the coins. She reached over Tyler, searching for the other half of the belt, and pulled out a frayed end that was missing a buckle.

"This seatbelt don't work."

"Well, you shoulda gone to Avis."

Tyler had ridden in the back seat of Bill's van many times before, but this was the first time Rennie had cared about belting him in. But this was a longer trip. And they would be traveling on a busy interstate. Her latent concern wasn't unreasonable but everything about this trip had him on edge—the long wait for Rennie, the tightness of his new boots, the way Wild Bill and Rennie seemed more excited than he was, and the fact that he had no earthly idea what awaited them in Cincinnati.

"What am I supposed to do, tie him in with a rope?"

"Maybe he should sit in the front," Crit said flatly.

She exhaled disappointment. "I guess I'm giving up shotgun." She told Tyler to move to the front and belted him in while he squirmed and she combed her fingers through his gelled hair. "You look awful handsome."

"I'm rich," Tyler said, and showed off his new dime and penny.

"Well, good for you. Somebody in this family oughta be. I'm gonna get a pop and take a final pee, anybody want one?"

Both Crit and Tyler said no to a pop and Crit told her they were already running late. She pretended not to hear him.

"I want my baseball and my fire truck," Tyler yelled after her.

"You can't have both, you can pick one, which one?"

"Baseball," Tyler said and frowned.

Rennie went back into her room. Wild Bill walked over to the grass and slid through a few t'ai chi moves. Rennie came back out soon enough. She brought out a twelve-ounce Pepsi and Tyler's softball. She handed off the softball to her son and Crit noticed that more of its leather surface was covered over with crayon squiggles and faces. He imagined Taylor's initials were now pretty much invisible.

Rennie held onto the van doorframe and swung up and in on her three-inch heels and plopped down on the back seat and pulled down her hiked-up skirt. She had trouble closing the side door and Bill had to go around to close it for her while she sipped from her Pepsi and burped.

"I guess I'll ride back here like a second-class citizen."

"If I have to wear a seat belt, he has to wear a seat belt," Tyler said looking at Crit.

"True dat," Rennie said.

Crit scowled and fastened his seatbelt so as to end all conversation about it.

Bill came around to the driver's side and looked at Crit funny.

"What?"

"Did you put something in your hair?"

"I think we all look fabulous," Rennie said and grinned at Bill. "You should come too. There's a picture of you in the show. We're both big stars."

"I'm part Indian. You paint me, you steal my soul."

"It's already stole, muthafucka."

"You said a bad word," Tyler said, and rubbed two shame fingers at his mother.

"If you say a bad word really fast it's not a bad word." She repeated muthfucka hyper fast and Tyler giggled and said it several times faster.

Crit was just about to turn the ignition.

When he heard it.

It sounded like trouble. Then he saw it. And it was.

His brother's F-series pickup turned off the highway and came up at them. Black-windowed and dark as a funeral limousine and pumping country rap beats with rhymes spat out about moonshine and hunting with coon dogs.

Crit watched his brother's approach on high alert.

Chrome pulled up and his window rolled down and he smiled and nodded to his music while pushing his palms up and down. He had on his favorite Raybans. His ear wasn't bandaged and a black scab clung where the lobe was missing. A silver Honda Accord followed Chrome in, driven by one of Chrome's bikers who had the Rolling Stones's "Beast of Burden" pulsing loudly. The two songs aggressively assaulted each other until the biker parked behind Bill's van and gave up the battle by turning off his ignition.

Chrome turned his music down but not all the way off and climbed out of his truck. He walked over and peered over the top of his shades at his brother.

"Lookin' good, Bra."

Crit said nothing.

"Big day, huh?"

He hadn't gotten an answer, but Chrome's chin nodded up and down several times as if he had. And then he cupped his hands to the glass and peered in at Rennie. "Hot, hot, hot, I look at you too long I might go blind. Way to represent."

Rennie crossed her arms to cover her cleavage. "How's your ear?" And she said it like she didn't care about his ear.

"Ouch, you want to go there. And I was accentuating the positive." His eyes moved back to Crit. "I'm here because I'm truly proud something good came out of these hills. I mean it. And you can tell that girl behind ya I'm proud of her, too."

"For what?" Rennie said.

"Somebody got their kid back. Somebody kicked their old ways to the curb," Chrome saluted Tyler. "Hey, Little Man, you're lookin' good, too."

"I'm rich," Tyler answered and showed off his dime and penny.

"Yes, you are." Chrome made an *O* with his lips and whistled. "That'll go a long way if you break down on the highway, but not all the way. I'm kinda worried."

"Worried about what?" Tyler asked.

"Driving all that way up to Ohio in Wild Bill's crap van. Kinda dangerous."

"Two hundred forty thousand miles and she ticks like a Rolex," Wild Bill bragged and knocked twice on the hood. "But she could use a new paint job and shocks."

"Well, I'm worried. I'm a worrier about the details. Plus it looks like shit and the guest of honor in a big art show deserves better. And that's why I'm lettin' y'all take one of my newer rides from the lot." He nodded at the Honda that the biker had parked. "Even put in a child seat."

Rennie turned around and looked at what Chrome offered with interest. The biker climbed out. He had on a leather vest and no shirt that showed off his tattoo-sleeved arms.

"All gassed up and I'm even donating travel money because I'm proud of my brother. Y'all can stop and eat someplace nice." Chrome pulled out two crisp hundred-dollar bills from his chained wallet and held them out.

Crit climbed out, gave his brother an onerous look, and then stepped past him and jerked open the driver's door to the Honda. He found the trunk release and punched it. The Biker had to move out of his way as Crit stepped around to the back and yanked open the trunk.

There it was.

The red tool box.

Wedged in next to a spare tire.

"No way," Crit said and slammed the trunk down hard.

Chrome came up beside him and stank of cologne and lowered his voice. "Easy Cheese. Somebody still works for me. And who would think to get clandestine at an art show. What's not to like?"

"No way," Crit said again. "We're takin' the van," he said loud enough for Rennie to hear. She had come out the passenger door to check out the Honda. She liked the child seat.

Crit started to move back to the van but Chrome grabbed his arm. And squeezed tight. Crit slung it off and nearly threw a punch. They burned eyes at each other and their foreheads touched and seared.

Chrome's lips leaked words like acid into Crit's bad ear. "I ate a lot of shit lettin' yer gal walk free and clear. You don't take the Honda our deal is off. She'll get hurt. Or worse." Then Chrome backed away and shrugged a little, as if what he'd said was an unpleasant, ordinary fact.

Crit shook no.

"So you're willing to risk it, two against one, muss up that nice shirt and make that boy an orphan over one little tool box?"

Crit's face muscles clenched. His prison stare didn't seem to dent Chrome's remorseless smirk.

"What's wrong?" Rennie asked and she was moving toward them.

"Stay where you are," Chrome said, and held up a hand.

Rennie stopped in her tracks. The biker stepped up to just behind Chrome.

A high-pitched whine like a bone caught in a grinder rose up in Crit's ear canal and sang in a language unknowable to any other. It was his own language and it told him he was alone and would die alone. That things rot and decay, and far from rising from the grave, he was still buried in his unshakeable, unholy past. A dog barked. Crit looked beyond his brother to the other side of the office and saw the balky pit bull dragged across the potted asphalt on a rope held by the heavy mother. Her kids, Trey and Brittany, were alongside and were complaining and carrying suitcases and plastic bags and stuffed pillowcases out of their room to their minivan. Brittany was sobbing. Crit heard

Wild Bill say *shit* out loud and then he jogged off toward the family and had a hot conversation with the woman about back rent owed.

Crit leaned closer to his brother's face. "That's the last threat you're gonna make against her on this side of the earth." His eyes lasered into Chrome's Raybans, but all he got back was his own reflection.

A smile pulled at the corners of Chrome's narrow lips and he reached out and slipped the two hundred dollar bills into Crit's gold-lariat-trimmed shirt pocket.

"I like it when you talk like the old you," Chrome said. And he poked the money down deeper with one finger.

Chapter 21

NOAH'S ARK

The highway curled through green hills and followed ancient streambeds. Past Bethany and Whetstone Branch. In books it says the Appalachians are amongst the oldest mountains in the world. Born of powerful upheavals within the terrestrial crusts and sculpted by the ceaseless action of water. Crit had not read those books. He drove fast in a bad mood. The Honda wheels cried on the curves and his ear buzzed angry. Systemic waves of self-loathing pounded his troubled mind. He had almost believed there could be a future separated from his past. As if what had happened before was just a nightmare he could wake from. He had almost bought the bluff. Fool's gold. He glanced at the sticky note on the Honda's dash. Sister Nikhael's tight cursive penmanship ushered Crit ahead and Crit drove ahead, mile-by-mile, drawing closer to what he knew in his heart and soul, as much as he knew anything, must surely be the impending disaster he deserved.

Rennie worked the radio, but was never satisfied and kept changing stations. She commented that the Honda had a new kind of audio input and she should have brought her phone charger so they could listen to some real tunes. Ten miles out of Jackson she even asked if they could go back for it.

Crit shook a hard *no*.

"Why not? Some teacher gonna give you a tardy?"

Tyler said being strapped in his child's seat was like riding in a space ship and he made a series of whistling rocket sounds.

They stopped at a Shell station in Campton before they got on the Mountain Parkway so Tyler could use the bathroom. Then Tyler said he was hungry. The Shell had a snack section and Crit picked out three dehydrated pizza slices off a tray under a heat lamp. Rennie got them sodas and napkins and they sat outside on an unpainted picnic table that someone had left ketchup blotches on. There was a steady hum and drone from cars and trucks crossing the Mountain Parkway overpass a hundred yards distant. Tyler and Rennie chattered on about the various cars and travelers who pulled up to the gas pumps. Their characterizations devolved into calling everyone either a *fatso* or *not a fatso*.

Tyler quickly wolfed down his entire slice. Rennie ate most of hers and left a few pieces of crust.

"Not hungry?" Rennie asked, blotting grease from her fingertips with a napkin.

"Not much." Crit had only taken two bites. He hadn't had any breakfast, either, but his stomach felt cold and tight.

"Tybo, go toss our stuff into that trash can," Rennie said. "And watch out for cars."

"He's not done."

"I'm done."

"Go on."

It took Tyler two trips to clear their table and while he was away Rennie asked, "What's wrong?"

"Nothing."

"What did he want from you?"

"Nothing new."

"I know he don't give out money for nothing."

Crit watched a Little Debbie delivery truck roll up to the gas station door.

"Are you doin' bad stuff for him 'cause of me?"

Crit thought about her question. The delivery man opened his rear compartment door, pulled out a hand dolly, and started loading it with boxes of snack cakes.

"You can be honest with me," she said and leaned in and her heavily made-up eyes studied his face carefully.

Crit turned away and shook his head. "I don't know why I'm doing anything."

Tyler came back with pizza stains on his shirt and hands.

"I ask you to do a simple thing and you come back a mess."

"There's a big fatso," Tyler called out loud enough for the large woman stepping out of a small car to hear him.

"Shush," Rennie said, and hauled Tyler off to the bathroom to clean up.

Crit got up and walked to the Honda. He got in and waited. He read over the sticky note. He squeezed and compressed the laced-leather steering wheel cover and hatched a plan to pull up to the next cop he saw. He would confess that he was a drug mule and name his brother as the kingpin. He would confess that they had killed Taylor fourteen years ago. He would toss out a few more names of the missing from the old days. He would confess to each and every corrosive offense he'd ever committed against the laws of man and God, and burn the map of his life like a trash fire. He and Chrome might end up processed together up at Roederer and he could catch him out in the exercise yard and there would be a reckoning with a shiv or a shank or a sock with a rock.

Rennie opened the back door and fastened Tyler into the child's seat. Tyler complained that he liked his front seat perch in the van better and Rennie sang out, "*You can't always get what you want.*"

The only drawback, Crit thought, regarding his plan, was that he couldn't do it with Rennie and Tyler in tow. They didn't deserve that.

"What are you thinking about, Einstein?"

Crit realized he'd been sitting frozen for some time after she'd climbed in. He turned the key. The engine started. He pulled out of the Shell station and looked for the ramp to the Mountain Parkway.

He found it and headed West.

They merged onto I-64 at Winchester, where the mountains receded and the country flattened out. He now passed horses grazing in groups or alone, standing in wide green pastures behind well-kept slat fences. Some of the biggest homes had lawns the size of football fields. Folks seemed to have nice things down here. He drove through it and the unbroken horizon started to irk him. This flat country seemed strangely passive and lacked *weight*. He'd spent his entire life, even most of his prison life, surrounded by formidable peaks, where shadows reached longer. Frost and winter clung on. No road was straight as the crow flies. Two days of rain, or a minor ice storm, and the entire county came to a standstill. Where a living had to be scraped out in ever-eroding valleys, or underground, or on the wrong side of the law. Upland people were tattooed with stubbornness and clannishness. They were unafraid to stand up and strike first. Like his brother. Like himself. Like every dirt-poor-raised motherfuckin' bastard he'd ever known.

He drove a semi-circle around Lexington's leafy suburbs and then found the exit onto I-75 North. Six lanes full and seventy miles an hour in both directions. Every time he crested a hill he could see an endless stream of cars and semis stretched out like a river to the top of the next low hill. The sun was off to his left and low, and just above the treetops. They passed the big Toyota plant near Georgetown that had its own exit and the dozens of tan and white-roofed factory buildings that took up more space than all of Jackson.

The I-75 corridor was flooded with cars from many different states that had license plates with birds or flowers or fish on them. He looked out his side window and watched strangers slowly pass or recede, depending on whether they were passing or getting passed. Many in the vehicles, the young and old, would turn and shoot him the briefest of glances. Crit wondered why he and they were drawn to eyeballing each other for such fleeting moments of wasted curiosity.

Tyler got bored with his softball and complained that he should have brought his fire truck instead.

"Well if you don't like it anymore, toss it out the window," Rennie said and that seemed to shut him up. Then she looked over at Crit and looked at him long enough for him to notice she was staring. When he finally said *what* she said, "You got something you want to throw out the window?"

He didn't answer.

"Because if you had told me you were gonna be cross as a bear the whole trip, I mighta made other plans."

She changed the radio from country to a rock station. It soon became apparent, when all the up-tempo singing was about praising *him*, that it was a Christian rock station.

"Bible thumpers should forget about rock and roll and stick to gospel," she said. "But don't tell Eldon I said so."

She turned off the radio and put her ear buds in and connected the mini plug to her phone.

And just then they passed a big highway sign advertising something called *The Ark Encounter* and *Creation Museum*. Crit remembered hearing about it from an inmate who had given himself over to God, that some crazy Australian had built a big Noah's ark up near Cincinnati. And here it was.

The highway gained another lane when I-71 to Louisville merged into it. Tyler said he had to pee again and maybe poop. Rennie told Crit to look for a gas station but what came up next was a big interstate rest area. Crit turned off and decelerated down the ramp and parked beside an idling RV with Wisconsin plates. There was a pavilion at the back that had a circular, domed roof that looked like a giant umbrella. The place somehow seemed strangely familiar.

Rennie unfastened Tyler and lifted him out. "You're gettin' heavier than a sack of potatoes."

In the grass beside their car two slender young men with long hair were kicking some kind of beanbag up into the air. Barefoot. Tyler watched them. They didn't seem very good at it. Rennie leaned back in the passenger window.

"You gonna be here when we come out?"

She said it as a joke but Crit felt like she was reading his mind. He had passed a trooper five miles back. Pulled over and parked in the center divider. Might still be there. He could head North to the next exit. Exit up to the crossover. Left. Left again. And get down to the business end of making things right in no time.

Her eyes stayed on him.

He blinked.

"I'll be here," he finally said.

"Okay, Mister Cranky."

She took Tyler by the hand and pulled him away from the men with the beanbag and toward the pavilion. Her high-heels clacked down the concrete walkway and her short dress caught looks and comments from a tourist couple who came out of the pavilion door just as she and Tyler went in.

Crit sat and stared through his windshield without seeing anything in particular and he was suddenly hit with the realization that he'd been here before. Right here. Liddy and he had pulled off the interstate to use the bathroom. He looked around. They probably parked ten feet from where he sat now. Or maybe he was parked on the same spot. He tried to figure in his head how long ago. It was a lot of years and the math tripped him up. Liddy had giggled and pranced off to the pavilion. They'd bought sodas and potato chips from the vending machines. Then what? They'd checked out a wall rack of tourist brochures. He remembered that it was a *Kings Island* brochure that caught Liddy's attention and that was the reason they had headed across the Ohio to the famous amusement park. Crit shook his head with heaviness and tried to stop remembering. But he could not and he could hear carnival bells and laughter and Liddy's smile burned into his mind's eye and watered his eyes. If only he could go back to there and not be who he was. If only she had met someone better. The RV beside him revved up and backed out and Crit came back to the present moment of the life that was entirely his.

Tyler had left his softball on the back seat and Crit reached over the backrest for it. It took him a few seconds to locate Taylor's initials underneath a smiling crayon-green face. He found it only by feeling for the cuts in the leather with his thumbnail.

What a dirty thumb.

He pressed down hard until his nail whitened and bent.

The young men stopped kicking the beanbag and walked to where they had left their sandals. They crossed the sidewalk and climbed into a Volkswagen Jetta, but they didn't pull out right away. Crit watched as they lit up a joint.

He pushed open his door and tried to climb out. His seatbelt held him. He fumbled for the release. Slid out. He stepped over to the Jetta and tapped the window.

He had come up fast and the young men turned to him, startled, like he had caught them doing something much worse.

He brought his finger and thumb to his lips and made a sucking sound.

They looked at him. They looked at each other uncertainly. The passenger shrugged. The driver smiled and rolled down his window and handed Crit what they were smoking. He had long black hair parted in the middle and resembled Jesus or that thin actor in the *Matrix.*

It was soggy at the tip, fat, and poorly rolled. Crit inhaled deeply. The fire end flared. He exhaled then took a second hit. Held the hot smoke longer and handed it back. He felt his lungs ache and tilted his head back and blew a stream of ash-colored smoke straight up at a murmur of crows or starlings crossing the sky.

"Gonna be a nice sunset," the driver said languorous and sucked a hit.

The sun was red and cut in half by low clouds and the light it gave was golden-red.

Crit felt a creeping dizziness. He lifted up Taylor's softball. And offered it.

The driver looked at the crayon-colored object through blood-shot eyes and slowly nodded. "Sure, Dude. Barter system beats capitalism."

Crit gave Taylor's softball to the strangers and walked back to the Honda. He climbed in and sat down.

He reached for and felt the keys in the ignition. He jingled them like a wind chime. He opened the glove box to see if there were any sunglasses. There were none. But there was a half-roll of Wintergreen Certs that someone had left on top of the owner's manual. He peeled back tinfoil and popped three small lozenges into his mouth. He waited. A pleasant fuzziness descended like a curtain of Vaseline. Rennie and Tyler stepped out of the pavilion and walked toward him bathed in yellow slanting light and followed by their shadows. Rennie's legs were bare and long and she walked with funny mincing steps on her high heels. She placed her hand onto her son's head so she wouldn't fall over.

"Sorry it took so long. We had a bathroom accident."

"Don't tell him about it," Tyler pleaded.

She got Tyler situated into the child seat and belted herself in. "What are you sucking on?"

He offered her the roll of Certs that was peeled back to nearly the end. She didn't want any. But Tyler did.

Fifteen minutes later they drove under a sign that said…

Florence Y'all.

And the sunset sky fissured and marbled, and the traffic thickened and slowed and they started down the long angled decline to the Ohio River. Crit stiffened his back and concentrated on the minutia of driving: How his fingertips caressed the wheel. The amount of pressure applied to the gas pedal. How the steering wheel never stopped moving. He focused intently on the layered auditory tonalities of his ringing tinnitus. There seemed a high-end hiss and simultaneously a low-end roar.

Shake, rattle and roll.

It was the end of rush hour and the outgoing lanes were bumper-to-bumper, heading out the way they had come. Several cars had their lights on.

Bright lights, Big City gone to my baby's head. I tried to tell my woman but she don't believe a word I said.

He changed the speed on the air conditioner fan until its frequency seemed to match the droning in his head. Rennie had her buds in, eyes closed, and was nodding and humming to her own thing.

They reached the bottom of the hill and came onto the massive Brent Spence Bridge. The traffic noise changed tone sharply as it echoed off the steel webbing. There were two distinct rumbling sounds. Cars crossing into Ohio filled three lanes on the bottom of the bridge and made one kind of noise. And the Kentucky-bound traffic overhead made another. He could see the skyline of Cincinnati winking through the side girders. Some of the more modern buildings had domed roof-points like silver bullets and their metallic and shiny glass surfaces shimmered. A crimson band of color clung to all sides on the horizon and in the western sky it was sapphire, amber and rust—the colors of a bruise. The turgid brown of the wide river spread out below like an oil slick. He passed the mid-point and he was no longer in Kentucky.

Rennie took out her buds and asked Tyler if he'd ever seen a bridge so big. Tyler didn't answer but watched everything with big eyes. She let out a whoop and pointed out the Cincinnati Reds baseball stadium that appeared huge and round on the far side of the river.

Bright Lights, Big City, went to my Baby's head.

Crit suddenly flicked his turn signal and moved into the right lane alongside the guardrail. He looked for it and found the red push-button with two white triangles. He depressed it and the hazard lights flashed. He then watched his rearview and lifted off the gas and put his foot on the brake. And slowed. And the traffic behind him backed up and slowed like he was the lead dancer in a conga line. He braked to a crawl. Behind him was honking confusion.

"What's wrong?" Rennie asked.

"Everything."

He stopped on the bridge just past the middle point. Traffic whizzed fast and dangerous on his left. Angry stalled drivers behind detonated horns.

Rennie asked him if it was car trouble. Crit didn't answer and punched the trunk latch and jumped out and almost got hit. Rennie watched concerned as he turned sideways and hugged their Honda to the trunk and lifted it open. He was hidden from her. Then he appeared on the other side of the trunk carrying a red toolbox to the guardrail.

"What's he doing?" Tyler asked. "Did he leave us?"

Rennie shook her head uncertainly.

Crit could feel the pulse of traffic in his boots. Before him was a wide empty space and then a vast purple sky. He flung the toolbox out between two girders. And it fell. He didn't see the splash a hundred feet below. And he didn't hear it. A driver yelled abuse out an open window. Horns blasted with frustration.

He moved back to the Honda and climbed in. But he didn't drive away. Not right away. He sat with his hands at two and ten as recommend in *The Kentucky Driver's Manual*.

Rennie looked at him with piercing eyes beneath heavily mascaraed lashes. "Did you smoke something?"

"Suppose I did."

"Those hippies at the rest stop?"

"Suppose we just go. We don't go back to Kentucky. We just drive ahead. Where we look at and what our eyes see, that's where we go. What we hear we hear. No plan. Just go." He raised his right hand and pushed it forward and aimed his fingertips at the end of the bridge.

She didn't answer for a moment and the honking was deafening.

"I got some money from working with Eldon. Back in my room and Bill can send it. Plus what I got in my pocket from Chrome. We can sell this car and get a cheaper one. And I can do what it takes when that runs out."

"Where do you want to go?"

Where do you want to go?"

"Everybody's mad at us," Tyler said.

"Chrome will come after us if we steal his car."

"He won't find us."

Rennie thought for a moment and she seemed unusually calm given where they were and the ferocity of the honking.

"Can we go to Florida, or maybe California? Someplace with an ocean."

"Sure. Just choose."

"Maybe Hawaii." Rennie leaned back into her seat and closed her eyes. She remained still for several seconds and then she opened her eyes and an untroubled smile bloomed across her sparkling red lips. "You know what? I know where I want to go more than anywhere."

"Where?"

"I wanna see your show. I didn't dress up for nothing.' Before we go anywhere else, we gotta see that."

He was trying to figure a way to get out of her request when a panel truck with a pest control sign on the side nearly rammed into them.

"These cars are gettin' way too crazy," Rennie said.

Crit put the shift into drive. Depressed the pedal. They were moving. He passed beneath a sign that said *Welcome to Ohio*.

Crit left the bridge and followed the instructions on the sticky note.

Right onto I-71.

The freeway split off toward Dayton and he stayed right toward Columbus. Tall buildings that were almost skyscrapers rose on the left and on the right were green trees in a park with a walk-path beside the river. The *Wintergreen Certs* had dissolved to nothing but had left a hint of their taste. Crit drove much slower than the impatient drivers who whipped past on both sides like their lives depended on getting somewhere fast. He drove under the walk-bridge to the Paul Brown Stadium and Rennie and Tyler made awestruck comments about the impressive home of the Cincinnati Reds that was right now right beside them. Rennie and Tyler even caught a glimpse of some of the high-up grandstand seats. Crit didn't bother to look at the stadium. He stayed focused on his sticky note and the street signs.

Turn left on Vine Street.

Crit saw the sign too late and had to jam his hand out the window and wave back traffic to get to the left. Horns blared. He turned and was now cutting North through the very heart of downtown. Men and women who were dressed like they lived lives very different from his own moved with speed and purpose down busy sidewalks. A pushcart vendor sold hotdogs. A construction crew jackhammered. Pulling good overtime after five, no doubt. A travel agency billboard advertised flights to faraway places. Maybe they could even fly him to Bulgaria.

He went through a yellow light changing to red and checked his rearview for cops. Saw none. They drove past a huge Westin Hotel with twenty floors rising. The sky was charcoal-dark with low-hanging cumulous clouds artificially illuminated by the glaring urban sprawl.

"You better turn on your headlights," Rennie said.

He did.

"That man has a raccoon on his head," Tyler said, pointing at a man with a long scraggy beard wearing a Daniel Boone coonskin cap in a line of scruffy men and women, some with shopping carts, lined up at the side gate to a church.

"I think that church feeds 'em," Rennie said.

"Can they feed us?"

"I think they feed you if you don't have a home."

"Can we pretend we don't have a home?"

Rennie looked at Crit. "Yes we can." She reached over and

circled Crit's arm with her finger and thumb and held on.

He felt her touch like he was feeling it for the first time and it gave him goose bumps. The noise in his head changed key. He had purpose. To keep driving ahead and make better things possible. He nodded forcefully. He would take care of this woman and her boy. He would beat his buzzard's luck to death with a crowbar if he had to, to protect them. He would break away from his brother. He would atone and wash the poison from his bones and veins.

"What?" She had seen him nod.

"Nothing."

"You think they'll have food at this thing?"

"We can't stay long. We can eat somewhere else."

"I mean if they got food, we can pack our pockets for the road," she said, giving his arm a squeeze. "We're on a budget, right? I'm thinking ahead." She released his arm and tilted the rearview to look at herself. She whisked her hair better. And then she opened her purse and brought out a tissue to blot her nose.

"Do you like the way I look? You never said." Some sparkles came off on her tissue.

"You're always gonna look a hell of a lot better than I do."

"Well, that's not hard." She chuckled and brought out a small can of Revlon hairspray from her purse. "Your hair dried out. You want me to spray you up, Mister GQ?"

He said no. But she sprayed him anyway. And he ducked and got some in his eye and said ouch. Tyler laughed at that.

They were no longer traveling under the tallness of downtown. They were passing through a neighborhood of stone and brick three-story townhouses and shops and cafes with outside tables, umbrellas, and chairs. They passed a leafy park where dozens of young men and women congregated in small groups and drank from coffee cups while their dogs scampered around a fenced-in square. There were no parking meters now and all the parked cars were Audis and Saabs and foreign, with the occasional hybrid electric.

Cross McMicken Ave. and the driveway to parking lot is 100 feet on left just past the Gallery.

They passed McMicken and came up on a four-story brick building with wrought iron fire escapes on their left. Each floor had large industrial windows and the sign on the front said *Over The Rhine Gallery.*

The name was in red neon letters like it was a bar or honky-tonk.

"That's it, I think."

Crit slowed to get a better look. Rennie leaned forward and watched a young woman in leather pants, combat boots, and a billowy white blouse, come out talking on her phone.

"I guess leather is back in style."

The car behind them honked. Crit slowed even more and flicked his blinker and turned into the gap between the gallery and a Mayan restaurant. They motored through the narrow driveway lined with graffiti-style wall murals of whimsical cartoon figures. They came out into a rear parking lot that was shared by several businesses and had recently been surfaced with new sealcoating. The parking spaces hadn't been re-lined yet so some of the cars were unevenly parked. Crit looked for a space when headlights flashed from a shiny black Tahoe SUV at the very back of the lot.

And then flashed again.

Crit's guts tightened. The Vaseline fogginess in his head burned away.

Rennie didn't notice the Tahoe. She was cantered around looking at the artwork on the walls and chatting with Tyler about the images and colors and characters used.

"I can draw just as good," Tyler said.

"I bet you can, Baby."

Crit turned and drove as far away from the Tahoe as possible. He was stopped by a concrete-block barrier wall. He looked around. The only way in and out was the way they had come in. He pulled forward and then backed up and parked, so as to keep his nose out.

Rennie let out a happy whoop and climbed out. "The stars have arrived."

Tyler had managed to unfasten the straps on his child seat—maybe even miles back—but Rennie didn't bust him about it. She opened the back door and repeated that the stars had arrived.

"Am I a star?" Tyler asked.

"You sure are, you're like a shooting star," she said and lifted him out in a big swooping arc, and then took a comb out of her purse and combed his hair.

"That hurts."

"Lookin' good always hurts."

Crit stepped out. He could smell the fresh sealant. His ear intoned warning. He glanced over the tops of the parked vehicles at the Tahoe. No movement. It sat there like a sleeping shark.

"Do we have to go around to the front?"

A middle-aged man with a gray ponytail and Elton John glasses climbed out of a mini-Fiat and stepped up to a back door. Beside the back entrance was a large sculpture that could be a horse or a dog and seemed welded together out of dissimilar scrap metal parts. Some kind of droning string music seeped out of the building when the man opened the door.

"I think you go in there," Crit said and turned back to look at the SUV and his brain reeled through two or three moves ahead.

Rennie held out her hand for him to join her. "This is about the closest I'll get to a red carpet, ever."

"Go on in. I'll be there in a sec," Crit said as calmly as he could with adrenaline sluicing through every capillary in his venous system. "I just need a minute."

"Nervous?"

"I've been sittin' too long."

"Okay, we can wait."

"Naw, go on in. Don't wait for me," he said, trying not to sound stressed.

"Well, okay, Mister Cranky, but don't take too long. We

don't know anybody."

Rennie took Tyler by the hand and played a cadence across the pavement with her stilettos. Just before she went in, she paused and pulled down her skirt and readied herself and then looked back and smiled and beckoned Crit to hurry up. And then she and Tyler went inside.

Crit watched the door closely and his eyes hung onto the empty space where they had been.

He turned to face the SUV.

The windows were dark and nothing happened. He was about to walk to it when the driver and passenger doors slowly cracked open. Two men stepped out and looked around. They appeared Hispanic. Both had on tracksuit bottoms and bold-colored sports jerseys and flat-brimmed baseball caps. They came with no hurry. They passed under a security light and he could tell that the larger of the two had the name *Messi* printed across his jersey. The other man was slender and walked slightly ahead and presented like he was in charge. They came up to Crit and looked around slowly and carefully, and then looked him over the same way.

Crit kept his hands outside his pockets where they could see them.

The heavier man stood off to the side. He had a wide nose and thick neck and biceps like he pumped. The slender man seemed smaller up close. He didn't weigh more than one-fifty and had dark, intense eyes and a thin-line beard.

"Chrome send you?" The slender man asked in a South-of-the-Border accent. Chrome had known inmates in prison rumored to be Mexican drug cartel. They stayed to themselves and no one crossed them.

Crit nodded.

"Where is it?"

Crit stuck his chin toward the Honda. "Where's yer money?"

"You first. Show."

Crit drilled eyes with the slender man. The bulkier man spread his legs for a better foundation and to show off the lump at his belt. Probably a 9 millimeter. The weapon of choice in the trade. It could fire twelve rounds as fast as you could pull the trigger.

"There." Crit nodded at the Honda.

The larger man stepped closer to Crit and raised up both his palms to show what needed to be done. He felt Crit for weapons. Made him turn. Even felt inside his Chinese boots. Then rose and nodded to his partner. The slender man nodded at Crit.

Crit walked. He glanced behind and the men were following, split out on either side. He moved through the warm, weightless air. His ear sang of danger and fear.

He came up to the Honda. He put his hand on the door latch.

"Hold."

Crit paused and the larger man came around and opened the driver's door and looked in and over every part of the interior of the car. Then he sat inside it. He opened the glove box. He even felt under the seat.

"I need to pop the trunk."

The bigger man nodded at the slender man.

"Go ahead."

Crit leaned in and found the button and pushed the trunk re-lease.

Click.

* * *

Rennie and Tyler moved through the gallery in a kind of curi-ous daze, as if they were traversing a strange planet. The floor was shiny-lacquered and reflected the mingling crowd. They saw an Asian musician in a tuxedo, playing a droning single note on some kind of bass fiddle. They saw stylish young men and women, and some older, laughing and drinking from wine glasses. About half the crowd were dressed like they had put a lot of thought into their attire and the other half wore grungy black T-shirts and hoodies and jeans. One African-American young man held a skateboard. Some moved in a slow clock-wise semi-circle around the walls, stopping at each painting and twirling their drinks. The chatter and music echoed off the walls. Tyler stuck close to his mother and watched everything and said nothing.

Rennie saw a female bartender with a high and tight haircut, pouring wine. She didn't see a food table, but she did see a caterer with a tray. And others seemed to be grabbing and eating from what the caterer offered. Rennie pushed Tyler over to her. She was tall, more than six feet, and completely bald, a large gold ring dangled from her nose, and her eyebrows seemed tattooed on. She had noticed their approach and lowered her tray.

"What's that?" Tyler asked.

There were seven or eight bread squares with brown paste and green sprouts on top.

"Lamb pate' on toast," the caterer said pleasantly.

"What's the green thing?" Rennie asked.

"Rosemary."

"You think you can eat one of those?"

Tyler didn't answer but made a squeamish face.

"I'll be coming back with Swedish meatballs, maybe he might like those instead," the caterer said to be helpful.

"Sure, thanks," Rennie said.

"How do you blow your nose?" Tyler asked.

"With a Kleenex," the caterer said, and moved away.

Rennie turned and scanned the room. Her eyes locked on something familiar. There on the other side of a chattering, middle-aged couple was the image of Wild Bill, performing his awkward t'ai chi.

She grabbed Tyler by the hand and pulled him through the crowd to where Bill was mounted and spotlighted by overhead track lighting. He looked like some kind of crazy mountain buck dancer inside a framed black border. She tilted her head and looked. She felt Bill had somehow gained prominence and worth here on the gallery wall. She felt prideful, as if she herself had somehow contributed to *this*. What all these people had come to see.

"That's Uncle Billy," Tyler said.

"Hell's yeah."

"Mommy look."

And Rennie looked to her right where Tyler was pointing and felt another jolt. There she was, also black framed, and likewise beautifully displayed: in the middle of all these college-educated wine-drinkers and caterers who looked like Amazon warriors from some futuristic TV show.

"Who are you talking to?" Tyler asked.

"You mean in the picture?"

"Uh-huh."

"Nobody that I remember."

She moved inches from it and inhaled to see if it still smelled like Breathitt County. But all her nose picked up was antiseptic clean newness. For the first time, she really studied how Crit had made her. It was a marvel. Negligible and densely packed dark slashes and unruly watercolor washes that seemed helter skelter up close found meaning and shape only when she took a step back. She looked at herself from a distance of one foot, then two, then three. She looked and studied the totality of what she had been at her very worst. It was as if the painting had distilled the entirety of her pathetic past into one terse, visceral, reactive pose. In scary movies, demon spirits sometimes left the screaming host and entered inanimate objects. She imagined her demons were now trapped in this two-by-three-foot square of framed drywall. She closed her eyes and said a silent prayer to never go back there again. Ever.

Then she took out her phone and told Tyler to stand next to it. He frowned and she told him to stand up straight and smile. She touched the circled dot and heard the synthetic shutter click. Checked it. The flash had gone off and her son's pale complexion glowed like an albino. She turned off the flash and took another snapshot and checked that. It was perfect. He was on his way to heart-killer handsome. He had her freckles and small nose and bluebird-blue eyes and full lips. She would now have this image of her handsome son and the promise of his future, standing beneath her demonic past. And she could look at it every morning, like a north star, to keep from drifting.

A couple in their early twenties stepped up to look at Crit's paintings and Rennie asked the man if he could take their picture. He didn't nod, smile, or say anything. But he handed his plastic wine glass to his partner and took her phone. *The Clash* was printed across his T-shirt. Rennie put her hands on Tyler's shoulders and told the man to make sure to get both paintings in. He took several seconds to artistically compose and then snapped it.

"You're the subject, right?" He handed her phone back. "You have the same hair."

"Yep, that's me, or was."

"It's good."

"It's fucking amazing." Rennie bragged.

"What do those little blue dots mean?" Tyler asked and touched a blue sticker on the information card next to his mother's image.

"It means it was sold," the young woman beside the man said. She had a clipped Northern accent, curly dark hair, and black glasses.

"How much?" Rennie asked.

"I imagine whatever the price was set at." The woman answered and she read the information card. "Nine hundred and fifty dollars."

"And the person who made it gets that?"

"The gallery always takes their cut."

"They do what they do," the man said with churlishness.

Rennie looked at the painting of Bill and it also had a blue dot. And the price was also set at nine-fifty. Rennie's eyes brightened and she looked toward the door. Crit needed to hear this and see this. He didn't have to work ditch jobs off the books or break the law to support their permanent vacation. All he had to do was sit in a motel room and do what seemed to come natural to him. What he'd been doing ever since she met him. And good money would roll their way like rain down a hillside ditch.

The young woman took a sip of red wine. "It says the artist took up painting while incarcerated." She turned to her partner. "I think that's awesome. There's a kind of authenticity and danger in every stroke."

***

The trunk clicked open, but just an inch.

Crit moved around to it and put both hands on it. The smell of fresh sealant wafted. The two men behind him spread out on either side. All three men looked down. He lifted the trunk.

What was revealed was gray carpet, an ice scraper, and a spare tire.

"Where is it?" The slender man asked.

Crit reached under the spare tire. His fist closed on a tire iron.

His brain screamed.

Crit whirled and cracked the heavy man on the side of his head, bending him over and knocking his cap off.

The slender man reached into his waistband and grabbed a pistol. Crit swung and snapped bones in the slender man's wrist. The pistol clattered off the bumper. The slender man made a dive for it. Crit swung again and split his skull open. A sickening thud. The slender man collapsed onto his face on the asphalt.

The heavy man was now struggling to get up. Crit kicked him in his temple with the point of his new boot.

Both men were now sprawled out seven feet apart and not moving. Four seconds had passed. Crit's tinnitus thundered.

In some small recess of his adrenaline-pumped brain, part of him was disgusted with how easily the moves had come back. But he shut down those unnecessary thoughts. He wasn't done. They weren't clear. He knelt and patted down the slender man and pulled out a white envelope. And it was thick with hundred-dollar bills. Blood trickled from the laceration atop the slender man's head and down the side of his face into his line beard.

Crit slipped the envelope into his lariat-trimmed front pocket and searched the pavement for the weapons. He found the slender man's Ruger Blackhawk underneath the taillights near the rear tire. He couldn't find the heavy man's pistol. He dropped to his knees and checked the body. He finally found a 9 millimeter Glock trapped beneath the heavy man's leg.

Crit jogged a short distance to the back of the parking lot and tossed the Blackhawk up as high as he could onto the roof of the three-story building next door. He then tried to toss the Glock up, but it clanged off the gutter and dropped back down into a lower basement area. Crit wasn't going down there and it would have to do.

He looked around. No witnesses. Thankfully.

He exhaled. He stepped back to the bodies. The Heavy man was moaning and twitching. The Slender man wasn't moving at all. Crit put his hand close to the gaped mouth and detected a faint rasp of air.

Good. He didn't want a homicide investigation.

Crit pulled the slender man out of the way of getting run over and turned him over on his back so he could draw air easier. These buyers had to crawl away on their own volition. The rules of their trade would dictate handling this theft in-house. Revenge and retribution would roll his brother's way. While he and Tyler and Rennie would be free and clear to destinations unknown. The envelope of cash in his pocket could get them through the first six months and beyond.

Crit jumped into the Honda and cranked it. He drove past the comatose bodies and up close to the back door of the gallery and nearly clipped the scrap iron sculpture. He jumped out and left his door open, the engine running, lights on, and rushed inside.

Crit hurried across the gallery floor and bumped into a man with a full beard and a black turtleneck and spilled the man's drink. Red wine splashed Crit's jeans and spattered the glossy lacquered floor. Crit didn't bother to apologize and moved away. Where were they?

And an arm grabbed him.

Crit turned into the beaming face of Sister Nikhael. She had a thick rainbow-colored shawl around her neck and her hair was different and she was wearing makeup, the first time he'd ever seen her with it.

"Yay. I was getting worried that you weren't going to make it."

She moved conspiratorially to his other side and nodded in the direction of an open door. Inside was a white-walled office with chrome furniture and two men in dark suits and ties were conversing.

"That's James Willet, the assistant curator at the Cincinnati Museum of Art. Dude on the left. With my own ears I heard him say you were a talent to keep an eye on. The guy he's talking to is a freelance art critic named Clark something. What we need to do now is lay the groundwork. We're going to walk over there and I'm going to introduce you and you don't need to give a speech, but I need you to nod and say *thank you* if either one of them says anything nice at all about your work. And they will. Got it? Here we go."

She tried to lead him toward the office door but he wasn't having it.

"Thanks for everything, huge and beyond. But an emergency came up and I can't stay. I'm just here to grab my people."

She didn't hide her disappointment. She looked like he had punched her in the face for no reason.

"Come on? Really. I went to a lot of trouble to get you here."

"So did I."

Crit left her sputtering and frustrated and he moved away and through the crowd. His eyes searched for red and blue hair.

He reached the back wall and felt rising panic. They weren't here. Not on the first floor anyway. Where were they? Time was ticking. The men outside may well be fully revived. Maybe he should have kept one of their pistols. He saw a set of stairs to the upper floors and headed for that. Halfway to the stairs he saw a glint of red and blue in the crowd and turned to it and felt a jolt of recognition.

There she was.

As he had made her.

Screaming into a phone. And Wild Bill beside her.

Both images had been professionally framed by someone else. He took a step closer. What he had made was there and looked different than it had in his motel room or his cluttered secondhand store. He got close to what he had done and what he saw was only half-familiar.

Someone took his hand. He turned and Rennie was smiling. "Yeah, wow, right?"

"We gotta go. Now."

"Okay, but that sister-woman was looking for you, she sounded anxious, did you see her?"

"We can't stay. Where's Tyler?"

"What's wrong?"

"Where is he?"

"In the bathroom. He wanted to go on his own and kicked me out. Now that he's seen the big city he's acting out all grown up."

Crit saw the restroom sign. It was mounted on a drywall rectangle pushed out from the far wall.

"But what's the hurry?"

Crit didn't answer and grabbed Rennie's hand and pulled her through the crowd and across the room. She almost fell and he caught her.

"Watch it, these aren't running shoes."

The restroom door was locked. It had three black vinyl figures stenciled on; one with pants, one with a skirt, one with half pants and half skirt.

He knocked.

"You look way worried."

"I'll tell you later."

Crit knocked louder, and called out Tyler by name.

"Maybe he's locked in and can't unlock it."

Crit tried the handle. Someone was attempting to turn the handle on the other side. Crit released and the door opened.

Tyler came out laughing and there was a hand on his shoulder with two black fingernails. The hand was connected to a face he'd known his whole fucked-up life. And the face secreted a bilious smile.

"I just found out if you say a bad word fast, it's not a bad word." Chrome chortled and held out a hand, and Tyler low-fived him. Then he winked at his brother.

Distress tightened Crit's face and eyes.

"Don't encourage him. What are you doing here?" Rennie asked in a straightforward tone. She wasn't yet as panicked as she would soon become.

"Love brought me here. The more I thought about it, I knew I couldn't miss out on m'blood's first ever big art show." He smiled louder. "This place is awesome, Bra."

"What do you want?" Crit heard himself ask through the shrill grinding.

"This." Chrome said and moved closer. Crit flinched back. Chrome reached and lifted out the cash envelope that Crit had taken off the Mexicans. Held it between his thumb and finger as their eyes seared. Chrome pocketed the cash and rubbed his thumb to the side of his mouth. "We do need to discuss some business outside. It's a little too noisy in here."

Crit turned sideways and looked behind. One of Chrome's bikers was at the back door. Another was standing between Crit and the front door. The stairs weren't blocked but where would that lead, anyway?

The strange fiddle music found a faster tempo.

Crit turned back to his brother, got close to his scabbed ear. "If I go out there, they stay here. Nothing happens to them. You leave them alone."

Chrome's smile leached away. "You're always negotiating from a shit hand, Bra. Nothing but deuces and weak threes." Some of his smile came back. "But sure. They can stay here because I want 'em to stay here."

Rennie caught the tension of the moment. "What's going on?"

"Not a thing, Darlin'. We're going outside and have a talk." Chrome smiled light and breezy and knelt to speak to Tyler at his level. "You and your red hot momma stay here and look at all the fancy pictures on the walls. Okay?"

"I've seen 'em all," Tyler said bluntly.

Crit said, "Well, maybe someday something you paint might end up on these walls, and I want you to go find the best place for it, okay?"

Tyler looked around and nodded.

Crit reached down and led the boy to his mother. Then he whispered to her. He told her that he would be fine. She and Tyler should stay inside where there were people around them. And she should have her phone ready to call 9-1-1 if Chrome came back inside alone for her. He said it all in a calm voice but her eyes grew more worried the more he spoke.

He tried to step away but she grabbed him and was holding onto his wrist and arm. Her eyes were intense and wild. It was a look he hadn't seen in her since her bad times. There was anxiety and fear in her face, but not for herself, it was all concern for him. It felt like something between them broke when he had to pull her hands off.

Crit moved toward the back door and noticed that Sister Nikhael was watching him. She shook her head and turned her back on him. There it was, finally. What he had always expected and deserved.

Crit moved past the caterers and through the crowd and the sound of the room hissed away like air out of a flat tire. He went through the back door. And the headlights of the Honda were on him and the engine was running. Chrome reached through the open door and cut the engine. Took the keys. And he nodded in the direction of the black Tahoe.

Crit saw them.

The men he had assaulted were bent-over and nursing their wounds and leaning against the hood of their SUV in the back of the lot. The slender man held his wrist like it was giving him immense pain.

"Let's go have a talk." Chrome said.

The heavy man straightened up with a grimace when he saw Crit and Chrome coming and he got his boss's attention. Both men's eyes burned with smoldering vengeance.

"You don't have it do you?" Chrome asked in a whisper as they drew closer.

"What?"

"You know what."

Crit shook his head *no*.

Chrome made a *tisk* sound.

Crit didn't like any of this. But he went along and followed his brother. The slender man had a dried blood rivulet from his hairline to his throat. The heavy man had a raw gash on his forehead like a third eye. Their SUV was parked in the shadows and their faces were dark and pitiless.

"He's gonna give yer money back and apologize," Chrome said with a casual shrug and held out the cash envelope. "He got greedy on his own. I'll deal with him."

What Chrome held out stayed untaken for ten seconds.

"Fuck that," the slender man finally sneered.

"Where's my pistol?" The heavy man grunted.

Crit stayed silent.

"He asked you a question." Chrome said.

Crit looked at his new boots and said nothing.

The heavy man stepped forward fast for a big man and sucker-punched Crit hard. It was a straight-line jab to his forehead that caught him unprepared and rocked his head back. He staggered back onto his heels and fought for consciousness and tried to keep from falling.

Neither Chrome nor his bikers moved an inch to help.

The two Mexicans spoke in angry rapid Spanish and then the slender man said to Chrome, "Give me him. And the money. And we can still do business."

The slender man's request seemed to echo and replay in Crit's fuzzy brain. He tilted his sagging head to see his brother's face. What he saw was Chrome was thinking and then nodding. And it hadn't taken all that long.

"Okay."

The slender man snatched the envelope from Chrome and said something harsh in Spanish. The heavy man answered in Spanish and then reared back and kicked Crit in the stomach and the ground came up fast and Crit was on it and the pain was piercing and he couldn't pull any air. He could only suck in croaking pain and the realization that he was never to fully breathe again. Somehow the heavy man now had a knife in his hand. And he stepped over and straddled Crit. Crit tried to paw up a defensive hand but he didn't have anything in his lungs to fuel him and his muscles wouldn't behave and the heavy man reached down and had him by his hair and was turning his throat up.

What happened next Crit wasn't sure. There was a percussive detonation and the heavy man let go and toppled beside him. Crit finally found some air that tasted like asphalt and managed to glance up to see his brother aim a pistol at the slender man's surprised face and pull the trigger.

Bap.

Blood spray and smoke and the slender man fell backward onto his SUV hood and then rolled off onto the mephitic asphalt.

Crit rasped and struggled up onto all fours. Shook his head like a dog. Coughed and spat. He heard his brother tell one of the bikers to get the truck and then his brother's square-toed and buckled boots moved to where he squatted and pulled the cash envelope from the clawed hand of the slender man. It was spotted with blood and brain matter. Chrome wiped it off on the dead man's tracksuit pants.

"Someone's comin.'" Crit heard one of the biker's say.

Both ears hummed unreliably. Her voice came like a train's whistle far away and got closer. She was calling his name. She was barefoot and had lost her stilettos. He thought of the first time he had seen her and she was barefoot. She was close and he saw her slow down when she beheld the bodies and blood and then looked at the man who had done the killing and halted with fear.

Chrome told her to shut up and keep quiet and moved toward her. He held his pistol at his side and she took a frightened step back and turned to run. But one of the bikers had moved up behind her.

"I told you to stay inside."

Her lips tremored. "I've got a son, please don't…

"I know you do."

She now looked at Crit so he might say that she was going to live. Crit said nothing. He was tapped out. Had trouble breathing. He felt mired in darkness and mud. He slumped over onto his butt and was impotent to say anything or do anything that mattered.

Chrome raised the blood-smeared envelope and offered it to her.

She looked at what he offered with confusion and fear.

"Listen. I'm gonna give you what this dingbat stole."

Her red and blue hair wobbled and she didn't understand.

"And you can take the Honda. Keys are it."

"To make me shut up?"

"That. And what's the chance yer boy is mine?"

Her lips somehow found a brave smirk. "50/50. Probably less."

"Well, that's fifty good reasons to get him as far away from me and him as possible." He slung a thumb at Crit. "We're bad people to raise a kid around. Don't come back to Jackson."

"You're wrong. He's not like you. Not anymore. And we have plans." She said and then looked down at Crit to get him on her side.

Crit wasn't looking or listening to those around him. He was in a room of hopelessness and echoing gunshots. His stare was moored on something fuzzy and far away. An out-of-focus mass of bad maps and bad roads that clung to him like flypaper. No matter how hard he swatted, and ripped away, their rank stickiness clung on. He blinked and now saw bright reds and yellows. Graffiti squiggles and shapes came into focus on the driveway wall. Some artist had gone to great lengths to create such things of whimsical beauty. The wind and the rain would come and time would dull and erase what was done until what was left was shabby and the building owner would paint over it.

"Get the fuck out of here." Chrome said to Rennie in a *don't-fuck-around-with-me* tone. And he jerked her away from Crit.

"I'm not leaving without him," she said stubborn, as only someone raised behind a shit-filled eight ball can be stubborn. "Stand up and tell him," she pleaded with Crit.

Crit didn't stand and said nothing like that. He said nothing at all.

"He has a date with his parole officer in the morning. And you wanna turn my brother into a wanted felon? Sure, that'll work out great."

Chrome's F-series pickup with the metal flake body and fancy rims pulled up and the driver got out. The bikers took out and unfurled two blue tarps and moved quickly and efficiently, and wrapped up the dead men like burritos. Chrome acted as lookout and had them pause when some hipster with dreadlocks came out of the gallery to unlock a bicycle and pedal away.

Rennie had her arms crossed around herself. "You ought to say something."

All he could say was…

"Go."

Chapter 22

WEST VIRGINIA

Crit rode beside his brother in the passenger seat. The bikers sat on the cramped jump seats of the extended cab. Somebody needed to shower. Maybe it was him. One of the bikers snapped a lighter and lit a cigarette. Smoke filled the cramped space. Chrome cracked his window and the night whistled in.

Chrome took the local Southgate Bridge that crossed into downtown Newport. At the end of the bridge was a roundabout and then the road straightened and headed South. No one spoke but *Slipknot* screeched through twelve consecutive rap-metal songs and then screeched back through every one of them again. Chrome didn't have a map or check his phone. He drove like he was freewheeling, making it all up as he went along, and they were soon traveling on highway 9 toward Vanceburg.

The road swung South toward Grayson. They drove through a half-dozen one-stoplight, nothing mountain towns that census takers could show were in decline and were hemorrhaging citizens. Chrome crossed under I-64 and went two miles farther, then seemed to change his mind about something and turned around in a Valero Gas Station and headed back the way he'd come. He took the ramp onto the interstate and headed East toward Ashland. During this part of the trip Crit didn't have his eyes open to notice anything. But he wasn't sleeping.

They crossed into West Virginia at Catlettsburg and Chrome immediately turned South onto 52 and hugged the east side of the Big Sandy for twenty curvy miles. It was dark country and the sky was dark and their headlights lit up only a small part of the world and their place in it.

Chrome suddenly turned off and went up a nameless mountain road that skirted a sheer drop-off into a ravine. Chrome stopped and cut the headlights and the engine. Crit managed to open his eyes and didn't know where he was but he was pretty sure his brother didn't either. Chrome climbed out so the bikers could climb out over his bent-down seat.

Crit remained in the cab and didn't turn around but he could feel the tailgate fall and the truck springs bounce as lifeless bodies were pulled off. A lone cicada trilled, looking for a mate. The woods would be thick with their collective screaming by the end of summer. The bikers moved into the trees and unfurled and rolled the dead down into the ravine. Chrome stood just outside Crit's window and watched the work and lit up a joint. He inhaled two tokes. He didn't bother to offer Crit.

"You got to pass a piss test tomorrow."

Too late, Crit thought.

Chrome put the joint out by pinching out the embers with his fingers.

"There weren't no drugs in that tool kit, were there?"

The window was rolled up but Chrome heard what Crit said and he turned to his brother with a peculiar smile and what he said was muffled but clear.

"We're scorpions, Bra."

They drove another twenty miles or so through West Virginia and Chrome again pulled over and had the bikers burn the tarps in a strip mine slag pit. Then they headed home. They crossed back into Kentucky at Louisa and Chrome finally checked his phone for directions and took Highway 23 toward Prestonsburg.

Sunrise found them fifteen miles outside of Jackson and momentarily lost. They had skirted the entirety of the Daniel Boone National Forest and were coming in from the East on narrow, twisting back roads over countless Appalachian ridge peaks, and past mobile homes with barking dogs and old cars and the occasional rusting tractor parked beside some rotting tobacco barn missing tin on its roof.

A rust-colored sky bloomed majestic atop dark undulating mountaintops. One of the bikers was snoring. Crit had one eye cracked open and one eye closed and took in the resplendent vista only because his heart pumped blood into his eye and brain. Taylor could only see things the dead could see if they could see at all, and Crit doubted that they could. Eyes, brains, ears, reproductive organs, the blood-fed organs that created civilizations; they were always the first things to rot away. Hair lasted longer. Bones and teeth lasted almost as long as tombstones. Crit wondered if Chrome had tossed Taylor down a ravine and likewise left him for wild animals to pick clean and his bones to scatter. But he didn't bother to ask, now or ever after.

EPILOGUE

Crit had gotten a splash of urine on his hand. He capped the beaker and sat it on top of the toilet and rinsed in the basin. He looked down at the deflated red balloon floating atop the toilet water like a comic-book turd. Like the red ski cap left in the grass by Tyler's friend. His brother had given him the balloon, filled with clean urine, and told him to hide it under his ball sac. Crit flushed, then took the beaker outside and handed it to Brenda Cowan, who was waiting with blue latex gloves on both hands.

"How'd your art show thing go?"

"Good." Crit said.

"Glad to hear it. So they liked your paintings?"

"I guess they did."

"Well good. But don't get in a habit of asking for favors like that."

"I won't."

"We're done here," she said and walked back to her office.

* * *

Once or twice in the months that followed, alone in his motel room, he flipped to a blank page of his sketchpad, and thought about making something grow where there was nothing. But all that seemed like a thin and empty ritual that someone else had done.

* * *

Crit unlocked and Eldon walked in and looked over all that was inside. Crit stood by the door. Eldon laid his hands on some of the newer household appliances and then he moved around the perimeter and looked at each and every one of Crit's paintings and drawings that were hanging on the steel fence and walls. He even went into the back room and looked at some of the paintings in there. And then he came back and told Crit what he saw in them was a cry for God's help, and that Jesus died on the cross so Crit didn't have to paint so darkly.

Eldon took over the payments on the store and gave Bill three hundred dollars for furnishings and inventory. He also told Bill he wanted him to play guitar in his church band, which lubricated the deal.

Crit borrowed Bill's Econoline and loaded up his artwork with the intention of hauling them all to the dump. Bill tagged along, and it took some coaxing but he managed to talk Crit into storing them in an unused motel room. And that's where they went —Stacked on top of each other on a bed frame with no mattress. *A hand slapping at a handball. A lunch bucket pulled up to a guard tower by a rope. Icicles on razor wire. Snow drifts drifting. Dead birds. Snow melting into puddles around a metal fence. April tree branches budding. A half-eaten grilled cheese sandwich. A Styrofoam plate. A mosquito sucking blood. A raised middle finger. A hand holding a bottle of Crown Royal. An Asian man fixing a bicycle chain. A boy throwing a softball.*

Lights out. Door closed.

* * *

Crit never heard from Sister Nikhael again, though he did get a check in the mail from *Over the Rhine Gallery Limited* for eleven hundred and thirty seven dollars. And later he heard through

Brenda Cowan that the good sister had stopped teaching her class on Wednesdays at Little Sandy.

Once or twice a week Crit made runs for his brother and did it without complaint.

August came hot and dry. The air trilled with grinding waves of cicadas. The Asian delivery man gave up his bicycle and started making deliveries on a moped with a milk crate strapped to his back seat.

Wild Bill gave up his daily t'ai chi and spent more time fishing.

***

By the middle of September the leaves started to yellow early due to the dryness and heat. And then the first week of October a storm blew in. It was the last rumblings of a Louisiana hurricane that had crawled up through Alabama and Tennessee, and the wind blew terrible all through the night. Crit woke when his room shook and he went out into the rain and looked up at a big limb that had split off a hackberry tree and was resting on top of Rennie's old room. Wild Bill came out in his mismatched Crocs and told Crit there was no hurry in fixing it.

But the next morning Crit borrowed a chainsaw from his brother and went up and cut the thick branch into fireplace-size logs and tossed them off the roof. Then he went up with a tar bucket and broom and brushed roofing cement into the lacerations the branch had made. He was up there and it was nearly noon when a Fed Ex truck rolled in off the highway. Crit could see only the top of the truck as it parked. He didn't see the driver get out.

Crit came down and cleaned his tools with gasoline and then moved through the pass-through by the ice machine and noticed a *Fed Ex* envelope leaning against his door.

His name and address was hand-printed on the label stuck in the plastic pouch. The return had no name but the address was from the room he had just fixed the roof on.

Crit sat on his brown and tan coverlet and tore off the serrated tab and pulled out a series of watercolor and crayon images. There was no letter or note inside. The first image was a blue ocean with a lone seagull flapping above it and a happy green fish dangling from the seagull's mouth. The next image was a stick figure mom with red and blue hair and a small boy with big sunglasses, standing on a yellow beach and waving at the viewer.

The last image was the mother and son buried under the sand. Only their smiling faces and their big feet were sticking out. There was a red beach umbrella on the left and a blue one on the right. *It's hotter than a pepper sprout* was scrawled on the sand by their feet and then at the top were words colored in with different colors.

We love you, we miss you, xo, xo.

Crit stared at this watercolor for a long time. He stared at it even after the sun lowered in muted increments across the mountain sky and night squeezed out the day. He stared at it long after his motel room was swabbed in darkness and shadows elongated and cars and trucks whooshed softly down the hill toward the blinking red light.

He sat there and he looked some more.

ACKNOWLEDGMENTS

Loud Water would not have been possible without the contributions of Charles Shouse, filmmaker and lifelong Breathitt County resident. Some parts of this story were originally knocked around by us as a movie idea. And this would be a different book entirely if not for my conversations with the incarcerated writers and artists of Voices Inside, a writing and performance program behind the razor wire. Keep your pens moving. My students at U.K. are always an inspiration, as is my home state of Kentucky. I'd like to thank Heather Henson, my sister and the superior writer in the family. Check her out. A big shout out to Pioneer Playhouse, where they still let me direct. Eric Campbell and Lance Wright at Down & Out Books, thanks a million. Perhaps the Covid-19 pandemic and its forced isolation should get some props for allowing for quiet time needed to write this. And lastly, I'd like to thank Lin for her inspiration in so many ways, including her unmatched gift at giving special names to wild birds.

ROBBY HENSON is a filmmaker, screenwriter, theater director, and arts-behind-bars instructor. He received his M.F.A. from NYU's graduate film school and has written and directed several documentaries for PBS as well as five feature films - The Badge, Pharaoh's Army, The Visitation, House and Thr3e. His films have been seen at Sundance and around the world and he is a member of the Writers Guild of America. He currently teaches screenwriting at the University of Kentucky and is also Artistic Director of Pioneer Playhouse, a regional theater in central Kentucky, where he runs their outreach program Voices Inside that instructs incarcerated writers in writing and performance skills so as to fight recidivism. This is his first novel.